GRAVE CONCERNS

A Dan Courtwright Mystery

Other Books by Paul Wagner

Dan Courtwright Mysteries
Danger: Falling Rocks
Bones of the Earth
Holes in the Ground
Granite Gorge
High Sierra Quarry
Vertical Exposure

Artisan Public Relations
Wine Sales and Distribution
Wine Marketing and Sales

Lecture Series:
The Instant Sommelier (Great Courses)
A History of Wine in 10 Glasses (Audible)

GRAVE CONCERNS

PAUL WAGNER

A Dan Courtwright Mystery

Published by Albicaulis Books

It was the third Search and Rescue mission that finally got ranger Dan Courtwright's full attention.

The first one was in early March, and Dan remembered how cold it was. They had met up at Dodge Ridge before dawn, wanting to be out on the trail by the time it was light enough to see anything. Sixteen people in the SAR team, all bundled up tightly against the freezing temperatures and breathing clouds of steam that billowed up in the kaleidoscopic emergency lights of their vehicles. Team members shaking hands through thick gloves, patting each other on the back, and stamping their feet to stay warm on the compacted snow and ice.

Angela got them all together, as she always did, and started giving out the assignments. Everyone had a laminated sheet of paper with a quick fact sheet on the missing man. Height, weight, what he was probably wearing, and what gear he had with him.

"His name is Danny Capra," she said. "Twenty-seven years old. Five foot eleven, about a hundred and sixty-five pounds. His girlfriend says that he is very experienced and has a winter tent, winter sleeping bag—all the right gear. And she says he is very determined, very disciplined. He's not likely to give up." She paused here. "But he didn't get back when she expected him. And his car is still here in the parking lot."

Dan considered this. According to the girlfriend, the guy was supposed to know what he was doing and had the gear he needed. That was if the girlfriend knew what she was talking about. And that was when he started, four days ago. Who knew what he might have now? A nasty fall was always a possibility, or an avalanche. It had snowed on and off for the past few days, so he might have lost track of the trail. And with cloud cover overhead, he would have had to use a compass for a sense of direction. Or a GPS unit.

Dan asked about that.

Angela shrugged. "His girlfriend didn't know if he had a compass or a Personal Locator Beacon. Which means he probably doesn't have one. If he had one, he'd have told her about it. At least the PLB. And we probably would have heard from him."

So he didn't have an emergency beacon. That meant that he could be in trouble, and nobody would know until they found him. It also meant that if he were lost, he wouldn't be able to call for help, or to figure out where he was.

"We don't even know if he needs help," Angela continued, "but he's a day overdue, and in this weather, we can't take a chance."

Angela had paired Dan up with Blake, a young ranger with boundless energy and long legs. Dan knew it was going to be hard work keeping up with the guy. But they would stay together. That was a given. The last thing anyone on a SAR rescue team wanted to be was the subject of a SAR rescue. And the surest way to avoid that was to stick with your partner and follow all the rules.

Angela handed out the maps and sent each pair out with a specific mission. Dan and Blake were to follow the road down to Crabtree trailhead, and, if they had time, work their way up to Camp Lake. It would make for a very long day, and at this time of year the days weren't that long to begin with.

Dan checked with Blake and made sure they had all they needed for the day. His own radio was on and inside the pocket of his parka, because it was cold enough to kill the battery if he left it out.

Dan looked around at the team. They were serious, confident, and tough. Dan liked this feeling of being one of the grown-ups. He trusted this crew. When the shit hit the fan, these were the people who stepped up. He was one of them, and it felt good.

Blake gave him a nod and gestured for Dan to lead the way. It was a nice touch. That way Dan could set the pace, one that he could live with. It showed Dan that Blake was thinking like a team—something that not all young men did in a situation like this. Dan gave him a smile, certainly invisible behind his goggles and scarf, a thumbs up which he could see, and hit the trail.

In front of him, his headlamp gave him a tunnel of light to follow. Off to the side, he could see Blake's lamp occasionally flickering off to one side or the other. Dan aimed his straight at the trail, hoping that he wouldn't lose it under the heavy layer of fresh powder snow.

The sky was just beginning to show some light. It would never get bright today—the clouds would make sure of that. But for the next half hour or so, they would still use their headlamps.

It felt good to get out, Dan realized. He had done some hikes in the foothills over the winter, but this was different. This was real miles, and at elevation. Through the steam of his breath, he could see the trees draped in blankets of white. Occasionally a lump of snow would tumble down out of one of the trees, glittering in the light of his headlamp.

He and Blake had the most strenuous job today, the longest section of trail to cover. Dan took that as a compliment—that Angela thought they could handle it. And it also meant that they would cover the most ground. Maybe that meant they were more likely to find this guy. He had to admit that there was a certain part of him that hoped he and Blake would be the ones.

As the forest turned from black and white to the slow gray of dawn, Dan started looking more carefully around them, looking for a splotch of orange that would be the guy's tent. Or yellow. That would be his jacket, according to the sheet.

It looked like there were some faint indications of tracks in front of him on the trail, but who knew if those were from four days ago, or a more recent hiker? And all of them had enough snow over the top to disguise them or hide them from time to time.

Dan led the way for what he thought might have been forty-five minutes, or an hour at most. His watch was buried up the sleeve of his jacket. But it felt like a good time to check in. He stopped and turned to Blake.

"You want me to lead for a while?" Blake asked.

Dan shook his head. "No, I'm okay. I just thought it would be a good idea to take a little break."

Blake turned away and scanned the forest around them. "This guy could be anywhere out here," he said.

Now that they weren't moving, Dan could hear how silent it was. They listened for a few seconds. Not a sound. Nothing but white, black and gray. A soft plop of snow falling off a tree branch.

Blake pulled out his whistle and showed it to Dan. Dan nodded his approval, and Blake gave a few blasts, then waited.

Nothing. They were far enough out now that the other searchers wouldn't cover this section.

"Remind me to stop every few minutes and give that a shot," Dan said.

Blake pointed to the trail ahead, encouraging Dan to take the lead again.

Now Dan was feeling the excitement. Maybe the hiker was nearby. The sky was lighter now, and they had turned off their headlamps twenty minutes ago. He and Blake continued on, out into the white silence of the forest, hoping they would be the ones to find this guy. That would be great. They pushed on with a purpose.

But in the end, they weren't the ones to find him. In fact, nobody found him. While the SAR team spread out to search along his reported route all morning, the missing hiker had other ideas.

Just before eleven, Dan's radio came to life with a call that Danny Capra had been found. He'd walked into the Dodge Ridge parking lot from the side opposite the trailhead and was in perfect shape.

It was only later in the day Dan learned that Capra had made a complete circuit around the back of the ski area, but it had taken longer than he expected. On the day he was planning to hike out, it started getting dark. Night began to fall, so he set up camp and slept. The next morning, while the SAR team spread out following his route, Capra had waltzed into the other side of the lodge, where someone recognized him.

He was suitably embarrassed about all the fuss and apologized profusely to Angela.

When Dan and Blake heard the news, they turned around and made their way back to the parking area. They didn't get there until the middle of the afternoon. By then most of the other team members had left. Angela treated them to coffee from the thermos and thanked them for their efforts.

Dan shrugged.

It had felt good to get out—to breathe hard in the mountains and feel that sense of solitude. But you couldn't help wondering what that guy was doing out there for four days in the snow, and with days that only had ten hours of sunshine. It seemed to Dan that it would have been a lot of time staring at the inside of a tent.

<h1 style="text-align:center">chapter 2</h1>

The second rescue was another story entirely.

For one thing, it was snowing all day. Dan drove up to the same Dodge Ridge search area through snow flurries that at times reduced the visibility on the road to about fifty feet, maybe less. He knew that searching for someone in those conditions would be brutal, and he was right.

They tried to stick to the main trails and forest service roads, hoping to find a footprint or a tent, and not finding anything at all. Of course, the footprints had been filled in hours ago with snow, and if there was a tent, it was almost certainly just a white lump in the forest by now.

But they kept at it, yelling and blowing their whistles, and hoping that somehow they would get a reply.

The guy's name was Antonio Gemmeli, and the call came in from his parents. They described him as a very bright and motivated student, always up for a good time, but also from a deeply religious family. But what they didn't say was whether he had any real experience in the wilderness, or with snow camping.

His roommates said that he had been working all week on a project on his computer. They invited him to join them for dinner, and he said he was too busy—that he was really close to figuring something out, some problem that he'd been working on. By the time they came home, he had left.

Apparently, his friends were surprised. He left abruptly on Friday night before the storm hit, and drove right up to the trailhead. They found his car there. No snow tires, and Dan's guess was that the guy probably didn't have chains, either. The car would be there for a while.

This time Dan was paired up with Ruben Arriaga from the Sheriff's Department. Ruben liked being out in a blizzard even less than Dan did. They spent the rest of the day carefully working through a tight search grid, and finding nothing at all. It was miserable. Visibility was limited. It was cold. And they didn't find Mr. Gemmeli.

By the next morning, Tony Gemmeli's parents were there, along with a group of his friends from college. The snow had let up, but there were still flurries from time to time, and Dan was happy that he didn't have to worry about organizing twenty-five volunteers in addition to the SAR regulars.

Angela hit on a simple solution. She paired up each volunteer with someone from the qualified SAR team and sent them out in all directions. Dan was introduced to his new partner, Tony Gemmeli's older brother, Marco.

Dan asked if Marco had much experience in the snow.

Not so much, Marco told him. But he said he was dressed for it, and ready to get to work.

Dan looked around and found Ruben Arriaga being paired up with a young woman who was surely not wearing enough clothes to stay warm. Dan didn't envy him, either.

At least Dan hoped he wouldn't have to worry about that. Marco was bundled up like the Michelin man. It looked as if the guy had put on every coat in his closet, with a scarf and woolly hat on top of everything else. Dan wondered if the guy would sweat too much and get hypothermia anyway. Not a happy thought. And Dan couldn't tell how much of the clothing was actually made for being out in the snow.

Dan made sure that Marco understood exactly what the day's activities would and would not entail, and then set off with Marco behind him, tracking down the grid. That way Dan was doing all of the hard work of breaking the trail.

It was a long, slow day. The clouds stayed in place all day, so the sky was a uniform gray, and the landscape was shaded from black to white. If he hadn't had his GPS unit, there would have been no real way to follow the search pattern. Dan carried it in one hand, checking constantly, and left most of the yelling to Marco. He figured that it would do the brother good to keep busy. That, and Dan could tell from Marco's voice when he needed a break. Meanwhile, Dan blew his whistle at each pause.

By the time they stopped for lunch, Dan could see, or hear, that Marco was getting frantic.

As they sat in the snow and ate, Dan told him the story of the previous rescue, how the whole team had been out in the snow, looking for the guy, and he just walked into the lodge as if nothing had happened.

Marco appreciated the story, but the worried look on his face didn't disappear.

And in spite of his bulky clothes, he looked cold. It was hard to tell, but Dan thought Marco might be shivering in there somewhere. He thought they'd better get moving again.

While they were hiking, Marco had been warm enough, but once they stopped, his chin was trembling, and Dan realized that he had another problem on his hands. He made Marco stand up and move around, and poured hot chocolate into him.

When Marco went off to pee, Dan radioed back to Angela and explained the situation. Marco wasn't going to want to turn around, but Dan knew that he had to get the guy back to the trailhead sooner rather than later.

He and Angela agreed. Dan and Marco would now aim for a new search section, one that was back towards the trailhead.

"Have they got anything?" Marco asked.

Dan shook his head. "We're just trying to make sure that we haven't missed anything," he said.

Marco looked off into the forest, blanketed with snow. "But what if he's out here?" he asked, waving a hand toward the forest beyond.

"The important thing is to be scientific about this, to follow the grid," Dan explained. "We can't just go off in every direction and hope that we find something. That leaves too many holes behind."

Marco considered this. He was still staring out into the woods. "Tonio!" he yelled. "Toni!"

Dan waited. There was no answer. He looked at Marco and bent his head towards their new search area.

Marco waited a moment longer, yelling for his brother. Then he turned and followed Dan.

Dan kept a close eye on Marco for the rest of the afternoon. By 2:30 he had seen enough. The man was clearly hypothermic, and Dan knew they still had a mile and a half to get back to the trailhead. He poured the last of the cocoa for Marco and gave it to him.

"We need to get you out of here," he said to Marco. "You're freezing, and I don't want to have to call for help."

Marco didn't argue. He was too cold to do that. But he did refuse to move. "I'm staying out here until we find my brother," he said finally. "I know God will protect me."

Dan walked over and stood in front of him. "No," Dan said. "You are walking out with me right now. And if you don't, I will have to call my boss and tell her that I've got a problem here, that you're hypothermic, and I need some people to stop searching for your brother so that they can come help me get you out of here."

He waited while Marco processed this.

"I can make it until dark," Marco said. His voice had an uneasy edge to it that Dan didn't like.

"At the speed you are moving, it is going to take us until dark to get back to the trailhead," Dan said. "We need to go now."

Dan reached out and gently tried to turn Marco to face the hike out.

Marco slapped his hand away. "Don't touch me," he yelled. "We're not leaving until we find my brother."

Dan took a deep breath and let it out slowly. He pulled out his radio and called Angela. In a voice loud enough for Marco to hear clearly, he explained the situation and asked if she could pull a few people off the search so that they could help him.

Marco Gemelli reached out and knocked the radio out of Dan's hands. "You son of a bitch," he said.

The radio squawked in the snow. Angela was asking for his position.

"If I don't answer, they'll send more people out looking for us," Dan explained.

Marco stared at him for too many seconds.

Dan slowly bent over and picked up the radio. "I think we've got things worked out here," he said to Angela, as he watched Marco's reaction.

Marco was stumping off into the snow, his curious gait accentuated by his heavy clothes.

"If you're heading for back out, that's this way," Dan said, pointing with his arm.

Marco stopped and turned around to look at Dan. Again he stared angrily, then started in the direction Dan had indicated.

It took them the rest of what was passing for daylight to get out.

Back at the command center, the mood was somber. As the family and volunteers clustered around the van, hoping to hear any news at all, the groups slowly filtered back, none with any sign of the missing hiker. Others were gearing up to head out into the night, hoping for better luck.

Dan drove home, looking forward to a warm shower and hot meal. Unless that night crew was lucky, he'd be going back out again the next day.

It wasn't until the middle of the third day that they found the tent, buried under thirty inches of snow, and well off any of the trails. But that glimmer of hope died almost immediately when they found that the tent was empty. Dan was two miles away when he heard the news and turned to follow up on the new search pattern. He spent the rest of that day with what was now an army of searchers, all spreading out from the location of the tent. By nightfall, they still hadn't found Tony Gemmeli.

That happened the following morning, about five hundred yards from the tent. Antonio Gemmeli's body was frozen solid. They could see no reason why he had left the tent. His clothes were not nearly warm enough for the conditions. Someone suggested that maybe he had needed to pee in the blizzard and had become disoriented in the dark and the snow. In blizzard conditions that could easily happen. It was also clear that he had been outside the tent for most of the snowstorm. He was buried under three feet of snow.

That was the end of the second SAR activity. Along with the

rest of the team, Dan packed up and left, leaving Marco sobbing and praying with his grieving family in the parking lot. Dan turned on the heat to full bore in his vehicle and drove slowly and carefully back down the mountain, all too conscious of how fast you can die if you don't know what you're doing.

On the drive down the mountain he thought about what it would be like to die like that. There was no satisfaction in finding Antonio Gemelli, only a deep sadness.

Dinner with Kristen was a rather somber event.

chapter 3

The third call came only six days later.

It was the same trailhead, and the same area. Dan wondered what the hell was so interesting about the backside of Dodge Ridge. Why did what appeared to be normal, sane people pack into here for miles in deep snow, for days?

The missing hiker was named Karl Rahm, an experienced backpacker, and somebody who was supposed to have all the right gear for this kind of trip. Dan considered that Mr. Rahm might be missing the one piece of gear that was most critical in the backcountry—common sense.

When Rahm had started out, three days ago, the forecast was for a few snow flurries, but generally good weather, given the season. But the minor flurries had turned into a much bigger storm, and for the past two days the snow had come down with real purpose. It would be miserable to hike around in those conditions. And it would be easy to get disoriented.

At the SAR command center, Angela looked at Dan and waved him over. "How do you feel about working with Blake again?" she asked.

Dan assured her that would be fine.

"Good," she said. "I think you're the only guy who has a chance of keeping up with him."

Dan grinned. "That's because I make him stay behind me," he

said.

Angela gave him a quick grin and laid out the map for them. Once again they were going to tackle the longest search, far down along the road, as far as they could get. Others would fill in behind them.

Dan looked at Blake. "We seem to be the lucky ones," he said. "To boldly go where no man…"

Blake laughed. "You up for this?" he asked. "It'll feel good to get in some miles today."

Dan agreed and allowed Blake to wave him forward as they set off down the trail. "I'm happy to let you lead sometime," he called to Blake over his shoulder.

"Nah," Blake said. "That's okay. This way I don't have to worry about leaving you behind."

Dan showed him his middle finger over his shoulder as he strode down the trail and set off at a pace that he hoped would give Blake just a tiny bit of pause.

It didn't.

An hour later they called a halt. Dan could hear some of the searchers far behind them, calling out and blowing whistles into the white forest.

He looked at Blake. "What the hell is going on?" he asked. "This is the third time we've had to come out looking for someone this month."

Blake shook his head. "No idea. Must be cabin fever or something."

"Some magazine or website must have done a feature on getting lost in the snow," Dan said. "And now all these guys think it's a great idea."

Blake was staring off into the forest. Dan followed his gaze.

"Do you see something?"

Blake shrugged, then shook his head. "Hello!" he yelled out. "Karl!"

They waited but got no answer. Dan blew his whistle for good measure, but that was still only met with silence.

"Ready to move on?" he asked Blake.

Blake nodded, but he was still staring off into the forest. Dan waited a moment longer. Finally, Blake turned and the two of them set off down the trail again.

Now they were well beyond the other searchers and were calling out and using their whistles at regular intervals. Hike for five minutes, stop, whistle and shout and listen for a minute, repeat as needed. Their job was to follow the snow-covered road as far as they could. Another five minutes, another stop and shout.

By the middle of the morning, they had stopped to drink some hot chocolate, and Blake laced his with a double shot of instant coffee.

Dan watched him do this, then asked if he was having trouble keeping up.

Blake laughed. "Keeping awake is more like it," he joked. "I just want to make sure I don't miss anything."

Dan was packing up the thermos when he heard Blake yell again.

"Karl! Karl Rahm!"

Amazingly, an answer came back from somewhere up ahead.

Dan and Blake looked at each other wide-eyed, then immediately started racing toward the voice. Soon they saw him, galumphing through the deep snow, thrashing along and waving to them.

Dan whipped out his radio and called in. "I think we may have found the guy," he said.

Blake was now ahead of Dan and had reached the man. He turned and waved to Dan. "It's him. We got him!"

Dan hurried to catch up, still talking on the radio. "Confirming that, we have found Karl Rahm," he said. Angela immediately wanted to know where they were, and what kind of help they needed.

While he gave Angela his position via the radio and PLB, Dan watched and listened as Blake checked out Rahm. The guy did seem to have all the right gear. He said he was warm enough and was still carrying his backpack.

"Are you okay to hike out?" Dan asked him.

"Sure," Rahm answered. "That's what I was planning to do."

"You're warm? You've had something to eat and drink?" Dan asked.

"Breakfast in bed," Rahm said with a grin. "And a lot of hot coffee."

Blake looked at him. "Did you get stuck somehow?" he asked. "What happened?"

Rahm shook his head. "Did you see the weather for the past two days?" he asked. "Snowing like a son of a bitch. That's one bet I lost. So I holed up in my tent and stayed warm until things got better."

"Which is today," Dan suggested.

"Yep," Rahm confirmed. He looked around. "This looks like a good day to hike out," he said.

Dan could see Blake grinning behind his mask. "Yeah, let's do that."

On the radio, the other teams were getting the news and clearing out, packing up. Angela was asking if they needed any help.

"I think we're good," Dan said. "But if you want to send a snowmobile out to pick him up, it might help."

Angela said she'd get a couple of them on the way. But it would be a while before they arrived.

Karl Rahm shook his head. "I don't need that," he said. "I'm fine. I'm okay to hike out from here. What is it, a few miles?"

"Something like that," Blake said.

As they hiked, Dan wanted more of an explanation.

"So what were you doing out here alone?" he asked. "Getting your merit badge for snow camping?"

Rahm laughed. "No, sorry. I sure didn't mean to create any trouble. I'm sorry. I should apologize for that."

"But you just thought…" Dan suggested.

"I took a chance on the weather," Rahm admitted. "I sure got that one wrong. But it wasn't too bad. I was warm enough in the tent. I just didn't think it was a good idea to hike around in that stuff."

"You got that right," Dan agreed. He considered mentioning the last SAR event, and the man who froze to death, then decided against it. "But you're the third time we've been out this month. Must be something in the water."

Karl Rahm looked at Dan and started to say something, then thought better of it. "I'm sorry," he said. "I really am."

Dan shook his head. "Nah, don't worry about it. Blake loves coming out here and getting his exercise in the snow."

They trudged along for a few more minutes. Twice, Dan started to make another comment about the situation, and then didn't. Finally, he stopped and turned to look at Rahm. But before Dan could speak, Rahm interrupted him.

"Hey, I'm sorry," he said. "I guess I owe you guys an explanation."

Dan met Blake's gaze and raised his eyebrows, not that Rahm could see them behind Dan's goggles.

"I wasn't just out here camping in the snow," Rahm continued. Then he looked at the two rangers. "Have you guys ever heard of Matthew McLeod?" he asked.

Dan and Blake exchanged glances, then shook their heads.

"He's a writer," Rahm explained. "He writes mystery novels about the West."

He waited. Dan shrugged. "Okay. And…?"

"There's a group of us who think that he might have hidden a treasure up here somewhere," Rahm explained. "Somewhere around here." He waved his arm at the forest around them.

Dan snorted. "And you think you're going to find it in the snow?" he asked.

Rahm gave an embarrassed grin. "Not really. I was just checking things out," he said. "Trying to get a head start, for when the snow melts and things finally open up."

Dan shook his head sadly. "Treasure, huh?" he said. He didn't think he did a very good job of hiding his disdain.

"Five million bucks," Rahm said. "I figured it was worth a shot."

And that was when they heard the snowmobiles.

chapter 4

"You have got to be kidding me." Steve Matson, the head of the Mi-Wok Ranger District, was not amused. And since Steve was Dan's boss, Dan knew enough not to smile—not that he wanted to.

"I am not kidding you," Dan answered. "That's what the last guy, Karl Rahm, told me. And I'm guessing that the other two guys knew about it, too."

"You mean the one who died?" Matson asked.

Dan nodded. "Toni Gemmeli. I talked to his brother. He found a bunch of this guy McLeod's books on his brother's bookshelves. And who knows? There may be more people out there that we don't know about."

"Give me an incident report," Matson said. "I want all the names and details. I want everything you can find out about the writer. What's his name?"

"Matthew McLeod," Dan replied. "Like the tool."

"Any relation?" Steve asked.

"To the guy who invented it?" Dan asked. "Not that I can see."

"If somebody died because of this guy, I want to know everything you can find out," Matson repeated. "And I'm going to call our legal team and see just exactly what our options are, if we can charge him with anything. It's irresponsible. Completely unacceptable."

Dan replied with a skeptical look on his face. "I'm not sure," he said. "There seems to be some doubt about all of it. Maybe it's real, maybe it isn't."

"If it's real enough for people to die out there, it's real enough for me," Matson said. "I want to know what this guy McLeod has said."

"From what I can tell," Dan responded, "it's all buried in his mystery novels. They're full of secret codes, hidden messages. There are whole websites dedicated to figuring out what they mean."

"So where does the treasure come in?" Steve asked.

"The fourth book, Death Zone," Dan said. "Something about five million dollars' worth of bitcoin hidden in the mountains."

"Five million?" Steve's eyebrows shot toward the ceiling.

Dan nodded. "Yeah. Enough to get people's attention," he said.

"Get on it," Steve ordered him. "Let me know if you need help." He rolled a pencil between his fingers.

"No, not at this point," Dan said. "I'll just spend a little more time on the computer and track down what I can find."

"So this stuff is all on the internet?" Steve asked.

"It's part of his fan club," Dan said. "They have a series of websites talking about his books. That's where it seems to have started. Some of the people there think he's hidden clues throughout all of his books."

"And what does he say?" Steve asked.

Dan's mouth twisted up on one side. "Not much," he said. "He just tells people to read all of his books. Which could mean he just wants everyone to buy all of his books."

"Or it could be interpreted to mean that the clues are all hidden in his books," Steve suggested. "Get what you can on this guy, and then I'll give it to our legal team. If he's playing games that involve people getting lost and dying in our forest, I want to put a stop to it right now."

"Will do," Dan agreed.

"And you might give the Sheriff's office a call, and see if they have any ideas," Steve suggested. "They might know more about this than we do."

Dan grinned. "Or less."

"Or less," Steve agreed. "You don't need any help reaching out to them?" he asked. Steve knew that Dan's best friend worked for the Tuolumne County Sheriff's Office.

Dan chuckled. "I think we're having them over for dinner on Saturday," he said.

Steve didn't like that answer. "Don't talk about this at dinner," he said, dropping the pencil on his desk. "And don't wait until Saturday. I want this official, and I want it quick."

"I know," Dan assured him. "Got it."

The two sat in silence for a moment. Dan wondered if Steve had more on his mind.

"Just a question," Dan began, then waited for Steve's approval to continue. Steve waved him forward. "How is this different from geo caching? I mean, they leave a tiny box or can somewhere, and then share the GPS coordinates. I know we discourage that, but the only thing we can ever find to charge them with is littering."

"Five million bucks won't fit in a tiny little can," Steve said.

"It's bitcoin," Dan explained. "It's computer code. It would fit on a thumb drive that's…smaller than my thumb." He held his thumb up to illustrate the point.

Steve took a deep breath and let it out slowly. "If people are dying to find it, I want it stopped," he said. "And I'm willing to get a judge who will agree that dangling a five-million-dollar carrot over the edge of a cliff is something that you can go to jail for. Or at least get you sued."

"Okay," Dan agreed. "I'll find out what I can."

"Good," Steve was shaking his head. "Where does a writer get five million dollars that he can give away?"

Dan shrugged. "His books are popular, but I doubt that he makes that kind of money," Dan said. "I don't think any of the books have been made into movies, if that's what you're thinking. But if he bought bitcoin when it first came out, maybe…"

"I thought that stuff all went into the toilet a couple of years ago," Steve said.

"Not all of it," Dan said. "But that might be something we could suggest."

"What do you mean?" Steve asked.

"That what used to be five million dollars of bitcoin might only be worth a tenth of that now." Dan said.

"So five hundred thousand dollars." Steve said. "Still a lot of money. 1 wonder if it might be better to reach out to the publisher and see if we can talk some sense to them."

"Whatever you think will work," Dan said. "I'd just like to see this settle down."

"You and me both," Steve said. "I'll reach out to a couple of people in our legal department and see what they think might work best."

Steve was checking his computer as they talked. "The publisher is Bolton Hall," Steve said. "They're famous, aren't they?"

Dan nodded. He wasn't sure he knew enough about publishers to answer the question, but he wasn't going to admit that to Steve.

Steve continued to click away on the computer. "It says here that they were acquired a couple of years ago by a venture capital firm." He continued reading while Dan waited. Steve gave a short chortle. "It doesn't sound like many people in the publishing world are happy about that."

He looked up at Dan, who waited expectantly.

Steve read from his monitor: "Another example of pure greed driving a treasured old house into the ground for the sake of the almighty dollar. They might as well change the name to Bullion and Hall, and just get a contract to print the US currency."

Dan smiled. "A rejected author?" he asked.

Steve shook his head. "The editor who quit a few weeks after the sale. She sounds like a firecracker."

"Maybe we could get her to help," Dan said with a grin.

Steve smiled back. "I'm not sure she's the one to exert any influence now. I'll get our legal team on it, for what it's worth."

Dan did not have a good feeling about this.

<h1 style="text-align:center">chapter 5</h1>

Five years ago, the first time that Dan met Cal Healey, the local Sheriff's deputy, Cal had pulled Dan over on Highway 108 for speeding.

After the usual pleasantries, Cal asked him why he was driving so fast, and Dan, in his official uniform, had explained that it was his first day at his new job, as a wilderness ranger in the Stanislaus National Forest, and he had underestimated how long it would take him to drive up to the ranger station. He was running late.

Cal listened to Dan, and then, without a word, handed back Dan's driver's license, registration, and proof of insurance. With a curt "follow me," he had flicked on his emergency lights—but no siren—and quickly led Dan all the way up to the Summit Ranger Station.

Dan was mortified. And it was even worse when Cal walked into the ranger station ahead of Dan and loudly introduced him to the rest of the staff.

Before Cal left, Dan thanked him quietly and swore that he would never speed again. The only sign that Cal had heard him was a twinkle in the Sheriff's eye as he walked out. That, and a quick "I know. Welcome to Tuolumne County, Mr. Courtwright."

It was four days later that Dan stood in line at the Twain Harte Market, behind a woman whose cart was overflowing with food. She took one look at Dan's meager collection of cans and frozen food and invited him to go in front of her.

Dan initially refused, but then she insisted, and Dan was happy to do so and thanked her.

And then she noticed his outfit.

"You must be the new ranger up at Summit," she said.

Dan admitted that he was. News travels fast in a small town, he thought.

The woman glanced at the food in his basket again, then looked back at Dan. "I'm Maggie Healey," she said, reaching out and shaking his hand. "I think you must have met my husband Cal the other day."

When Dan gave her a look of confusion, she continued. "The Deputy Sheriff."

Behind his trim black beard, Dan turned a brilliant shade of red.

Maggie took one more look at the items in his basket and asked him if he lived alone. Dan admitted that he did, at which point Maggie invited him to dinner on Friday night.

Dan stumbled out an apology about how he might be busy, and Maggie laughed out loud. "You can't escape me, Dan Courtwright," she said, reading his name on the nametag on his shirt. "About 6:30."

The line in the store had moved forward and it was now Dan's turn to pay. While he quickly put his credit card into the reader, he heard Maggie talking to the checker as if the woman was an old friend—which she probably was, Dan realized.

And before he could walk out the door, Maggie had handed him Cal's business card with their address written on the back.

"Don't be late," she said. "I don't like my food to get cold."

The checker in the store had smiled at that.

Dan nodded obediently and asked if he could bring anything to contribute to the dinner.

Maggie gave one last look at his grocery bag and assured him that no, he could not.

The dinner had been delicious. Dan later learned that Maggie had a well-deserved reputation as a gourmet cook. And she had at least acted delighted with the flowers Dan had decided to bring as a hostess gift.

Cal, meanwhile, had waited until he had everyone's attention before he told the story of how he and Dan had met. To chuckles and outright laughter, Cal explained that his actions had involved less paperwork and were almost certain to be more effective than giving Dan a ticket.

One of the other guests had asked Dan how his coworkers had responded to the whole thing.

Dan gave a painful smile. "They'll get over it, in time," he said. "I'm guessing it'll take a couple of years."

This was greeted with even more laughter.

"Let me know if you need any more help up there," Cal offered, his eyes wide with innocent appeal, a grin on his face.

Dan grinned. "I will certainly do that," he said. "Right now, I think you've given me all the help I can handle."

The rest of the evening was spent talking about Dan: where he had gone to school, what had brought him to Sonora, and how long he expected to stay. Dan's answers seemed to have been met with approval, and he was invited to a number of upcoming social events.

As the dinner party wound down, Cal asked Dan to stay for a few minutes more. Once all the guests had left, Cal invited Dan to sit down while Maggie wandered into the kitchen to start cleaning up.

"This is a small town," Cal said. "I think you could see that from the conversation tonight."

Dan nodded in agreement.

"That means you need to be a little careful," Cal continued. "The guy you flip off on the highway just might end up being the guy who chairs the meeting you are driving to attend."

Dan smiled and nodded. "Point taken," he said.

"And if you need anything," Cal continued, "and I mean anything at all, I want you to call me."

Dan looked directly at Cal and was surprised to see how serious and sincere the expression on Cal's face was.

"I mean it," Cal added.

"Thanks, I will," Dan assured him.

"Where are you living?" Cal asked. When Dan told him, Cal explained that he knew the landlord. "Let me know if he gives you any problems," he added.

Dan explained that with his new job, he would be looking for a place to buy, so he wouldn't be living there long.

"Good," Cal said. "If you need any recommendations on a realtor, I can help. If you want."

Dan agreed that would be great.

Just then Maggie appeared with a package of leftovers from dinner.

"You must be way too busy with getting settled in to do much cooking," Maggie said. "This will help. We need more people like you up here, Dan."

Dan had thanked her profusely and finally managed to get out the door. He set the food on the floor in front of the passenger's seat in his truck and climbed into the driver's seat. And then he sat there for a good minute, not starting the truck, just sitting there until he was afraid that Maggie might come out of the house and ask him if there was something wrong.

There was nothing wrong. Dan had just found out that he was now part of a community. And he was both grateful and a tiny bit scared.

But five years later, Cal had become Dan's best friend, and Steve Matson knew it. Which was why he had asked Dan to call the Sheriff's office to ask for their help.

Cal listened while Dan explained his theory about Matthew McLeod and the mysterious treasure hidden somewhere in the Sierra. When Dan had finished, Cal had only one comment.

"Great," he said. "So now we've got all sorts of knuckleheads climbing around the backcountry looking for a thumb drive worth five million dollars. And in under less than optimum conditions."

"To go with all the usual knuckleheads that find their way into trouble back there," Dan agreed. "All year round."

Cal considered this for a moment. "I say we go after them with a RICO indictment," he suggested.

"What the hell is that?" Dan asked.

"Organized crime," Cal said. "Racketeering. A conspiracy to commit crimes. We pull in the publisher of the books, his literary agent, every bookstore that sells them, and take their ill-gotten assets. This would be worth a lot of money. And we'd get to keep some."

"Are you serious?" Dan asked.

"Well," Cal admitted, "the way I see it, it's either that or maybe handing the guy a two-hundred-dollar fine for littering. If we can find the damn thumb drive."

"It may not be a thumb drive," Dan explained. "It could be a safe deposit box key, or even a piece of paper with a URL printed on it."

"Okay," Cal agreed. "Maybe only a stern warning for littering."

"So you haven't heard anything about this?" Dan asked.

"Nope," Cal replied. "But I have a bad feeling that is all going to change. I'm just not sure what we can do about it."

chapter 6

It was the first true dinner party that Dan had ever hosted. Although it was really Kristen who was hosting it. She informed him that his job was purely to manage the front of the house. As a catering chef, she would take care of everything else. Now that Kristen had moved in with him, and they had even remodeled the kitchen to her liking, it was clearly time to pay back some of those social favors. Actually, it was well past that time.

There was no way that Dan could ever repay Maggie and Cal for the many times they had invited him to their house for dinner, even if he didn't count the number of times that Maggie had played matchmaker and invited Kristen as well. And somehow he and Kristen had always ended up sitting next to each other. Cal and Maggie were obviously first on the guest list.

And Dan had invited his elderly neighbors, Ruth and Walt Sorenson. Once they had learned that Dan liked to solve crossword puzzles, they religiously sent over their copy of the New York Times once they had finished with it. And at least once a month Ruth showed up at Dan's door with a plate of cookies or cinnamon rolls— usually as an icebreaker to a conversation about one of the many local issues that Ruth and Walt took on. While Ruth was a tiny ball of energy, Walt towered over her, although his posture was stooped, as if he were trying to make himself smaller and less imposing. If Ruth was a bright and lively wren, Walt was a lumbering stork. And in conversation, Walt was as taciturn as Ruth was voluble.

Kristen had also invited her friend Carol, who worked in the county planning department. The two had met when Kristen opened her catering business in town, and Carol had become both a valued client and a good friend.

To round out the party, they had invited Dan's colleague Doris from the Summit Ranger Station. Doris was decades older than Dan, but he was technically her supervisor. It could have been quite awkward if Dan hadn't immediately recognized that Doris knew most of the area like the back of her hand, and she knew everything about everyone within ten miles of their office. But Doris had called the day before to say that she wasn't feeling well, and was concerned that she might have COVID, despite being both vaccinated and boosted.

So it would be only seven around the table.

With that cast of characters, the conversation over a glass of wine in the living room began carefully. Ruth and Walt weren't sure quite what to make of Carol, and cautiously avoided any sensitive topics—the most obvious of which was the new Yosemite North development that was proposing to build a massive resort on the way to Yosemite National Park.

But by the time they had sat down to dinner, the wine had taken effect, and the conversation opened up. Cal tossed the first ball into the air by asking Dan if he'd heard any more about that treasure hunt in the mountains.

Of course, everyone wanted to know the details, and Dan quickly outlined what he knew—that a writer seemed to have written a series of mystery books about the Sierra, and some of his readers were convinced they had found a secret code that would lead them to a five-million-dollar prize hidden somewhere in the Sierra.

Dan was barely finished when Cal snorted out a response. "Stupid sonofabitch," he said. "If, and that is a very big if, he really did it, then he's a jerk and an asshole."

In the uncomfortable silence that greeted that remark, Ruth asked, "What makes you say that?"

Cal couldn't hide his scorn. "The kind of people who are going to go looking for that money are going to be completely unprepared for what they get into," Cal said. "We've already had one guy die out there—froze to death last month." He looked to Dan, who confirmed this.

Carol asked Dan if he thought that was really the author's fault. "I mean, three years ago we had someone die up at Dodge Ridge, and last summer somebody drowned in the Clavey River. People do have accidents, and sometimes people do stupid things. Flatlanders."

Cal looked at her. "Yeah, they do," he said. "I'd just as soon they not get any extra encouragement."

"But I want to know about these books," Ruth said. "Who wrote them? What are they called? I think this is interesting."

"A guy by the name of Matthew McLeod," Dan said. "It's a series, I guess. And people think there are clues hidden throughout the books."

It was then that Walt broke his silence. "Not very different from Forrest Fenn," he suggested. When many of the group looked confused about the reference, Walt explained that Forrest Fenn had hidden a treasure chest somewhere in the West and generated a lot of publicity for his books about it.

"Did they ever find it?" Maggie asked.

Walt nodded. "After Fenn died, someone eventually did find it. But I think there were people who got into trouble over that one, too."

"I think it sounds kind of fun," Maggie said, looking at Kristen. "How many books are there in the series?"

Dan shook his head. "Six or seven, maybe more," he said.

"Ten books," announced Carol, who was staring at her phone. "And there is a whole community online about this."

"Oh, great," Cal grumped. "Now we'll get the selfie crowd."

"So what?" Ruth asked. "If we get more people visiting the Sierra, and they see how beautiful it is, maybe we'll get a few more votes to protect it in the future. And right now we need every vote we can get." She glanced over at Carol, who smiled politely.

"Well, let's hope they know how to push a lever on a voting machine as well as they know how to hit the SOS button on their locator beacon," Cal said. "I am not looking forward to a summer filled with search and rescue for a bunch of flatlander yahoos."

Dan chuckled. "Cal, they should put you in charge of the tourism office," he said.

"It isn't going to help tourism if people keep getting lost and dying up here," Cal answered.

That's when Maggie put her foot down. "Stop being such a grump, Cal," she said. "I think it sounds like fun, and I am going to see if the library has some of these books. Anyone want to join me?"

Kristen nodded and smiled, which Maggie took for a yes.

Ruth raised her hand. "I'm in. Maybe we girls can tackle this puzzle and show the men how to really solve a mystery."

From the far end of the table, Dan saw Kristen catch his eye. "I guess I should probably read at least one," Dan said carefully. "That way I won't have to admit complete ignorance when I talk to some of these people."

Walt didn't offer to take a look at the books. "You know," he said quietly, "if you really like mysteries in the mountains, there are certainly more interesting ones than an artificial one like this."

That brought silence to the table. As they sat and looked at Walt expectantly, he shrugged.

"Oh, go on, Walt," Ruth told him. "You might as well tell them what's on your mind."

Walt's shoulders went up again, and he looked around the table, as if he was hoping someone would get him off the hook.

Nobody did.

Walt took a deep breath and let it out slowly. "Well, there are some real mysteries, not just ones created to sell some books. I prefer those."

chapter 7

Walt looked around the table again, and then continued. "It's kind of a long story," he said. "You might not want to hear all of it."

Dan chuckled. "Walt, I don't think you're going to talk your way out of this," he said. "I've learned that when you talk, it's a good idea to listen. So why don't you tell us the whole story?"

Walt checked again, and found a number of the other guests nodding and agreeing with Dan. Then he looked down at his plate for a moment, as if to collect his thoughts. "I don't suppose any of you have heard of a man by the name of Norman Bollinger?" He paused here and looked around the table again. Nobody responded, other than a few slight shakes of the head.

"He was a high school biology teacher down in Manteca," Walt explained. "Interesting guy. Probably way overqualified to teach high school biology." He paused here and wiped his fingers across his lips. The rest of the table waited patiently for him to continue.

"But he had a kind of sideline," Walt said. "He was fascinated by the old Sierra juniper trees."

"Oh, I love those trees," Maggie interrupted him, then quickly stopped and held up her hand. "Sorry."

Walt smiled and shook his head, as if to accept her apology. "He loved them, too," he went on. "And he spent about fifty years on a quest to find the oldest juniper in the Sierra."

"The Bennett Juniper!" Maggie cried. "Cool! Have you guys

seen it?" she asked the group.

A number of the people around the table began to answer, but before they could finish, Walt had held up his hand. When things quieted down, he continued.

"The Bennett is the biggest," he said. "At least as far as we know. But it may not be the oldest." When he looked around the table, he could see people were confused. "Sometimes the oldest trees have lost limbs, or even parts of their trunks, so the oldest isn't always the biggest."

Maggie interrupted again. "Dan, is that true?"

Dan shrugged and agreed that it could be, then turned to Walt. "So did he find an older tree?"

"Nobody knows," Walt said. "This was all decades ago. I think Bollinger died sometime in the late fifties, early sixties? The only reason we know about all of this is that he kept journals with detailed records of every trip and tree he took."

Cal's brow was furrowed. "So why don't we know?" he asked. "Can't you just look in the journals?"

Walt gave Cal a tight smile. "You would think so, wouldn't you, Cal? But according to his daughter, he never completed the report on his last trip. And that wouldn't have made anyone think much, except for one thing. When she visited him in his last days—this was long before we had anything like hospice care, so he was just in the hospital, waiting to die—she asked him about that. She had decided that she wanted to publish his journals as a kind of tribute to him, and they had been working on that together. So she asked him where the last trip was, and what he found."

Walt paused to take a sip of water.

Maggie was getting impatient. "So what did he say? Had he found it?"

Walt shook his head. "He wouldn't tell her. He just smiled at her and patted her hand and said that sooner or later, everyone would know. She came away convinced that he had found it."

Maggie wasn't letting him stop there. "But does she know where he went on that last trip? Hasn't anybody checked it out?"

Walt nodded. "Sure, people have tried. They don't know where he went, but they know all the other places he went, so there's a group out there that has narrowed it down by a process of elimination. Remember, though, this is long before GPS and exact locations. So all we have are his descriptions of how to find these places."

Maggie sat back in her chair, clearly disappointed. "Well, if they've done all that, I'm sure they would have found it." She looked around the table for confirmation.

There were murmurs around among the guests expressing opinions both in favor and against Maggie's conclusion. But they quieted down when Walt held up his hand again.

"But that's not the mystery," he said.

Now he had their full attention. Walt took another breath and folded his hands in front of himself. He took a moment to collect his thoughts, and then started up again. "Bollinger kept detailed notes, not just of the junipers he found, but of everything he noted of interest. He identified old mining camps, interesting geological features, and other kinds of trees that got his attention. And he covered a lot of ground. He was amazing."

"It sounds like they would make a great guidebook, Dan," Maggie suggested. "Everything to see and do in the Sierra."

Dan smiled at her to show his agreement, but he didn't want to sidetrack the conversation. He turned back to Walt.

When Walt saw that he had Dan's attention, he went on. "There were all kinds of interesting notes in those journals, including archeological sites."

Walt stopped there and looked around the table. All eyes were on him.

"Oh, get on with it, Walt," Ruth muttered at her husband in exasperation.

Walt's eyebrows shot up at this remark, and he unfolded his hands and held them up in surrender. "Okay," he said meekly. "One of those archeological sites is in Tuolumne County, and it's never been explored, never been studied."

Cal gave a mild snort. "Where is this, Walt? I can already see it's going to mean more work for me."

Walt smiled and shook his head. "I doubt it, Cal. It's pretty hard to get to. It's well down in a canyon, and a bit of a hike from any trailhead. The only way down is a steep old logging track."

Dan vaguely remembered seeing something about an archeological project in the Stanislaus National Forest, but he couldn't quite pinpoint the file in his memory banks.

Walt looked at him. "Dan, you might have seen something about this," he said. "The dig was approved quite a few years ago, but nobody ever had the funds to get a team in there to do it."

Dan shook his head to show that he didn't know much about it.

"Well, we finally got the funding," Walt said. "As soon as we can get in there, we're going to explore the place for the first time in who knows how many years?"

"Wait," Maggie said. "You're doing this project?" The skepticism in her voice was apparent.

Walt dipped his chin to one side, then looked up at Maggie. "Not me. An assistant professor from UC Merced. But I've signed up as a volunteer to work on the project."

Maggie looked slightly disappointed. "And that's the mystery?"

she asked.

"We don't know quite what Bollinger saw there, but he certainly thought it was important. He mentioned it twice in his journals." Walt said. "With notes that it was something of special interest."

Carol was shaking her head. "How did they ever get funding for something as fuzzy as that?" she asked. "You should see the kinds of forms I need to fill out to get any funding at all." She looked at Cal. "Cal, you know what it's like."

"Oh, yeah." Cal gave her a short chuckle. "But we can always claim it's in the interests of public safety."

Dan looked over at Walt. "How did you get involved with all of this, Walt? How'd you find out about it?"

"An old friend of mine used to be a professor at Berkeley," Walt said. "This kid at UC Merced was one of his last grad students. When she came up with this idea, he put her in touch with me as a local contact."

Dan noticed that Kristen was staring at Walt, a slight frown on her face. "Walt, are you funding this dig?" she asked.

Walt gave a short laugh. "Ha! Not me, Kristen. No, thank you. But it turns out that Willoughby Partners—you know, the guys behind that big new Yosemite North resort? They seem to have decided that they need some good local PR. And I think they're hoping that we'll find something exciting that will draw some attention to the area."

"And to their damned resort," Ruth said with some bitterness. "It's just like greenwashing, only with archeology. What do you call that? Dustwashing?"

"I think it's cool that you're volunteering, Walt," Kristen said. "Good for you."

Walt smiled. "Well, I'm retired, so I have the time. And I've always been interested in that sort of thing. You see, it is kind of a mystery—a puzzle. We'll be discovering the pieces. And maybe we can figure it out."

Ruth let out an angry breath. "I don't care about that," she said. "But I want you to keep an eye on those damn developers. I don't trust them for a second."

Walt grinned at her and gave her a wink. "That's just a side benefit," he said. And he gave a little shrug. "Admittedly, it's a pretty good one."

Dan was curious. "What have you found so far, Walt?" he asked.

Walt paused. "Well, we're just getting started," he said. Just when Dan thought he wasn't going to say any more, Walt continued. "We've laid out the grid lines. And we've done some basic passes with a ground radar machine. The next step is to determine where we start digging the first trench."

chapter 8

May 12, *Tuolumne County Record*: The Tuolumne County Sheriff's office called off the search for two young men from San Bernardino, who had been reported missing three days ago by relatives. The boys were located safe and sound in a Jamestown restaurant earlier today. The Sheriff's Department had no further comment on the situation, other than to recommend that travelers file a trip plan with an emergency contact.

A week later, as the month of May was running out of days, Doris was getting fed up. As Dan's assistant at the Summit Ranger Station, Doris handled most of the incoming phone calls, and she was getting far more than usual. Doris, who loved to talk to people, had now suggested to Dan that they direct all calls to the voicemail system.

"And then what?" Dan asked. "Are we going to return all the calls?"

She looked at him with what passed for anger in Doris. "Maybe we only return the calls of people who are interested in hiking, and not in buried treasure. I mean, what is the deal?" she said peevishly as she looked up at Dan. "We've posted on the website, and we've sent out press releases that the trailheads are closed and won't open until the snow melts and the roads are stable, but that isn't enough, apparently." The curls of her short gray hair were quivering with indignation. The overhead lights in the office were flashing off the wire rims of her glasses.

"More calls about the famous buried treasure?" Dan asked.

Doris was just a couple years short of a full retirement, but Dan sure hoped that she would stay on. He had come to value her knowledge of both the local area and the locals themselves. And while she wouldn't be his first choice to help out on a trail, he had a legitimate fear that the entire ranger station would sink straight into the earth without her ability to understand USFS regulations and make them work—a rare brand of common sense combined with the ability to understand those who speak, or write, in bureaucratic tongues.

"That must be it," Doris agreed. She waved her hand at a tall stack of paper. "And people are writing in to get wilderness permits. Writing in!" she emphasized. There were no quotas for permits in the Emigrant Wilderness, and anyone could get a permit simply by walking in the door.

Dan nodded and gave her a sad smile. "It's going to be a busy summer."

"Look at this!" Doris held up a wad of the papers. "Here's a guy who wants three different permits, one right after the other, all for the same place. What's he going to do? Hike it over and over until he gets it right?"

She handed the papers to Dan, who looked them over.

Dan gave a short laugh. "I know this guy," he said. "Karl Rahm. He's definitely looking for the treasure. We had a SAR team out looking for him six weeks ago."

Doris rolled her eyes and grabbed the papers back from Dan. "Oh brother," she said. "And now he's coming back again. If he gets in trouble this time, we should send him a bill."

Dan was going to respond, but the phone rang again, and Doris picked it up.

Dan took advantage of the distraction to drift back into his own office and see if he couldn't find some emails to answer, or a report that needed writing. It was no fun talking to Doris when she was on a roll like this.

His email folder was filled with memos from various agencies, all informing him of a new policy, the importance of recognizing an existing policy, or a request to review a policy that was currently under consideration. Dan carefully moved them all to his archive folder, where he could forget about them for all time. Doris would tell him which ones really mattered. He had learned long ago that any response from him would either lead to the original sender ignoring him completely or putting him on a committee that would meet endlessly into the future.

One email caught his attention, a message from Steve Matson, his boss, requesting that Dan give him a call when he had a few minutes to talk.

Dan cocked his head to hear what Doris might be doing in the front office. When he heard her voice beginning to rise in volume on the phone, he knew he could call Steve. Doris would never do that if there were visitors at the counter, and it sounded like she might be on the phone until she was good and ready to get off it.

Dan allowed a small grin to flash across his face and called Steve Matson.

Sara answered the phone and told him that Steve would be right with him. Then she asked him how things were going up at the Summit Ranger Station.

Dan started to answer, then had Sara interrupt him to say that Steve was ready for his call.

"How are things going up at Summit?" Steve asked.

"I think we're okay," Dan said. "Doris is just about ready to pull the phone out of the wall because of all the calls we're getting, but other than that, things are fine."

"Is this still about that treasure hunt?" Steve said.

"As far as we can tell," Dan said. "I have to admit, I have never seen anything like this. Some of these people are nuts."

"Nuts in what way?" Steve asked him.

"We had a guy last week who was convinced that we knew where this treasure was, and we owed it to him as a taxpayer to tell him where it was," Dan said.

"Oh, Jesus," Steve commiserated with him. "What did you tell him?"

"That as far as I knew, there wasn't any treasure, but if he wanted me to help him look for it, I thought we should start on the big island of Hawaii."

Steve chuckled. "What did he say to that?"

"Nothing nice," Dan admitted. "He hung up on me."

Dan could hear Steve take a deep breath on the other end of the line, and took advantage of the break to pose a question. "What did you find out from the legal team?" he asked. "Can we go after this guy and get him to call these people off?"

"I guess our legal team was able to contact the publisher, Bolton and Hall, but they just got redirected to a big Wall Street firm that pretty much laughed at them," Steve answered. "No interest in discussing the issue, and no, they didn't feel any responsibility, all hidden behind very expensive lawyers who used really big words."

"So we're screwed?"" Dan asked.

"Pretty much," Steve said. "They were really pessimistic about our options. Basically, if we can prove the guy left something in the wilderness, then we can prosecute him. But maybe only littering, something minor at best. And that's only if it exists. There seems to be some question about that. The publisher did suggest that we might try contacting the writer or his agent."

"Okay," Dan said. "So are we going to do that?"

"Already on it," Steve said. "They have a call with her today."

Four hours later, Steve was back on the phone to Dan.

"The agent was very nice and understanding," Steve said.

"And?" Dan prompted him.

"And there is nothing she can do," Steve answered. "She suggested that we might talk to the publisher."

Dan snorted. "We know how that turned out."

"Yeah," Steve agreed.

"Maybe we need better lawyers," Dan said. "Hire some shark that sues the crap out of people."

"Well, our guys did get one concession from the agent." Steve said.

Dan waited. Finally, he responded. "I'm listening."

"We really have very few options here," Steve said. "We can't even prove that the guy hid anything up here. And unless we can prove that…" He didn't finish the sentence.

"And to do that, we have to find it?" Dan asked.

"Exactly," Steve said. "At which point it is no longer a hidden treasure, and the whole thing goes away."

Dan started laughing. "Hey Steve, do you want me to go find the treasure?" he asked. "I'd be happy to spend the summer looking for it. On the other hand, I'd love to see how you would budget those hours."

Steve did not join in the laughter. "Yeah, trash removal, maybe? Solitude monitoring?" he said sourly. Then his tone changed. "But I do want to ask you to do something, Dan. That's if you're willing. I don't like the way this is playing out."

"I like the way you ask me to agree before I know what it is." Dan said.

"It's kind of a big ask, Dan. But it just might help."

"Okay," Dan said guardedly.

"How would you feel about getting a hold of this writer guy, McLeod, and seeing if you can talk a little bit of sense into him."

Dan did not like this idea. "Like what? Tell him that his massively successful PR campaign is making Doris angry, and would he please stop it?"

"I was thinking of something a little more subtle," Steve said. "Maybe suggesting that this was a safety issue, that people were putting themselves in danger, and we wouldn't want him to feel guilty about it if someone got hurt. But do it in a friendly way."

"I'm not the right guy for that sort of thing, Steve," Dan said. "I'd be too tempted to tell him to take his books and shove them up his ass. Why not have your legal guys do it?"

"Yeah, well, don't tell him that," Steve said. "But I was thinking that it might work if it came from you instead of some government legal beagle. You know, the 'Ranger Sherlock Holmes' that he's read about in those magazines. He might even be flattered that you called him."

Dan refused to be convinced. "The only thing he cares about, as near as I can tell, is selling his books. And this whole thing is working like magic for him."

"I hear you, Dan," Steve said. "But let's look at this another way. You call him. You have that conversation. He thinks it might be even better publicity if he tells people about the call he got from Dan Courtwright."

"Oh, great!" Dan said. "So now I'm helping him sell books?"

"Maybe," Steve admitted. "But once your name is connected to this, we can use that to get our own message out about being careful, sensible, and making at least some effort to stay alive."

Dan thought about this for nearly a second.

"Why don't we just say that anyway?" he asked. "Why give the guy any more attention?"

"Because he'll also give us more attention," Steve said. "You know how often our announcements and press releases get ignored? But it doesn't seem like his do."

Dan had a twinge of reaction when he remembered what he had done with all those official USFS emails. "Yeah, okay. I take your point. So you just want me to call him up and have a chat?"

"Well, we'll try to give you a little training first," Steve said. "To make sure you are prepared. And we'll have someone sit in on it with you, just in case."

"Sounds like you have it all worked out," Dan said. He could see that Steve was not going to give up on this easily.

"Are you up to it?" Steve asked. "Want to take a shot at it?"

Dan shrugged. "How could it hurt? Sure, I'll give it a try. Do you know how to reach this guy?"

"Funny you should mention that," Steve answered. "As a matter of fact, we do. We can do it from my office here, but just in case, I'll send you his number."

chapter 9

Dan was surprised to learn that the first part of getting himself prepared for his conversation with Matthew McLeod was to read one of his books. At least it would allow him to keep the promise he'd made at the dinner party. The book got delivered to his house just two days later. He suggested to Steve that he could take some time off work to read it. Steve didn't bite.

"After hours is fine," Steve had said. "I don't even think you have to finish it. Just read enough to get an idea of what the guy writes about, and maybe something you can mention when you talk to him."

Dan explained the situation to Kristen, who had just started one of the books herself.

"This is great," she said enthusiastically. "Now we can read together and see if we can figure out the mystery. Maggie's reading the first one."

Crevasse was the third book in the series, according to the dust jacket. Dan was amused that the government apparently bought hardback books for things like this. Dan would have gone for a paperback. Kristen certainly had.

All of the books had alpine names: Avalanche, Bergschrund, Crevasse, etc. Dan liked that concept. He also thought that it might limit the total number in the series. He couldn't think of any alpine terms that started with the letter X. or Q, even J for that matter.

From the description on the back cover, Crevasse sounded as if it was going to keep him up at night. It was thrilling and spine-tingling, as well as intensely suspenseful.

Dan cleared his throat, sat back on the sofa, and cracked open the book.

Within a few pages, Dan was already getting worried, and not in a good way. The hero, Jack Pulaski, was all man. Ex-military, with a slight drinking problem, a terrible relationship with his ex-wife, and ready for action at the drop of a hat. He quickly rescued a dog that had been hit by a passing car and then got into a fistfight with the guy who hit it. Dan figured that was just to make sure we understood what kind of guy Jack Pulaski was. Pulaski took the dog to a vet and put the guy into the hospital.

And that was all in the first chapter. There was certainly more to come.

Dan looked over at Kristen. She was curled up on the far end of the sofa, her blond hair backlit by the reading lamp behind her shoulder. She quietly turned a page, then sensed that Dan was looking at her.

She glanced up. "What?" she asked. "How's your book?"

Dan grimaced. "Not great. How's yours?"

She made a little face. "Too soon to tell," she said. "Kinda violent, though."

Dan nodded. "Fistfight?" he asked. "Or explosions?"

She shook her head. "I shouldn't tell you. You might want to read it."

He grinned. "I don't think there's much chance of that."

She laughed. God, he loved to hear her laugh.

"Well, old Jack certainly gets into a lot of trouble," she said.

Dan grinned. "Yeah, in my book I think the guy would have ended up in jail for assault, and maybe sued by the guy he hit, all before we get into the second chapter. That would be right before he got fired."

"Testosterone poisoning," Kristen said. "There's a lot of that going around." She turned back to her book, adjusting one foot underneath herself on the cushions.

Dan watched her for another moment, then returned to his reading. Occasionally he could hear Kristen turning a page at the other end of the sofa. It was just enough to keep him there, sitting next to her.

Dan finished the next two chapters and then put the book down. The plot had thickened. Jack Pulaski was on the trail of drug runners on one hand, and on the other hand he was fending off a crooked sheriff who was trying to kill him. And his own boss, the head ranger, seemed to hate Jack Pulaski with a passion, but had to leave him alone because Jack was so damn good at his job. And Jack took every opportunity to be insolent right back at the boss. It was all very exciting, but Dan couldn't help thinking how little it connected to the way he did his job in the forest service.

Dan looked over at Kristen again. She was still reading, but her eyes were only half open as she scanned the pages.

Dan smiled. "From where I sit, it does not appear that your book is spine-tingling," he said.

She marked her place with a finger and looked at him. "Oh, it's fine. I'm just tired. And I don't care about any of the people in it."

"Not even the heroic Jack?" Dan asked.

"He's kind of a jerk," she said. "And if the country were really as full of other jerks as this book is, I think we'd all move to Canada. Or Sweden."

Dan slid over to her on the sofa. "You know how it's going to end," he said. "Jack will save the day, heroically. And he'll do it despite his nasty boss and the crooked cops and everybody else."

She smiled at him. "You really can see into the future, can't you?" she said with mock amazement. "And does he marry the girl?"

Dan checked the title on her book. "Bergschrund." He shook his head. "I don't think so, or she'd be around for this one." He held up his own book.

"Maybe she dies, leaving him with a broken heart," Kristen suggested.

"Or leaves him for a guy who finds a way to stay out of so many fights," Dan said.

Now it was Kristen who shook her head. "No, that's part of his charm, apparently," she said. "Getting into fights, and then having scars to show for it. She likes that part. She gets to be the mom and take care of him, just like Wendy in Peter Pan."

Dan leaned over and kissed her on the side of the head. "Figured out the treasure clues yet?" he asked.

Kristen closed her book and held it down in her lap. She leaned into him. "I'm not sure it's worth it," she said.

"Five million?" Dan asked.

Kristen frowned and looked at the book in her lap. "How many of these do we have to read?"

Dan laughed. "Not me," he said. "I only have to make headway in one of them. You and Maggie and Ruth have to read them all."

Kristen gave a sigh, then picked up her book again. "Twenty more pages, and then I am calling it a night."

Dan picked up his own book. "Two more fights or one more dead body," he said. "Let's see who gets there first."

<h1 style="text-align:center">chapter 10</h1>

When Dan drove into the parking area at the district ranger office in Sonora, the first thing that caught his eye was the car. There, among the usual bland white and pale green pickups and dusty SUVs of the USFS and its staff was a gleaming midnight blue rental car, and not one of the small ones, either.

Dan took in the reflections in the car's finish and concluded that it lived in a garage—something that none of the other vehicles in the parking lot did. The dark color would make it an oven in the summer, and in the winter the thing would slide all over the icy roads like a bejeweled hockey puck. But right now, on a warm sunny day in late spring, the thing looked like an advertisement for expensive watches, fur coats, or cologne.

Dan could just imagine the driver: perfectly cut hair, a suit that would cost more than Dan's car, Italian shoes, and a manicure. Absolutely wearing a tie. And definitely not Dan's kind of guy.

And he was right about that, except for the tie. Steve Matson introduced him.

"This is Dan Courtright," he said. "Dan, this is Martina Guzman."

Dan was right about the suit and the hair. Heck, he was even right about the nails, which were exactly the color of her lipstick, and shinier than her car outside. She was wearing an impeccably tailored charcoal gray suit and a white blouse that looked as if it were still in tissue paper in the box. And yes, the suit was every bit as expensive as Dan's old Subaru.

Martina shook his hand with a firm grip and indicated a chair in Steve's office. "Have a seat, Dan," she said. "We have a lot to cover this morning, and the call is only a couple of hours away."

Dan looked at Steve for help, but his boss just nodded to them both and indicated that they could use his office all morning. He would use the time to make a run up to Pinecrest and see how things were going.

Dan sat down in the chair and looked at Ms. Guzman. Her shoes, he noted, matched the nails and the lipstick. He wondered how many colors of nails and shoes she had, and decided he was probably underestimating by a huge factor.

"I've read up on you a bit," she began. "It's an impressive resume."

She didn't add "for a ranger," but Dan knew that was what she meant.

He gave a shrug that he hoped indicated modesty, and maybe just a touch of ennui.

She hefted a large leather bag onto her lap—the dark mahogany color somehow went perfectly with both the suit and the shoes—and pulled out two stacks of documents held together by enormous black metal paper clips. The leather of the bag was just as polished as everything else about the woman.

"One for you and one for me," she said with a humorless smile. And then she got to work.

Page by page, she talked Dan through the key points of their conversation with Matthew McLeod. She told him what he could say, and what he should never say. She had him read sections of the documents out loud, so that she was sure he understood what they meant.

She had him practice answering questions that McLeod might ask, and then had him do it all over again as she asked the questions a different way. She quizzed him on the key points, then wrapped up the first hour by suggesting they take a short break.

Dan sat back in his chair and let out a long sigh.

She caught that and smiled. "You're doing great," she encouraged him. "You're a natural at this."

Dan gave a weak smile. He was reasonably sure that she was lying about that, but he didn't have the heart to argue.

"And don't worry," she added. "I'll be right next to you for the whole call."

They stood up, and she asked if there was a restroom. Dan pointed her in the right direction, but he could only imagine what she would think of their facilities. At least he was reasonably sure that there would be toilet paper and paper towels. He stepped outside the office and chatted with Steve's assistant Sara. After the small talk, she asked him how things were going.

Dan just shook his head sadly. "Got me," he said. "I think I'm out of my league here."

Sara smiled at this. "You'll do great," she said. "If he gives you any trouble, just threaten to send Doris down there to straighten him out."

Dan chuckled, then stopped suddenly when Martina Guzman reappeared. "Who's Doris?" she asked.

Sara blushed and turned to focus on the screen of her computer.

"One of my colleagues up at the Summit Ranger Station," Dan explained. "Only dangerous when protecting her grandchildren."

Martina gave a tight smile. "Well, then I suggest we leave her out of this," she said, and led Dan back into Steve's office.

After another forty minutes, Martina Guzman finally called a halt.

"Do you think you have this?" she asked Dan. She seemed to imply that he should.

"Yeah," Dan admitted. "But this whole thing seems like a bit of a long shot. We don't really have any legal options here, unless he admits there really is a treasure hidden on government land, right?"

"Right," Martina agreed.

"And if I were him, I think I'd know that." Dan said.

"Oh, we're sure he knows that," the woman agreed. "And he's smart enough not to admit that."

"So this is all just kind of a charade," Dan said.

The attorney sat back in her chair and looked at Dan. "Think of it as sending a shot across his bow," she said. "You're right, we don't really have anything we can charge him with, but we can let him know that we are very concerned and are going to be looking very carefully at this situation."

"So I'm supposed to scare him with implied threats?" Dan asked, not liking the idea even a little bit.

"No," she assured him. "That's my job, and it may not even happen on this call. Your job is to make some kind of human contact with him and hope that he will be moved to help us without the threat of legal action."

"And if I'm not successful?" Dan asked.

"Then he's all mine," she said. And for the first time that morning, Dan thought there was an expression he hadn't seen on the face of Martina Guzman; a genuine smile.

<h1 style="text-align:center">chapter 11</h1>

Dan watched as Martina Guzman set up the Zoom call on her laptop. Once she had everything set, she got up and gave Dan her seat. She sat near him, just out of sight of the laptop's camera.

Dan waited until she indicated she was all set, then opened up the call. Within seconds the image of Matthew McLeod appeared on the screen—with a bushy red beard and mustache that covered most of his face, a plaid wool shirt and a Bass Pro Shop ball cap on his head.

"Good morning to you!" McLeod greeted him. Dan murmured something similar in response, and McLeod continued. "Your reputation precedes you, Mr. Courtwright. It's an honor to meet you."

"Good to meet you, too," Dan answered. "Before we start, can I ask your permission to record this? It's just to make keeping track of what we say easier."

"You are way ahead of me. I was going to suggest the same," McLeod answered.

Martina tapped the "record" icon and Dan waited for it to announce itself.

"To what do I owe this signal honor?" McLeod asked. "I understand that you would like to discuss my books. It would be a privilege to do so with someone who has achieved such fame, if not fortune." This last with just the tiniest hint of a smirk.

Dan was getting tired of the flowery talk already, and he could see Martina shifting in her chair.

"I was hoping to talk to you about the treasure you may have hidden in our National Forest," Dan said. "I think we'd like to get some clarity on that."

Ms. Guzman nodded her encouragement.

A huge grin lit up McLeod's face. "Hah!" he exploded. "So you believe it, too!"

Dan shook his head. "It doesn't really matter if I believe it," he replied. "I've only read one of the books. But a lot of other people believe it." Dan was happy to let the man believe he had finished Crevasse, which he hadn't.

"Good!" McLeod answered. "That means I've done my job."

Dan shook his head again. "Not good," he said. "We're getting swamped with people up here, and a lot of them don't have any idea what they're doing. We have some grave concerns. It's unsafe. One guy died."

McLeod's face became quite serious. "Mr. Courtwright, surely you can't hold me responsible for that. It's a sad fact that people die in the mountains every year, many of them because they are completely unprepared for the conditions. And they will continue to do so, whether I write books or not. Thoughts and prayers and all that."

Dan had to admit this was true. "Yes, but a lot of the people this year are specifically mentioning your books," he said. "And we'd like you to clarify exactly what's going on. If you have placed something, hidden something, in the National Forest, then you are required to notify us and receive permission."

"I understand," McLeod agreed. "But we're talking about my books, are we not?"

Dan nodded. "Yeah."

"Mr. Courtwright, I write fiction. You know what fiction is, don't you?" He paused here to wait for Dan to react. Dan tried hard not to do so. "It means I make it up. It's a product of my imagination. Just like it says in the beginning of every book. All the characters are fictional."

"But you base your books on reality," Dan countered. "You mention specific places in the Sierra."

"Ah! But which Sierra would that be, Mr. Courtwright?" McLeod replied. When the look on Dan's face conveyed confusion, McLeod continued. "There are many Sierras. You know this as well as I do. There is the Sierra of a topo map. But you and I both know sometimes that is not the experience we have on the trail. There's the Sierra of Bierstadt's paintings. But you and I both know that he saw things differently than you and I do. So which Sierra are we talking about here?"

"We're talking about the one where people read your books and then come up here and get into trouble," Dan said.

"But my books are fiction," McLeod reiterated. "They are only as real as the reader makes them. Let me give you an example. In one of my books, the characters meet at Silhouette Lake near Brown Bear Pass. Now, Mr. Courtwright, is there a Silhouette Lake in your Sierra?"

Dan shook his head. "No."

"And yet there is, in mine," McLeod continued. "And do you know what is strange about that? I have had quite a few readers tell me that they not only recognized Silhouette Lake, but that they had visited it on a backpacking trip."

Dan glanced over at Martina Guzman, who rolled her eyes but said nothing.

"So I ask you again, Mr. Courtwright. Which Sierra are we talking about?"

"The one where people die after reading your books," Dan said. He was getting angry.

A grimace flashed across the face of Matthew McLeod. "That's unfair, and you know it," he said. "People read the rules and regulations of the US Forest Service, and they die in the mountains, too. Are you having a similar conversation with the poor souls who write those regulations?"

"Those are written to try to keep people out of trouble, not get them into it," Dan said. He was pleased with that answer.

"And yet," McLeod was now holding up a single finger to the camera in front of his face. "And yet people read those and they still die in the mountains. Maybe the Forest Service should try to find better writers. Maybe they could find a writer who writes believable fiction about people, some of whom die in the mountains. Maybe that would be a better way to communicate the message."

Dan took a deep breath and let it out through his nose. "We would just like you to clarify if there is a hidden treasure or not. And if there is not, we would like you to make that clear. For safety's sake."

McLeod was smiling again and shaking his head. "In which Sierra, Mr. Courtwright? In the Sierra of my books, there is a Maxwell Lake in the Emigrant Wilderness. Should I clarify that such a lake does not exist, to keep people from dying if they try to find it?"

"I think five million dollars is a lot more interesting to most people than an imaginary lake," Dan said.

"Quite possibly," McLeod admitted. "But I defy you to point to one of my books and show me where I say there is a five-million-dollar treasure hidden in the Sierra."

"But there are hundreds, if not thousands of people who believe that you have done just that," Dan said. "Hidden in the text of the books you've written."

"And I should be punished for being a good writer?" McLeod asked. "Because people believe my stories? Because they are so captivated by my ideas that they bring their own analysis to them? There may be a treasure hidden in my Sierra, but that doesn't mean that there is one in yours, does it?"

"So it's just fiction?" Dan asked. "There is no treasure?"

McLeod took a moment to answer. "Mr. Courtwright, let me put this another way. You are a real person. I am sure if I went to the town where you were born, I would find a birth certificate with your name on it, and those of your parents. Isn't that right?" He paused here, and Dan shrugged, then nodded.

McLeod continued. "And I am sure that if I went to Humboldt State University and checked their records, I would find evidence that you attended that school, and received a degree from that institution. Is that correct?"

Dan nodded again, a little unsettled that McLeod knew where he had gone to school.

"And yet," McLeod continued. "I can assure you that there is no record of Jack Pulaski being born in Cody, Wyoming. There is no birth certificate for Jack Pulaski at all. There is no record of his military service. He doesn't exist, because, unlike you, he is fictional."

Martina Guzman was getting impatient. It was clear they were not going to be successful with this phone call.

"Now, what you need to understand is that people believe in Jack Pulaski," McLeod was still talking. "They know him better than they know many people in their own lives. They know where he lives, and what he likes to drink. They know how he got that scar over his right eye. In so many ways, he is very real to them. That's my job, and I'd like to think I do it well."

"And if they get into trouble, do they call Jack Pulaski for help?" Dan asked. "Because if they do, they are going to be disappointed. They might even be dead."

McLeod shook his head. "Not in Jack Pulaski's Sierra. Because in Jack Pulaski's Sierra, he would always make sure they got out. That's what Jack does."

Dan started shaking his head. "I don't think there is any reason to continue this," he said.

"Mr. Courtwright, you called me," McLeod replied. "You asked me questions, and I answered them as best I could. But you need to understand the fictional nature of what I do. I tell stories. I hope people believe those stories, because that's what good writing is."

Dan looked at Martina Guzman. She shook her head with disgust.

"We'll be in touch," Dan said. "I was hoping you might be willing to do something to help the situation. To keep people from dying up here. Clearly, you're not. I am going to have to leave it to people way above my pay grade now."

McLeod wouldn't let it go. "I understand, but I am not sure you understand, Mr. Courtwright. I know that you are a real person," he said. "But I don't think you realize that I am not. I am not real. There is no Matthew McLeod. It's a nom de plume. There is no birth certificate for Matthew McLeod. And Matthew McLeod didn't study creative writing at New Mexico State, any more than he studied forestry at Humboldt State. But without Matthew McLeod, Jack Pulaski wouldn't exist."

"So who are you?" Dan asked. "In real life."

Matthew McLeod leaned back and smiled. "I think we've covered this already," he said. "In your real life, or in mine?"

Dan shook his head in disgust. There was no way to deal with this guy. Dan was about to sign off when he remembered something. "One last question," he said. "Your books are in alphabetical order, all named for phenomena in the Sierra, except for the fourth one, Death Zone. That doesn't exist in the Sierra. It's only at much higher elevations, above twenty-some thousand feet."

The man posing as Matthew McLeod smiled. "That's in your Sierra, Mr. Courtright. But maybe not in mine."

Dan took a moment to consider this, then glanced at Ms. Guzman. "I guess we're done here," he said.

"So it would appear," McLeod replied.

They exchanged telephone numbers as a formality, and then, after a pause, McLeod added, "Do be kind enough to send me a link to the recording, if you would."

Dan nodded. "Yeah, I'll do that."

chapter 12

Martina Guzman closed down the window, and looked at Dan.

"That was a fucking waste of time," Dan said to her.

She tried to give him a smile, but her heart clearly wasn't in it. "You did fine," she said. "But he was ready for us."

"Yeah," Dan agreed. "He seemed to enjoy the whole thing quite a lot."

"It will probably appear as a fictional conversation in one of his books," Ms. Guzman admitted.

"So now what?" Dan asked her.

Now the smile came more easily to her face. "Now you're off the hook," she said. "Now we turn it over to my team and see if there isn't another way we can convince him to shut this down."

"Is there any legal way we can do that?" Dan asked.

Ms. Guzman shook her head. "Probably not," she said. "But that doesn't mean we can't make him uncomfortable enough that he might want to do something."

The way she said it made Dan grateful that she wasn't thinking the same thing about him.

After the Zoom call with McLeod, Dan left Sonora and drove up to get back to work at the Summit Ranger Station. It was a perfect sunny day, warm enough that he thought about rolling up the windows and turning on the air conditioning in his truck, cool enough that he left them down and let the mountain air blow through the cab, wafting in the scents of the forest.

He followed a string of four or five cars behind a guy pulling a boat, and allowed his mind to wander as they slowly wove their way through the curves of the highway. Even with the sun high overhead, there was plenty of shade from the towering pines along the road.

A huge logging truck came roaring past him in the other direction, and behind it he saw Steve Matson's vehicle. He gave a quick wave as Steve shot by, which Steve returned by raising a finger off the steering wheel. Dan guessed that Steve would get a full report from Martina Guzman.

Doris greeted him with a big smile when he walked in the door. "How did it go?" she asked expectantly.

Dan shook his head. "Not great," he said.

Her face fell. "Oh, rats. I was hoping we could put an end to this."

"Apparently not," Dan said. He was in no mood to relive the Zoom call.

Luckily, the phone rang just then, and Doris turned to answer it. By the time she had finished the call, there were three people at the counter, all wanting to ask questions. And Dan was happy to immerse himself in issuing permits and pointing out destinations on the topo map.

At least none of them mentioned Matthew McLeod by name.

The next day, for some reason, was better. Doris greeted him with a big smile, and immediately informed him that she had news from her grandson, Travis. Travis, now finishing up his first year at Cal Poly SLO, would be home in less than two weeks. It was enough to get Doris humming.

Dan had a full chart of trail work that needed to be scheduled for the summer, and only one of the three employees he needed to get the work done. He spent half of the day trying to make it all fit into the calendar, and then took another two hours to try to track down potential employees through the Byzantine federal hiring system, including a phone call to a nameless office in DC.

Just when he was ready to tell the HR bureaucrat on the other end of the line exactly what he could do with his phone, Doris tapped on the door to interrupt him. Dan hung up abruptly and looked at her.

She gave him a shrug. "A Bruce Spielman is on the phone for you?" Her eyebrows shot up as if to say, "Is that someone you know?"

Dan slumped in his chair. Bruce was his sister's ex-husband. One of a number of mistakes she had made in her life. Dan knew that Bruce never called without needing something that he thought Dan should be able to provide. He nodded to Doris and punched the button for the other line.

"Bruce!" he said cheerily. "What's up with you?"

"Hey, Dan," Bruce said. "How're you doing?"

Dan assured him he was fine.

"Got a minute?" Bruce asked.

If there was one thing to be said in Bruce's defense, it was that he did like to get to the point. Dan told him to go ahead.

"Well, I guess you know about Matthew McLeod and the treasure," Bruce began.

"Oh, yeah," Dan assured him.

"Well, I think I've figured some of it out." Bruce explained. "It's a kind of code in the books, but I think I've got a pretty good idea of how it works."

"Cool," Dan said, making no effort to hide his lack of

enthusiasm.

"Yeah, so I think I know how to figure this stuff out," Bruce continued. "The only thing is, I don't know the mountains. Or at least, I don't know them well enough."

Dan waited. He was not going to make this any easier for Bruce.

"So I've got most of this code figured out, but I was wondering if you could help me a bit with the geography part," Bruce continued.

Dan stayed silent.

"I mean, I'd share a part of the money with you, Dan," Bruce said. "That goes without saying."

"I appreciate the offer, Bruce," Dan said. "But I don't think I'm interested."

"Oh, come on, Dan!" Bruce argued. "You're a natural at this stuff. You're great at it. And I've got most of it worked out."

"Yeah, I just don't think that's the way I want to spend my time, Bruce," Dan explained.

"Look, I'm not asking for a lot of time," Bruce began to plead. "I just need a few pointers on the geography."

"Nah," Dan said. "I think you're going to have to find somebody else to help."

"Okay, wait." Bruce was begging now. "I just need one thing right now. Just one thing." He paused.

Dan waited in silence.

"Okay," Bruce continued. "What place in the Sierras shares a name with a president?"

Dan closed his eyes and gave an audible sigh. He let the silence linger, then began. "Kennedy. There are two Kennedy Meadows." He thought some more. "And a Roosevelt Lake. Wait, two of those, too."

Bruce was silent. Dan thought he was probably writing this all down.

"And there is probably a Lincoln somewhere, but I can't seem to remember where right now."

"No, that's okay," Bruce assured him. "But you're sure there are two Kennedys and two Roosevelts?"

"Yep," Dan said. "One Kennedy Meadows up here on the way to Sonora Pass, and another one down by Mt. Whitney." He waited while Bruce thought this over.

"And two Roosevelts?" Bruce asked.

"One right over the pass here, and another one in Yosemite," Dan said.

"Shit," Bruce said.

Dan smiled. "Sorry, but you asked."

He could hear the disappointment in Bruce's voice. "Yeah, no. Sorry, Dan. I mean, thanks."

Dan could almost hear the wheels spinning in Bruce's head. It wasn't a sensation he enjoyed.

"Wait, weren't there two Roosevelt presidents?" he asked.

"Yeah," Dan agreed. "Teddy and FDR."

"But only one of them died in office, right?"

"FDR," Dan answered. "And no, I don't know if the lakes were named for Teddy or FDR."

"No, that's okay, Dan." Bruce seemed to have come back to life. "I think I can check that out, online or something."

"Is that all you need?" Dan asked.

"Uh, well, yeah. Thanks, Dan. I can take it from here, I think." He paused. "Oh, wait. One more thing. What's a lollipop?"

Dan waited.

"I mean, I know what a lollipop is," Bruce continued. "But what's a lollipop in the mountains?"

"Some people call a trail that goes out for a few miles, then takes a loop, and then follows the first trail back again a lollipop, because it makes the shape of a lollipop on the map," Dan said.

"Oh, man, that's perfect," Bruce said. "That's a huge help. I guess there are lots of those?"

"You can pretty much make them up as you go, anywhere you want," Dan said.

"Yeah, that's what I figured," Bruce said. "This is great, Dan. And I promise, I'll share the money."

"Great," Dan said woodenly. "Glad I could help."

"No, this is great, Dan," Bruce was now fully enthusiastic. "Really great. I mean it. And if I find the treasure I'll make sure you get your share. I mean it."

Dan smiled sadly. "Talk to you later, Bruce." As he hung up the receiver, he could still hear Bruce thanking him. Dan stared at the phone for a moment, then got up from his chair and walked out to see how Doris was doing.

She was talking to a couple of young men about permits. And he heard them asking her something about presidents.

Dan turned around and walked back into his office. He flicked on the computer screen and stared, one more time, at the chart of trail work that needed attention. The day had taken a definite turn for the worse. Maybe he could find a little respite in the list of trail projects.

chapter 13

On Friday morning, Dan heard Kristen calling to him as he was showering. He took a quick rinse in the hot water and turned off the shower.

"Are you talking to me?" he asked.

She stuck her head in the bathroom door to remind him that she was expecting Ruth and Maggie to come over after dinner to discuss the Matthew McLeod books they had read.

When Dan took the towel and started drying off, she waited until he looked back up at her.

"Nice," she said appreciatively, and then walked out, leaving the door open.

Dan finished drying off and followed her into the kitchen.

"You're welcome to join us," she suggested. "But you might want to wear more than that tonight."

Dan re-wrapped the towel around his waist and got himself a bowl of granola. "Have you figured anything out yet?" he asked.

"Not really." Kristen didn't seem concerned. "Ruth said she has been doing some research online and has some things for us to think about."

Dan, his mouth full of cereal, shook his head dismissively.

Kristen caught the motion and held a hand up. "I know you think it's all a waste of time," she said. "But Ruth and Maggie are really having fun with it. And I am having fun with the two of them. They are really fun. Think of it as entertainment. Better than a movie."

Dan held his hands up in surrender. "I can't argue with that," he said. "What time are they coming over?"

"Around seven, so we'll have to eat a bit early tonight."

"Fine with me," Dan assured her.

"I haven't finished my book yet," Kristen said. "Maybe we'll just get a pizza?"

"Also fine with me," Dan agreed.

"Have you finished your book?" she asked.

"I'm working on it. I'm maybe halfway through it."

"Well, if you want to hear what Ruth has found out, you can certainly listen in," Kristen said. "I know they wouldn't mind."

Dan nodded and took a healthy swallow of his orange juice. "Thanks," he said, "I might. Or maybe I'll just wait and get your summary later."

"Don't count on me to remember it all," Kristen warned him. "You're better off just talking to Ruth."

But Dan had forgotten about this conversation by the time he got home that evening. After a day filled with phone calls and emails from what seemed like half the population of the American West, he was sick and tired of Matthew McLeod. The last thing he wanted to do was to talk about Jack Pulaski and the treasure in the Sierra Nevada. He was still angry about the Zoom meeting with the guy Monday morning.

It was the pizza that reminded him. That, and the fact that Kristen had tidied up the living room and moved all of his gear into the spare bedroom. He wolfed down his pizza, helped Kristen clean up the kitchen, and was just reaching up to put the two wine glasses into the cabinet when he heard a knock on the front door.

"Come on in!" Kristen called out.

Dan put the glasses away and turned to see Ruth and Maggie walk in the door.

While Kristen greeted them, Ruth looked over Kristen's shoulder and saw Dan heading down the hall to the bedroom.

"Looking for a place to hide, Dan?" she called out with a laugh.

Which stopped him, and he turned around and assured them all that he was not looking for a place to hide.

"Oh, good," Maggie said. "Cal refuses to even listen to me about this stuff. I'm so glad that you and Kristen are working on it together."

Kristen gave him a sweet smile and gestured to the sofa in the living room. "We can all sit in here," she said.

"Which book are you reading?" Ruth asked him.

"Crevasse," Dan told her.

"Oh, good. That means we've covered all of the first four," Ruth said. "We're almost halfway through."

Kristen caught Dan's eye and grinned. "So is Dan," she said.

"No matter," Ruth said. "We've got a good start going. Now, who wants to start?"

The other three quickly avoided her gaze.

"Haven't you been doing some research and stuff?" Maggie asked. "Maybe it would be best to start with that."

Ruth looked around the group and found that they all seemed to be in agreement.

"Fine," she said, "but before we get into that, did anyone notice an obvious pattern in these books?" She waited for the others to answer.

Nobody did.

"Well, it's pretty obvious to me," she continued. "From what I read in my book, and what I saw online, they are all simply rehashing the old Hercules/Heracles myth of the ancient Greeks."

She looked up triumphantly to see the others seemingly lost in the woods.

"Heracles!" she repeated. "The Greek warrior hero! Eats more than any man. Drinks more than any man. Has more women, well, and maybe a boy or two, than any man. And is the biggest, meanest, toughest, nastiest fighter of them all. And by succeeding at seemingly impossible tasks, he earns immortality."

"Herculean tasks," Kristen added. Dan noted she seemed happy about that.

Maggie was nodding. "That sure is how he comes across in this one," she said, holding up Avalanche.

"He's that way in all of them," Ruth insisted. "It's a classic, and I do mean classic, formula."

Ruth looked around expectantly. "What else?" she asked.

Dan knew he was in way over his head, and kept his mouth shut.

"Is Hercules always so sure of himself?" Kristen asked, holding up Bergschrund. "I mean, in this one he gets all sorts of expert advice, and then ignores it and goes off his gut instead. It's like he's trying to prove everyone else is wrong."

"Ha!" Ruth was almost shouting. "Pure Emerson. 'Truth comes from within, and not from listening to the majority of people.'"

"Are you taking notes, Dan?" Kristen asked him, her eyes smiling.

Dan shook his head. "No, but I'm listening."

"He had a Zoom call with the author on Monday," Kristen explained to Ruth and Maggie.

Ruth snorted. "Well, I wouldn't mention any of this to him," she said. "This stuff is all straight out of formulaic Hollywood, as far as

I can see. Of course, maybe that's his point. Write books that read like movies, and maybe they'll make a movie out of one of them. Although you'd never get me to see it."

"Ruth, I had no idea you knew so much about this,'" Maggie said.

"Pffft," Ruth dismissed her. "I used to teach English. This is high school stuff—freshman year high school stuff."

Dan certainly couldn't remember much from his high school English class, and from the looks on their faces, neither could Kristen or Maggie.

"Enough of that," Ruth called them to attention. "Let's take a look at these different systems I got off the internet."

She laid out a few sheets of paper on top of the old chest that Dan used for a coffee table. "There are at least four different systems people are using to come up with solutions to the riddles," she said. "It might be best if we tried to just lay everything out in some kind of a grid, and see which ones make the most sense."

chapter 14

The email to Dan from Steve was short and to the point. "You've probably heard about the new archeological dig down in the canyon," he wrote. "We've had a couple of complaints about it, mainly impacts on the ecosystem and hunters worried about scaring the wildlife. Why don't you take a hike down there on Sunday, and just see how things are going?"

It was the kind of invitation that Dan couldn't resist, especially since it was the dig Walt had been working on. Anything was better than spending another day in the ranger station, listening to people try to pick his and Doris' brains about the famous hidden treasure of Matthew McLeod.

The sad thing was that there were still quite a few hikers who had not heard about it all, and who were there because they simply wanted a backpacking permit. He felt sorry for them as they had to wait in long lines of people who were sure that everyone else was trying to steal their ideas on where the treasure truly lay. Dan noticed a couple of groups who simply bailed off the back end and went hiking. And he didn't have it in his heart to try to stop them.

Sunday morning, he was up before it was fully light, leaving Kristen sleeping softly in their bed. He ate a quick breakfast of granola and juice, grabbed a daypack and some snacks, and was out the door before she stirred.

The old logging road into the canyon was not in the best

condition after the winter, and there were a few places where Dan had to pick his way along, carefully edging along on the high side, while keeping his SUV from getting stranded in the ruts. It had been a wet winter, and the roads had suffered. He drove a good three miles down, before coming to a section that was both steep and muddy.

Dan stopped the SUV and got out to look. The rains had eroded deep ruts in the road, and the combination of red clay and sand was more clay than sand. He tested his footing on the stuff, slipped a little, and decided that he could probably get his vehicle down it without problems. And he also guessed that he wouldn't be able to climb back out until at least a couple of weeks later, when the soil dried out more.

He got in the SUV, slowly backed up about seventy-five feet, wheels slipping, and found a place where he could park next to a blue pickup truck with a UC Merced parking permit on the bumper. He hoisted his daypack, locked up the SUV, and started down the road, carefully picking his way to avoid the worst of the clay.

As he hiked down, he noted what looked like ATV tracks in the mud, and guessed that was how some of the people got down to the dig. There were also footprints here—sometimes showing him the best path down, sometimes showing where someone had slipped. Those were mingled with deer tracks and those made by either somebody's dog or a coyote.

The sun was out, sparkling clean in the warmth of spring. Overhead, a few towering sugar pines had dropped their massive cones, littering the floor with them. He knew Kristen would have wanted to collect a couple to put on their dining room table as a centerpiece and decided that he would pick some up on his way out. He was sure he would remember.

Down below in the canyon, he could hear the river roaring in spring run-off. And maybe those were voices? Maybe it was just the water. He wasn't sure how much farther he had to hike, but he guessed it wouldn't be more than a couple of miles.

The abandoned road zigzagged through a series of tight switchbacks, each one steeper than the last. Dan knew his SUV could never have made it down here anyway. And then the road turned straight downhill. Now it was less a road, more a rocky streambed, muddy in spots, with ruts that were two and even three feet deep. Dan could see where the ATVs had tried to climb one side of the road, chewing up the mud with their knobby tires. It would have taken a cool hand to drive down this, with the ATV tilted at a crazy angle.

And there was poison oak. It was just beginning to leaf out, bright and green, but Dan recognized the familiar glossy leaves and the three-leaf pattern. He made sure to give that a wide berth.

Now he could see the river, roaring white in sections, with some deep green pools in between. The road ran along the river for another quarter of a mile, a hundred yards up the side of the canyon. And then Dan came to the last switchbacks and saw the camp below him.

It was the usual flower bed of bright tents, blooming in between the trees and large boulders of the canyon. From what Dan could see, there wasn't a lot of flat space left, if anyone wanted to join them. And off to the right, out in the sunlight, he could see people working, walking around the yellow tape lines of the dig's grid.

His attention on the dig, he slipped and nearly fell on a particularly slick section of road. He jerked himself upright and surprised himself by not ending up on his ass. Still, and he wasn't sure, but he hoped he hadn't hurt something in his back.

Dan gingerly stepped off the end of the road and walked through the camp. It wasn't perfect. He would have liked to see better food storage to keep the bears at bay, but it didn't seem to be the kind of problem that would encourage others to complain. Dan walked out to join the crew in the meadow.

Dan saw Walt, standing off to one side with a young woman in a khaki outfit and a big floppy khaki hat, and he walked over to say hello.

They had their backs to him, and Dan was within ten feet before he called out. "Hi, guys. How's it going?"

Walt turned, and his face lit up when he saw it was Dan. "Well, well. Look who's here!"

Dan grinned and shook his hand. Walt looked good. He was wearing an Indiana Jones-style hat that looked ancient. He was enjoying himself, and it showed.

"Dan Courtwright, I'd like you to meet Dr. Erica Fisher."

Dan shook her hand and noted the hard calluses. This was a woman who was accustomed to using a shovel.

The two men loomed over Erica—she couldn't have been more than about five foot five, Dan guessed. And her loose khaki outfit left most of her shape to the imagination, but judging from her belt line, she carried more than average weight. From beneath her huge hat a big smile sent creases across her face, and her freckled skin and blue eyes helped explain the minimal amount of skin she left exposed. Dan guessed she was younger than he was, but not by much. Maybe in her early thirties.

"Welcome to the dig," Erica said. "What brings you out here? Not that we aren't happy to see you, but I didn't think we'd get an official visit so soon."

"Just thought I'd check in with you and see how you are doing," Dan said. He was looking around at the dig, taking note of a small group of workers who had now stopped what they were doing to look at him.

"Sure," Erica said. "Want the tour? There's not much to see yet, but we're making progress."

Dan didn't want to interrupt the work, but she seemed genuinely glad to show him around. "Sure, that would be great."

She left Walt with a clipboard and shovel, and started walking around the meadow. "We've laid the gridlines out, and we've done some basic scoping with metal detectors and the beast."

Dan gave her a quizzical look.

"Ground radar," she said. "Actually, the hardest part was getting it down here." She pointed to a machine a little larger than a lawn mower under a nearby oak tree. "The real bitch is going to be getting it back out again."

She walked him over to the edge of the grid. "You can see the cobbles over there," she said, pointing to an area closer to the river. "That's mining tailings from when they worked the river."

Dan blew out a lungful of air. "Man, that looks like hard work."

Beneath her hat, Erica smiled. "And now we get to do it all over again."

Except for Walt, everyone else on the dig seemed to be under thirty. Some looked like teenagers, but then Dan realized that college kids these days were likely to be about half his age. It made him suddenly feel much older.

One of them called out to Erica. "Can you take a look at this?" He was on his knees, working the edge of the new trench.

Dan joined Erica as she walked over to look at what the young man held up in his hand. Erica peered at it carefully.

"Bone," she said. "Could be human. Bag it and tag it."

The young man gave her a smile. "Thanks!"

Erica tapped him on the shoulder and gave him a grin.

chapter 15

Erica turned to Dan. "We're really just getting started here," she said. After showing Dan the grid and the first few tentative trenches on one side of the meadow, the tour finished up back at the camp. "And this is our home away from home," Erica said. "The Stanislaus Luxury Suites."

Dan looked around. From what he could see, there were no real issues with the camp. He asked to see the latrine, which was well away from the river up above the camp, and made a few suggestions about storing their food. Erica noted them down, and called over a couple of the students and explained his concerns.

They immediately began cleaning up the campsite, and one started rigging a line to hang more of their food.

"Got time for lunch?" Erica asked him. "I'm buying."

Dan laughed. "Sure, if you have enough, I'd love it. What's on the menu?"

Erica walked over to a large plastic bin and opened it. "Take your pick," she said. "We have just about every kind of energy bar, about six different kinds of chips, and more dried fruit than you can possibly eat."

"Looks like a backpacking menu," Dan grinned.

Erica shot a look at him. "Have you seen that road?" she asked. "Anything we eat has to come down that. And the less traffic we put on it, the better."

Dan selected a couple of energy bars and a bag of chips, and pulled out his water bottle from his daypack. He joined the rest of the group at what Erica called their dining room, a small clearing underneath a large live oak. Some of the branches were low enough to the ground to serve as benches. A few folding chairs rounded out the seating.

Dan turned to Walt and asked him if they had found anything interesting yet. He noted that Walt checked with Erica before answering.

"A few things from what looks like might have been a mining camp," Walt said. "Mostly bits of old metal. A couple of cans. Part of a shovel."

"A few old handmade nails," a young man added from across the way. The conversation went around the lunch group, each student making a self-introduction.

One of the young girls on the team had a small tattoo on her face and a nose piercing, and was sitting across from Dan. She smiled at him and said, "I'm Florence. When I first saw you, I thought you were another one of those treasure guys."

Before lunch was over, Dan learned that there had been at least four people who had walked down to the dig in the search for treasure. And he promised to try to discourage any more who asked for permits for this area in the future. If they asked. Because it wasn't a wilderness area, no permits were required.

"It's not really a problem," Erica said. "At least, not right now. But it could get to be a distraction, and you never like having lots of people traipsing through your dig."

But Florence said it more succinctly. "One of the guys was an asshole," she said. "They're such losers." Then she stood up and walked back out of the shade and into the sunlight of the dig.

Dan looked at Erica. "The kids didn't appreciate that he arrived well-armed," she said. "Assault rifle over his shoulder. But he just looked around and left." She stood up as if to say that it was time for her to get back to work.

Dan stood up as well, stretched, and took a look around the canyon. The trail back up to his SUV was going to be steep and hot. The nearby river was in full spring flow, rushing and roaring, sending a fine icy mist into the air where it raced over boulders and through white water.

He had never explored this part of the canyon. And he had all day. Down river, he could see a series of rapids and pools before the river turned the bend. He went down to the edge of the river, found a quiet spot, filtered two bottles of water, and slipped them into his day pack.

With a wave to Walt and Erica, he started walking down the canyon beside the river, picking his way over the river-rounded rocks and through the alders along the canyon floor.

It was hot out in the sun, and the light glared off the white granite of the cobbles of the river. Dan aimed for a spot further downstream where there were a few trees for shade, and picked his way along.

The river continued to rush past him on the right, the power of the water like a liquid steamroller, filling in the holes, crashing over the rocks, and carrying branches and small trees on its back. At times Dan thought he could almost feel the vibrations of the water through his feet, a steady thrum that was hidden by the splashing of the surface.

The river turned now, and Dan was up against a steep wall of black granite on his side. Across the way, the river had left a wide swath of rocks and sand on the inside of the curve. Later in the summer, it would have been possible to get across, maybe even rock hop there, and continue down on that side. But not now, not with this kind of flow.

He turned uphill and worked his way up a small tributary creek, trying to follow what might have been a deer trail. It got him up above the steepest part of the granite; then he peeled off and looked for a route to follow downstream, now higher above the river.

It occurred to him that the logging road was probably only a few hundred feet higher, but he chose to stay below it, sometimes scrambling over a downed tree, other times pushing through the branches of manzanita. At one point he stopped in front of a poison oak bush and backed up to locate a new way forward.

Sure enough, he was able to get back out onto the top of the granite wall and could see the river below him. When he looked upstream, he could see the archeological dig, looking much smaller and less important now. He turned his back on it and followed a granite ledge until it petered out, then found another one and was soon slowly navigating through rocks and brush to another small creek that led back down to the river.

When he got there, he called a halt and sat down on a large boulder in the shade of another big oak. He pulled out a water bottle and took a swig, his teeth hurting slightly from the intense cold of the water that had been snow only hours before.

A quick glance at his watch told him that he had left Walt and Erica only thirty minutes before, but the sense of solitude was overpowering. He was alone; the river surging by him helped underscore how hard it would be to get anywhere in a hurry down here. And how hard it would be for him to hear if anyone called for help.

Now past the black cliffs, the canyon led him onwards with the promise of relatively flat terrain for the next few hundred yards.

He wound his way around alder thickets, wondering if they might be cover for a bear. The deer would be higher up, in the shade now, waiting for cooler temperatures.

His mind went back to what the young woman had said—that the treasure hunters were losers. He thought about them coming down to this canyon, and what they might find. And that reminded him of Matthew McLeod. The memory smacked him like a nasty shock. He pushed the thought away.

He could see across the river, where the canyon walls stretched up into the intense blue sky. At the bottom, near the river, the trees were a dense blend of oak and pine, but higher up the pines took over, with only a few granite knobs sticking out to challenge them.

Dan continued down river, working his way back and forth between the open rocks of the canyon bottom and the shadier slopes of the trees just above it. The next granite wall loomed in front of him, and here the river narrowed, forcing the water into a churning mass of white chaos in a tight gorge.

Dan picked his way up the side of the gorge, using the fault lines and ledges of the granite to stay above the water. There were massive manzanita bushes here, glowing in the sunlight, their trunks a deep blood red. Some of them were ancient, maybe a hundred years old.

Dan began to descend again, to get closer to the river, and found himself once again on granite ledges. There was enough mist in the air to make the rock slightly wet, and he became intensely aware of the danger of slipping here. Falling into that mass of foam would be fatal, and he began to test each step, even while he leaned over to add his hands to the effort.

Ahead of him he saw that the ledge ran out, from six inches to two inches, to nothing.

Dan stopped and looked around. There was no easy way up or down. He would have to back up. He checked his watch and saw that it would probably be after four o'clock by the time he got home. That was if he turned around right then.

He eased himself back along the ledge until it was wide enough to turn around easily, then sat down, his feet on the ledge, his butt on the granite slope above it. He slipped off his pack and set it on the rock next to him. He took a deep breath and looked around.

Far above him in the canyon, he could see a hawk soaring overhead. His eyes followed the canyon down, the river showing deep dark green in the pools in the shade, and searing white with the rapids in the sunshine. Downstream, beyond the gorge, he could see that the canyon opened up again. Miles further along, he knew this monster of a river lost its momentum and faded into a massive reservoir, complete with houseboats, bathing suits, and vacationers on jet skis.

But here it was unadulterated power, driving itself inexorably down the canyon. In the white water of the gorge, he could see the trunk of an enormous tree, wedged against huge boulders, trapped there in the current. It was impressive to think of the power it had taken to carry it there, and then trap it forever.

A tiny movement in the trees across the river caught Dan's attention, and he froze. A fisher, the size of a cat but somehow more sinuous, crept out from the trees and stared into the water. Dan had never seen one in the wild before.

It paid no attention to him. It was only focused on the water and what might be in it. It gently padded up the gorge to inspect the pool above.

Dan smiled, and somehow the fisher sensed him. It stopped still, slowly turning its head to look across the river. Dan stayed motionless, but the fisher was not fooled. It met his gaze for a moment, considered the chances of Dan getting across the river, and then continued on its way, loping down to inspect the pool.

Dan took that as his signal to get up and get moving. He slipped his pack back on and walked back up the canyon toward the dig.

When he got to the first tributary creek, he decided to bushwhack uphill to the road, making sure that he gave one thicket of poison oak a wide berth. He could see where the road ran. It was a clear gash in the forest, but the last forty feet up to the graded surface was a steep and slippery gauntlet. He was gasping for breath by the time he took his last few frenetic steps off the incline and landed on the road.

He paused there for a minute, catching his breath, and smiling. It had been only a few hours, but the adventure into the canyon had cleared his mind and refreshed his soul.

The road seemed even steeper on the way back up out of the canyon, and Dan had plenty of time to think about what he would say to Matthew McLeod if he ever spoke to him again. That's when he wasn't thinking about where to put his feet, or how hard he was breathing.

When he got back to his SUV, he had forgotten the sugar-pine cones for Kristen.

chapter 16

Back within cell range, Dan's phone beeped to indicate a missed call, but he was not expecting to hear that it was a message from the Stockton Police Department. An officer there wanted Dan to call him back.

Dan waited until he was sure he had consistent cell coverage, and then dialed the number.

"Gregory," a serious masculine voice answered his call.

Dan identified himself and explained that he was returning a phone call.

"Got it," Gregory agreed. "Give me a minute to get my notes."

While Dan waited, he could hear fingers clicking on a keyboard.

"Here we go," Gregory announced. "Mr. Courtwright, what can you tell me about Nathan Petrovski?"

Dan ran a quick check through his memory. "Sorry," he said. "I don't think I know him."

"Are you sure about that?" Gregory pressed him.

Dan thought some more. "Is he a hiker? Is he missing? We've sure had enough of those."

"Not a hiker," the policeman answered. "At least, I don't think so. But yes, he's missing. Are you sure you don't know him?"

"Nope," Dan said. "Doesn't ring a bell."

"That's strange," Gregory said. "Because we found your name on his calendar just last week."

"Last week?" Dan repeated. "Nope. Sorry. Did he come up to Summit and talk to someone there?"

"We're not exactly sure," Gregory said. "We were hoping you might be able to shed some light on it."

"Sorry," Dan said. "I don't think I can help you."

Gregory was not going to let Dan go. "Maybe you can tell me where you were on Monday?" he asked Dan.

"At work," Dan said. "In Sonora and then the Summit Ranger Station."

"And you can verify that," Gregory asked. "Were there other people there?"

Dan chuckled. "Oh yeah, plenty of those," he assured the policeman. And then, with a note of incredulity he asked, "Do I need an alibi?"

Gregory didn't answer right away. And as Dan waited, an awful realization came to him.

"Wait a minute," Dan said. "Monday?"

Again, Gregory didn't help him with a response.

"I did have a phone call Monday," Dan explained. "With an attorney from the Forest Service and a guy by the name of Matthew McLeod. He writes mystery novels."

"This isn't a joke, Courtwright," Gregory scolded him.

"I'm not joking," Dan explained. "A writer named Matthew McLeod."

"And this was on Monday," Gregory asked.

"Yeah, you can check it out with Martina Guzman. She's an attorney with the Forest Service and was the legal counsel on the call with us. She'll even have a recording of the call."

"Okay, well, thank you for that," Gregory said. "Can you get me Ms. Guzman's contact info? I'll need to check that out."

Dan agreed to text it to him once they got off the phone. "Do you want me to check our permits to see if we issued him a permit?" Dan asked.

"Sure, that would be great," Gregory said. "At least we could check that box. But I don't think he's hiking."

"Why is that?" Dan asked.

"He didn't take his car keys or his wallet," Gregory explained. "He seems to have vanished. Do me a favor. If, for any reason, you do hear from him, would you give me a call?"

Dan agreed. And his opinion of Matthew McLeod took one more turn toward the bottom.

When he got home that evening, Kristen had rearranged the furniture in the main room, and Dan noticed a stack of books on a table near one end of the sofa.

"Ruth and Maggie are coming over after dinner," Kristen called out to him. "You can join us if you want."

Dan told her about the call from the Stockton detective.

"That's weird," she said. "Do you think it's the same guy?"

Dan shrugged. "I don't know, but I guess it could be."

"And now he's disappeared?" Kristen's eyes met Dan's. "Seems pretty suspicious to me. I bet he just took to the hills after you talked to him."

Dan chuckled and walked over to her and put his arms around her. "That's it?" he asked. "One word from me and he goes underground?"

"He disappears, just like the treasure," Kristen said. "If it even exists."

"Who knows," Dan answered with a light shrug of his shoulders. "And I don't know what we can do about it. I guess I should call

Steve."

"What if it is the same guy? Then what?" Kristen asked.

"No idea," Dan admitted. "I'll let Steve make that call."

Steve Matson wasn't happy to get Dan's call.

"All supposition right now," he said to Dan. "Thanks for letting me know, but I think we wait for Stockton PD to figure out what exactly they've got. In the meantime, we still have way too many people running up here without any idea of what they're doing."

"Without McLeod, or whoever he is, I don't see any way to stop that," Dan said.

"Well, there's one way to put an end to it," his boss replied. "Find the damn treasure, and everybody will go home."

"If there is one," Dan replied.

"If there is one," Matson agreed.

Dan hung up the phone and turned to Kristen.

"I guess you heard that?" he asked her.

She nodded. "Do you really think there is five million up there?" she asked him.

"I have no idea," Dan said. "And frankly, I don't want to think about it, either."

They had just finished dinner when they saw Maggie and Ruth walking up to the front door.

"Oh, hell, they're already here," Kristen moaned.

Dan jumped up to let them in, and Kristen quickly shared Dan's conversation with the Stockton Police Department.

Ruth's face furrowed into a frown, and she looked at Dan. "So the heat is on," she said. "We need to get to work."

As Dan prepared to drift into the back of the house, Ruth grabbed his sleeve. "Now Dan, this is girls only tonight," she said.

"But under the circumstances, I think we can consider you an honorary girl. We need you."

Dan shook his head and tried to pull his arm away, but Ruth wasn't letting go.

"Maggie, help me out here," Ruth said.

While Kristen watched in sympathy, Maggie explained that they now needed to be even more determined to solve the hidden treasure puzzle. "Cal is being a pain in the patootie," she said. "He won't even talk about it or read any of the books. But I think we can work this out. Only we could really use your help, Dan."

Dan tried hard not to react.

"Just in some of the place names and things," Maggie continued, "That's all. You just know these mountains better than anyone."

Dan's will was wavering. The women were not backing down.

Ruth still held him by one arm, but with the other she held up a paper bag. "This should seal the deal," she said. "I've got cookies."

Dan burst out laughing, gave a shrug of surrender and allowed himself to be led back to the sofa.

"Now," Maggie said with great seriousness. She pulled out a stack of papers from her purse and set them on the table. "I've got all our notes here, organized by each book. We just need to work out a plan on how to get started."

Ruth gave a quick glance around at the other three. Then she gave a pointed look at Dan. "Girls," she said, pointedly, "here's what we need to do."

chapter 17

Dan sat down on the end of the sofa and listened to them explain what they had learned. He looked around at the three of them. Ruth leaned in, intensely focused. Maggie sat further back, but held a stack of papers in her hands, and thumbed through them, looking for something. Kristen gave him a quick glance, then turned her attention to Maggie.

"I've spent hours on the internet on this," Maggie said. "There are quite a few groups that are posting things, but I think only a couple of them are really making any progress. Or at least, are sharing their progress. It's a lot of the same stuff, over and over."

"Of course," Ruth cautioned, "that's if they were telling the truth, and not trying to send us on a wild goose chase. I don't think we should post what we find." She looked around at the others, who seemed to agree.

"I thought of that. I tried to track each theory against what I could find in the books," Maggie said. "So I was able to eliminate some of them that were obviously off base."

"Did anyone else notice that there are chapters that don't really have anything to do with the plot in their books?" Ruth asked. "It's like the Cetology chapter in Moby Dick."

When the others looked at her in confusion, she explained. "There was one chapter in Moby Dick that went on and on about whales. It was something that really didn't have a role in the story.

Melville wrote an entire chapter about whales in Moby Dick."

"And in your book, what was it?" Maggie asked.

"Rocks," Ruth said with disgust. "It was about geology. Not even geology. It was about the number of places in the Sierra that are named for rocks."

"There must be a million of those," Kristen said. She looked at Dan.

Maybe that was his cue. "Granite Lake, right up the road here," he said. "And there are Granite Domes and Red Slate Mountain, Andesite Peak. Yeah, there are a lot of those."

Kristen was leafing through one of the books. She stopped and read for a moment. "Okay. In this one there is a section on how places are named for where the early settlers or miners came from," she said. "It's a whole history of places named for states."

"Virginia City!" Ruth exclaimed.

"Or Nevada City," Kristen reminded her.

They both turned to look at Dan. He shrugged. "There are the Alabama Hills, down on the east side," he said. "And maybe Washington Column? That's a rock formation in Yosemite. But I'd guess it was named for the president, not the state."

"Oh, that's good," Maggie was writing all of this down. "You know what? I think we're onto something here."

"I'm sure there are some mining areas in the foothills named for the states the miners came from," Dan said. "But I can't think of any right now."

"Okay," Maggie agreed. "We'll check that out." She made more notes on one of the pages she was holding.

Kristen had moved on to a second book. "In this one there's a chapter on the age of inventions, and how they changed the world," Kristen said. "It doesn't seem to have much to do with the rest of the plot."

This time the three women were quiet. One by one, they turned to Dan.

"Lake Thomas Edison?" he suggested. "And I guess you could include Whitney—although it wasn't named for the inventor. But it's the same name. And there are 'Bells' around, like Alexander Graham."

Maggie stared at Dan. "So there are fewer of those?" she asked intently.

Dan nodded. "Seems like it."

"Okay, that's good. Maybe we should start there," Ruth suggested. "My books were a lot more complicated. But that's why I mentioned it. I noticed the same thing in mine. One of the chapters was about girls' names. I could think of a bunch just on my own: Mary, Dorothy, May."

Dan smiled. "Yeah, there are a lot of those up by Dorothy, too. Stella, Marie. And in Desolation Wilderness there are a bunch, too: Velma, Suzie, Gertrude, Maud. And I guess the most famous is Florence Lake down further south. Lots of those places."

Maggie let out a deep sigh and started writing. "Give me a second here," she begged. When she was done, she looked up. "Okay, let's put that one on the back burner for a while. What else do we have?" She looked at Ruth.

Dan chose this moment to tell them about his conversation with Bruce Spielman, and the list of presidents who had died in office.

Maggie had now filled out two sheets of paper and was looking a bit overwhelmed. "Slow down," she said.

"Did you get the girls' names?" Kristen asked.

Maggie gave another long sigh and filled out another sheet of paper. The rest waited patiently for her to finish up. When she was done, she looked up expectantly.

"It's your turn," Ruth said to her. "What was in your books?"

Maggie held up the book. "Indian tribes," she said. "There are a ton of those."

"Miwok," Ruth suggested.

"And Paiute," Dan added. "Lots of those up and down the Sierra. Chowchilla's another one. What about Washo?"

"Okay," Maggie said. She was looking down at her notes now. Her face formed a frown. "And in this one there was a chapter about Satan and the devil."

The room was silent. Then Ruth shouted, "Devil's Postpile!"

The others congratulated her.

"Devil's Peak, Devil's Crag, and there's a Devil's Punchbowl further south," Dan said. "And I think there's a Devil's Dance Floor in Yosemite, but I'm not sure if that's an official designation."

"Devil's Slide," Ruth said. "But that's over on the coast. I don't think we can count that."

"Okay," Maggie agreed. "What else have we got?"

Dan thought about the book he had read. "Metal," he said. "There was a section in my book about precious metals in the West. That would give us Silver Lake, Silver Fork, and Silver Divide."

"Copperopolis," Maggie added.

"Don't forget Coarsegold," Ruth suggested. "And El Dorado."

When the others looked at her in confusion, she explained. "It means 'golden' in Spanish."

Maggie was now spreading out the papers in front of her. She counted out the pages. "Good. We're only missing two books," she said.

"Which ones?" Ruth asked.

Maggie consulted her notes. "Six and ten," she answered.

"Frazil Ice, and Jumar."

"And what are they supposed to be about?" Kristen asked. "I mean, the themes for the clues?"

Maggie picked up one of the books and began to leaf through it. Ruth picked up the other one and did the same. The rest waited.

"Frazil Ice looks as if it might be about trees?" Maggie said. "I think we'll have to read the whole thing to make sure."

"And Jumar has a section on the American novel," Ruth said. "Boy, that seems really out of place."

Dan snorted. "Well, trees as a theme is ridiculous. There must be a million of those."

The others murmured in agreement, but Ruth was silent.

"Novels," she said quietly, almost lost in thought. "Like what? I can't think of any. Tom Sawyer? The Old Man and the Sea?"

After a moment, Dan spoke quietly. "What about Huckleberry Lake?" he asked. "Would that work?"

Ruth smiled triumphantly. "It certainly would, Dan. That's excellent! But the obvious one is right here," she said. "Twain Harte."

"That would explain a lot," Dan said. "If that's a key part of this, no wonder everyone is coming up here to look."

"We might be living right on top of it," Kristen said. "That would seem to give us an advantage."

"We'll have to read those last books," Maggie said. "Just to make sure. I can do one of them." She looked at Ruth.

"Sign me up," Ruth said, holding Jumar up for all to see. "I'll do Jumar, whatever the heck that is."

"Great. And I'll do the ice one," Maggie said. "And then we'll need to put all of this together into some kind of order. There must be a way to lay this out so that we can see a pattern, or a system."

"A jumar is a climbing tool," Dan explained to Ruth. "It helps you climb up a rope."

"What we need," Maggie continued, "is a plan to organize all these ideas."

"A grid," Ruth suggested. "Like at Walt's dig. A grid where we can see everything and see how it relates to everything else. And a map, too. We need to see how all this goes on a map."

"I'll put it all into a spreadsheet," Maggie said. "And I'll send it out to everyone so that we can all work on it."

Dan stood up and walked over to his bookshelf, where he pulled out a large folded map of the Sierra. "This might help," he said. "It's not a great scale, but it has the whole range on one map."

They laid out the map and Dan began to point out a few of the locations he had mentioned. At one point he looked over at Ruth. "How is the dig going?" he asked. "Is Walt having fun?"

Ruth gave a dismissive chuckle. "How should I know? I haven't heard a peep from him since he started there. I assume that means that he's loving it. If he were miserable, he'd be complaining. But you can ask him yourself in a couple of days. He gets to come home and clean up then."

chapter 18

Dan was delighted to spend the next couple of days checking the trails out of Clark Fork with a shovel in one hand and a bow saw in the other. His thoughts of Matthew McLeod and his fictions slowly faded behind him as he walked up the Arnot Creek trail and began to work up a nice rhythm of breathing hard and pushing his pace up the steep trail to the top of the ridge.

He took a break to saw through a tree that had fallen across the trail, and by the time he had sawn through a second tree he had forgotten about Martina Guzman, too. The third tree presented a real problem: three trunks, each about eight inches in diameter, lay across the trail. Where they joined together, they were too big for him to cut with his bow saw. And yet they were close enough together that he couldn't see a way to cut each of them separately. The tree was far too big to move by himself.

With some creative angles and postures, he managed to get through enough of the smallest of the three trunks that he could consider walking down to the free end and bending and twisting until it broke. One down, two to go.

He decided to try the same approach with the second trunk, but it was bigger, and he knew he wouldn't get all the way through it. He got as far as he could, the saw now only traveling a few inches with each stroke, and when he had sawn through six of the eight inches of the trunk, decided he would try his luck again.

He walked down to the free end of this trunk and tried to move it. No luck. It was still too well connected to the main trunk, despite a couple of fearsome efforts on his part.

He walked back up to the trail and looked at the third trunk. There was a clear fracture there, but it was obviously still connected somehow. He gave the trunk a good kick, but it didn't budge a millimeter. Damn.

Dan climbed up above the trail and sat on the main trunk to think. Mainly what he thought about was how much work it would be to come back out here a second time with a larger saw, but he also had a brief flash of wondering just exactly what McLeod would think about this one. Jack Pulaski would certainly have a solution.

Dan got up and walked back over to stand on the trail and study the trunks again. Maybe if he could budge the far end of that last trunk, it would rotate the tree enough to give him a better angle at the second one.

He scrambled down the slope below the trail and grabbed the end of the third trunk. He was ready to give it a mighty heave when he noticed that the trunk was curiously easy to move. With the leverage he had gained, the other end pulled free of the trunk. He hoisted his end up and shoved it sideways, then rolled the whole trunk out of the way. The extra leverage at the far end had made it simple, and Dan couldn't help but laugh.

He was still smiling when he went back to cut through the final section of the second trunk, chuckling for minutes afterwards about how easy it had been, once he had the leverage. He could show Jack Pulaski a thing or two.

And that was the last time he thought about Matthew McLeod on the whole, two-day trip.

As he was hiking back to the trailhead at the end of the second day, he met three young men hiking in. Dan took one look at their overloaded packs, complete with a blue tarp strapped on top of one of them, and their blue jeans and T-shirts, and stopped to have a conversation.

No, they didn't have a permit, but they didn't think they needed one for this trail. Or maybe they didn't need one so early in the season. Whatever, they would just pay the fine and keep going.

Dan insisted that they hike back out a mile to the trailhead, and then drive back to the ranger station to fill out the paperwork.

As he followed them out, he questioned them about their gear. Most of it came from a discount store, and the guys had not tested any of it in advance. They didn't know what the rating of their sleeping bags was, but they were pretty sure they were warm enough. After all, they were going to be sleeping in a tent.

Yes, they had lots of food, but they hadn't brought a stove, they were just going to cook on an open fire. When Dan asked, they admitted they didn't have a campfire permit.

Dan made sure they made it to the ranger station, and even went in to encourage them to spend one night in a campground first, where they could test their gear, and still bail out if it didn't work. He wasn't sure they would take that advice, but at least he had made an effort.

He half-expected to get another SAR call on that group, but at least he would know where to start looking for them.

When he finally got back home late that day, Kristen had left him a note saying she would be working late that night, but she had left his dinner in the fridge. Before he could inspect it, he heard a car outside, and saw Walt drive up and park across the street.

Walt looked over and saw Dan, then waved to him. Dan waved

back, noting that Walt was now moving not toward his own house, but toward Dan's. The older man looked tired and filthy, but he had a big grin on his face.

Dan smiled and walked over to open the door for Walt. "You look like you've been having fun," he said.

Walt grinned. "You can say that again," he agreed. He reached out and shook Dan's hand. "I'm beat to hell and aching in places I never knew I had, but I am having the time of my life out there."

"Finding anything interesting?" Dan asked.

"Ha!" Walt exclaimed. "We're not supposed to say anything about it yet, but you'll hear about it soon enough. Hell, you'll probably be the one they send to check things out."

Dan raised his eyebrows. "Wow, Erica Fisher must be happy."

"On cloud nine," Walt agreed. "She's asked us to keep a lid on this for a few days, until she can verify some of the stuff, but yes, she is elated."

"I look forward to hearing about it, or reading about it," Dan said.

"Oh, I think you'll do more than that, Dan," Walt said. "She wants to make sure that a few of the powers that be around here feel like they are part of the discovery. She's going to invite a bunch of you down in a few days to see what we've got."

"I'm in," Dan said with a big grin. "I'd even be willing to pick up a shovel if that would help."

"We're past the shovel stage already," Walt explained. "We're down to little trowels and toothbrushes—the good stuff."

The old man was standing with a twist in his spine, leaning oddly on the porch post. "How are your knees doing?" Dan asked him.

"They're killing me," Walt admitted with a chuckle. "That's

how I know I'm alive. At my age, if it doesn't hurt, it ain't working."

Dan laughed. "Hell, Walt, I feel that way now."

"You're a kid," Walt answered. "Trust me, it gets a lot worse." And with that, he wished Dan a good evening and turned to walk to his own house.

Dan watched him go. "I can hardly wait," he called after him. Walt waved his hand over his shoulder to show that he had heard, and Dan went back to see exactly what dinner Kristen had left in the fridge.

So it didn't surprise Dan to receive an email from his boss Steve Matson asking Dan to hike down to the dig again on Thursday morning. There was going to be a meeting at ten in the morning, and Dan would be representing the Forest Service there. Now that he knew the way, Dan decided to spend a lazy morning at home, and cut the timing of the hike close.

The parking area was packed with cars this time, and Dan noted that one of them had a Willoughby Partners logo on the door—the developers funding the dig. And he was surprised to see that one was from the Tuolumne County Sheriff's office. More cars pinched the sides of the road, making parking more complicated, and Dan was disappointed to see that he had to back up the road to find a place to park. And it was tight. By the time he was done, he checked his watch and was embarrassed to find that he was now running late.

He locked up his vehicle and quickly strode off down the steep trail. His long legs quickly started to make up the time, and it was all downhill. He soon saw the river below him, still roaring in flood stage. The snow melt in the mountains higher up had only increased the flow.

He was so interested in the river that he almost missed the

snake.

Dan initially thought it was merely a stick on the trail until he saw it moving. A nice sized rattler, it was doing what snakes usually do—trying to get out of the way. Dan waited while it slowly slithered across the road, from right to left, with its head always pointing back at Dan, ready to defend its body with a strike if Dan decided to attack.

Dan watched as it reached the edge of the road, then almost magically disappeared into the leaves and brush by the side of the road. He gave it plenty of room and struck off down the trail again.

Once around the last corner, Dan was surprised to see a small canopy tent shelter set up near the campsite, and a group of at least twenty people clustered in its shade. As he scanned the sunny dig site he noted that there were no workers out there now. They must all be part of the meeting. And three ATVs were parked down there as well.

Down at the bottom of the old road, Dan saw Erica Fisher, her back to the river, facing the group and apparently speaking. She caught sight of him out of the corner of her eye and stopped briefly to give him a nod and a smile. A couple of people in the group turned to look. Dan crept forward, trying not to draw attention to himself.

Dan slipped in the back of the group. Walt was over to one side, somewhere between Erica and the rest of the group, and he was surprised to see Cal sitting in a folding chair in front. A few of the students were off to the side, and Dan recognized Florence, the young woman who had chatted with him last time. Another one of the volunteers was busy, snapping photos as Erica spoke. And unless he was mistaken, that woman in the front row was a reporter from the local paper. There were more there he didn't recognize.

It took him a few minutes to begin to hear what Erica was

saying.

"A significant find, from what we can see," she was saying. "Not just a few bones, but we have many human remains. There are bones from several individuals, of various ages here."

The reporter asked a question too quietly for Dan to hear.

"We don't have a confirmation of the dating," Erica answered. "But right now we are working on the assumption that these are between one and two hundred years old, based on the strata and context. We'll have more accurate dating once we get these fully analyzed."

Another question from the reporter, too quiet to hear.

Erica Fisher gave a grimace. "We don't really have a complete timeline on that. I can tell you that we sent material to various labs and should have something back in the next couple of weeks. But I can't make any promises about exactly when."

The reporter turned to Cal Healey and asked him something that Dan couldn't hear, either.

Cal shook his head and pointed to Erica Fisher.

"The Sheriff is not currently investigating this," she said. "As far as we can tell, these are historical remains, not the subject of any current investigation. But we invited the Sheriff's Department here both officially and as a courtesy."

The photographer kept snapping away, from one angle and then another.

Erica asked for questions. A tall man in a golf shirt and slacks raised his hand, and Erica nodded and smiled to encourage him.

"Do we have any idea how many people we are talking about?" he asked. "You've mentioned various individuals."

Erica was nodding as he listened to his question. "Yeah, we don't really know the answer to that," she said. "We think we have the remains of at least three individuals, possibly four. That's pretty clear, based on the size of the bones. But that reflects only a small portion of the site. We may find more as we continue the dig."

"Any idea how they died?" the man asked.

She shook her head. "No, not really. Not yet. That's a much more complicated process, and we will need to see if we have enough of the remains to determine that."

"Do we have any idea who they were?" he continued.

"Again, it's certainly too soon to make any conclusions about that," Erica said. "It may take weeks or even months to pull everything together. We may not know even then. And before we do that, anything I say would just be speculation."

A man in the front row raised his hand. Dan saw the long black hair, pulled into a ponytail, the broad shoulders, and the jewelry on his hand, and guessed he might be a member of the local Native American population of Tuolumne County.

"Why did you drag us out here, if you can't tell us more than this?" he asked. "And if what you have found is more than a hundred and fifty years old, then it is none of your business. Those are part of our heritage and our culture and need to be respected."

"That's exactly why we asked you all out here," Erica responded. "We are sensitive to these issues and want to involve all the interested parties as we move forward." She looked directly at the man. "The goal here is for us to have complete transparency."

"If these remains are of my people, you need to stop this digging right now," replied the man. "These aren't bones, they are our sacred heritage."

Erica nodded once more. "I completely understand and support that position," she said. "That's why we have stopped our work here until we can more effectively date the remains we have found."

"Can't you figure it out from the other stuff that you've found?" the man in the golf shirt asked. "I mean, haven't you found other stuff that would show you?"

"We have found some artifacts here that are probably from Native American sources," Erica answered. "But we've also found European artifacts as well. The site has both. That's why we are trying to study this more carefully. We just don't know."

There were some murmurs among the crowd at this, and the group seemed to become restless. The man with the ponytail was now standing up and speaking directly to Erica in a terse voice. Dan couldn't hear what he was saying, but it didn't look like fun.

Dan caught Walt's eye and gave him a nod. As the conversation with Erica deteriorated into smaller groups talking among themselves, Walt slowly walked over and shook Dan's hand.

"Sure beats looking for phony treasure," he whispered. "Doesn't it?"

chapter 19

Back at the front of the group, Erica Fisher was trying to pull the meeting back into order.

"Could I have your attention, please?" she called out. "People? Hey, folks, I need your attention up here."

Few in the group paid her much attention. They were too involved in their own local conversations. Walt and Dan continued to stand in the back. As Erica struggled, Walt suddenly clapped his hands loudly and yelled out, "Hey! Quiet! Listen up!"

Dan watched as the group turned to look at Walt, startled. Then they turned and sat back down to listen to Erica Fisher.

Walt gave Dan a wink and turned his attention to Erica. Out of the side of her mouth, he muttered to Dan, "Once a teacher, always a teacher."

By now Erica was thanking everyone for listening again. "I want to emphasize that we are not sure what we've found here, but we're stopping the dig until we have more information. Is that clear? Any questions about that?"

She waited until the group finally sat quietly.

"No? Then I also want to recognize some people here who have been working really hard on this." She waved her hand toward her team. "Would you guys come up here?"

A dark young man with a huge white smile quickly walked up to join Erica, waving to some of the others to join him. He stood at the front proudly, grinning at the group. Walt stayed standing next to Dan.

"Come on, Jacob," Erica called out. "And you, Florence. Where's Walt? And Kurt?"

Dan gave Walt a little nudge, and smiled as his old friend picked his way over to the side and around up to the front of the group.

Erica turned to the first young man. "These young people are all graduate students at UC Merced," Erica explained. "Alberto Leon is such a wonderful guy, full of fun. He's always ready for a new challenge, and if anything needs to get done, he's the first to stick his hand up in the air. He did his undergrad work at Penn State. We would not have managed any of this without Alberto."

Alberto gave a big grin and waved. "It's been great, guys. You should come and join us!"

Erica turned to the next young man, whose sunburned pink face was evidence of hours in the sun, perhaps without the appropriate protection. His hand swooped up to wipe a shock of black hair from his face. A shy smile flashed across his face when Erica addressed him.

"Jake, Jacob Turnbull, you are such a rock," Erica said. "Jacob Turnbull came to us from the University of Colorado. Go Buffs!"

Jacob smiled and nodded to the group.

"Jacob is also a great cook," Erica continued. "He always finds a way to make our meals more interesting by adding a little something. And with some of the stuff we start with, that's really saying a lot."

"Yeah, but he needs to use more salsa," Alberto called out with a big smile. He punched Jacob lightly on the shoulder.

Next in line was the young woman who had talked to Dan on his last visit.

"And Florence, Flor, nobody has energy like Florence Watters," Erica said. "First up in the morning, and by the time the rest of us are up she's always already at work. Sometimes we have to slow her down to get all the notes caught up, but she is a dynamo, and she loves to tackle anything that means hard work."

Erica paused there, and Alberto murmured something to her.

"Oh, yes, Flor came to us from Tulane," Erica explained. "We're hoping we can convince her that the weather is better here than in New Orleans."

"It is in the summer," Florence agreed.

"And where's Kurt?" Erica asked. The others pointed to the photographer, who was now at the very back of the crowd, standing near Dan, and still taking photos.

Erica waved him forward. "Put that camera down and get up here," she called to him.

Kurt waved back but didn't move.

Erica continued with her introductions. "From TCU, isn't that right, Kurt?"

He waved again, still behind the camera.

"Kurt Stingley has been a lifesaver on this dig, documenting every step we've taken with that camera of his. Sometimes I forget what he looks like, because all I see is lenses." Erica waved him up to the front again, and some of the others did the same. "Come on, Kurt. We need you for the group photo."

Kurt waved back, still behind the camera. "Who's going to take it? We'll get it later," he called back. "Don't worry."

There was a pause. Dan saw that Erica was thinking about how hard she wanted to push the issue. But then Alberto mentioned Walt, and Erica spun around.

"Oh, my gosh, how could I forget Walt?"

Dan could see Walt telling her not to worry.

"Walter Sorensen is one of you guys," Erica said. "He's a local. I think many of you know him. He's retired now, and decided one day that he would give me a call and see if I needed any help."

She turned to Walt and continued. "I have to tell you, Walt, that when you first called, I was ready to tell you 'no' right off the bat. But then I kept talking to you, and listening to what you had to say, and all I can say now is that I am so glad I didn't do that. You are an amazing person. I have leaned on you so many times, and your wisdom and advice have meant the world to me."

Walt shook his head. "You're the one who has done it," he said. He looked to the other members of the team, then spoke to the audience. "I think you can see why we all work so hard for Erica. She is exactly the right person to lead this dig."

Erica looked as if she was going to tear up, but turned to Walt and gave him a quick hug. The five posed for a few photos by Kurt, and then Erica spoke again.

"That's the team here," she said. "We have been working really hard, and we're anxious to keep going. But we've put the whole thing on hold until we can analyze the remains we've found. Please keep that in mind. And please don't add anything to what we've said here. If we haven't said it, it's because we don't know."

She waited a moment, looking at the crowd. Nobody said anything.

"Okay, then, that's it," she said. "That's all the news. Thank you for coming."

Dan stayed in the back while the group broke up, first talking in small groups, then continuing their conversations as they began to hike back up the hill. He wondered how well some of them would make it on that steep trail.

Dan noted that the guy in the golf shirt and Cal were still with Erica, listening as she spoke to the local reporter.

Walt walked over to stand by Dan.

"I can see why you like working with her," Dan said.

"She's great," Walt replied. "Smart as hell, and manages these kids just right. They're a good bunch. I hope we get to keep going."

"Who's the guy in the golf shirt?" Dan asked.

"Willoughby Partners," Walt answered. He lowered his voice. "For safety reasons I haven't told Ruth about him."

Dan chuckled. "His safety, or hers?"

"Exactly," Walt answered.

They watched as the man climbed on board an ATV and started it up. He motioned for the reporter to climb on behind him. She struggled awkwardly to get on board, put her arms carefully around his waist, and they roared off up the trail.

Cal walked over to Dan. "Want a ride back up?" he asked. "I have room, if you don't mind hanging on."

"Nah," Dan said. "I think I'll walk."

"Riding is a lot quicker," Cal suggested.

"Yeah," Dan agreed. "But my way is a lot quieter."

chapter 20

Cal climbed aboard his ATV and turned back to Dan.

"Did you get that all cleared up with the Stockton PD?" Cal asked him.

"I haven't heard back from them," Dan admitted. "Are you helping them out?"

Cal shook his head. "Not really. They wanted some kind of character witness for a ranger up here named Courtwright, and I told them those felony arrest warrants were all just a big misunderstanding."

Dan smiled. "Yeah, I bet you did. And have they found Petrosky, or whoever he is?"

"I am not at liberty to discuss the case," Cal said. "It's in the hands of the Stockton Police Department, and we will provide such assistance as they require."

"Which means they haven't told you a damn thing, and you are flying blind, just like me," Dan said.

Cal smiled and turned to Walt. "Good to see you having fun, Walt," he said.

"Oh, I am doing that," Walt said. "Nothing like an honest day's work, especially at my age."

Cal laughed. "I thought you were retired."

"That just means I get to do what I want," Walt said. Then gesturing at the dig, he said, "And this sure meets the definition."

"I wish I could say the same," Cal replied.

There was an awkward silence, and then Walt surprised Dan by asking Cal if he ever thought of running for Sheriff.

It took Cal a while to answer. He sat back on his ATV and took his hands off the bars. "Thought about, yes," Cal said. "But sooner or later you're going to make plenty of enemies. You decide to charge somebody and let somebody else go. Either way, people think you're crooked for the other side."

Somehow, Dan didn't expect that answer. "Can't you just go by the book?" he asked. "Isn't that what it's for?"

Cal grimaced. "Yeah, but that damn book has lots of pages," he said. "And there's always somebody who thinks they know better."

"Well, you should think about it," Walt said. "You've got a good reputation in this county, and I think a lot of people would vote for you. I know I would."

Cal smiled. "Thanks, Walt. At least, they might vote for me the first time. Then somebody they know would get into trouble, and they'd get mad about how I handled it. Or they'd be mad I handled somebody else differently. And sooner or later, that somebody would have enough money or power that they'd make a stink and try to get rid of me."

Walt shrugged. "I think you're underestimating people."

Cal smiled. "That's because you see people on their best behavior, Walt. I usually see them in different circumstances. Trust me. But thanks for the thought."

Walt nodded, and Cal started up his ATV. He gave a quick nod farewell and roared up the old road. To Dan's way of thinking, he went faster than he needed to.

"He's a good man," Walt said to Dan. "We need more people like him."

"Yeah," Dan agreed. "But I think he's happy flying just a bit under the radar."

"Well, he's probably right," Walt conceded. "I bet he gets more done that way."

Dan nodded, still looking up the road. He could hear the noise of Cal's ATV growing fainter as it climbed up out of the canyon.

"Still," Walt said. He left the question hanging.

Dan laughed. "Good luck, Walt. I don't think he's interested."

"The good ones never are," Walt answered.

Dan took his leave from Walt and Erica and began to hike back up the trail. The ATVs were long gone, and as he climbed back up the canyon Dan kept an eye out for his rattlesnake. He could see where the ATV's had struggled for traction in the steep spots, sometimes chewing up the side of the road. A month later the clay of the road would have turned to dust, but now it was moist and sometimes slick.

He picked his way from one side to the other, trying to stay out of the deepest ruts. He was breathing hard now, matching his breathing to the pace of his steps, inhale one step, exhale the next. It was how he tackled the steepest trails, at least at this altitude.

It felt great to feel his body working hard, the sound of his breathing like a steam engine, huffing and puffing in time with his legs. He had given up looking for the rattler. It would have been long gone by now anyway.

A quick check of his watch told him he could make it out by lunch time, just as his stomach growled to encourage him to pick up the pace. It was just a few minutes after twelve when he arrived at his truck. He had time to stop for lunch on the way to the ranger station.

The other vehicles were gone now, even the two with the trailers for the ATVs. They must have loaded those up quickly. The ground in the area had taken a beating, and the road back out was bound to be even muddier.

Dan tried to kick some of the clay off his boots, but it clung to his feet like thick glue. He walked over and picked up a dry stick and tried to scrape some of it off, but gave up when the job was only half done. Giving the boots one more kick each against his front tire, he climbed into his truck. As he was turning around in the road he noticed one more vehicle, a jacked-up metal gray pickup in the trees off to his right, well off the road. It didn't seem like the kind of vehicle Erica would drive, or any archeology grad student, for that matter. Dan noted the "Insured by Smith and Wesson" bumper sticker on the side.

Dan wondered if a truck like that could make it all the way down into the canyon. Or, rather, could make it back out again. As he drove off, he decided that he would ask Erica about the truck later.

chapter 21

Dan could see the line of visitors extending out the door of the Summit Ranger Station when he drove into the parking lot. When he walked in the door Doris greeted him with a curt nod of her head to show that she could have used his help about an hour ago.

He immediately stepped in behind the counter and asked the next person in line what he could do to help. The steady flow of tourists and backpackers didn't let up until late in the day.

That was when Dan apologized for not arriving earlier.

"What was that all about?" Doris asked.

Dan explained about the archeological dig and the human remains.

"At least it's not more nonsense with that McLeod fellow and his hidden treasure," she said.

Dan laughed. "You know, Doris, until you mentioned it, I had completely forgotten about that guy."

"Oh, he's got everyone worked up about it," she said. "Travis says that the kids at college are all working up ways to find it, and there's even a class about it at the JC down there by one of the teachers."

Dan told her about Maggie, Ruth and Kristen working together. He didn't mention his own role in the group. By the time he finished, she had a sour look on her face.

"I could think of better ways to spend my evenings," Doris said.

"If it weren't for Travis, I wouldn't even think about it."

Dan shot her a questioning look.

"He's got a group of computer kids down at Cal Poly who think they can solve it," she said. "They are using a computer to analyze the books, and have come up with all sorts of solutions and things. You know that poor boy, Antonio Gemmeli, went to school down there. But Travis says they might need a little help with the geography."

Dan smiled. "And what grandmother wouldn't want to help out her grandson on a project like that?" he asked.

"Well," she said, apologetically, "they are very bright kids."

Dan told her about Ruth's background and the fact that she had some interesting insights she had shared about the books.

Doris' mouth was set as she listened. "I would have to ask Travis about that," she said. "Those kids think they might be able to do it on their own."

"With a little help from Grandma?" Dan asked. "But I'm not suggesting anything. I'm just letting you know who some of the players are."

A few hours later Dan looked at the clock and noted the time.

"Know what time it is, Doris?" he asked.

Her face softened into a smile. It was a tired old routine between the two of them. "It's time to get out of here," she said.

Dan reached over to turn off one of the computers, and that was when the phone rang. Dan and Doris carefully regarded the device. Doris followed his lead, but then couldn't resist and finally answered it.

After listening for a moment, she said, "He's right here, Erica," and handed the phone to Dan. "Your friend from the dig."

Erica didn't waste any time on the call. "I know it must be the end of the day for you, but I wanted to thank you for attending our meeting today, and to make sure we are both on the same page about all this stuff."

Dan assured her it was no problem.

"I really want to clarify that we won't be doing any work at all down here, not even a photograph, until we have clarified the nature of the remains we've found," she said.

Dan again assured her that he understood that.

"But I'm concerned that others might not feel the same way," Erica continued. "And I'm worried that someone else might disturb the site."

Dan asked if she had talked to Steve Matson about it. "He's the guy who has the authority to close the area, if you want to do that," Dan explained.

"Of course, and I've talked to him about it," Erica said. "But as you know, closing the area won't necessarily stop everyone from coming down to the dig."

Dan agreed with that, but didn't offer any solution to her.

"We're going to have someone down here 24/7," Erica said. "I think that's the only way to make sure. The team is going to take turns."

"Sounds like a good idea," Dan said. "Just make sure you let Steve know about it."

"Already done," Erica said. "And he's given us his blessing."

She paused. Dan didn't know if she expected him to say more, but he had nothing to add.

"We've had a few problems already," Erica continued.

"Like what?" Dan asked.

"People coming down here, poking around. Some are just curious, but it's not a great situation."

"Did any of them give you any trouble?" Dan asked.

"A couple of them didn't want to leave, after they'd walked all the way down here," she said. "That's understandable. But I've asked Steve Matson if we can be a little more direct in discouraging people at the trailhead."

"Yeah," Dan agreed. "Not a bad idea. A warning at the top is worth two at the bottom."

"Exactly," Erica said. "So we're on that. Steve said it was okay. I just wanted you to know."

Dan chuckled. "Oh, I'll know. Steve will send out an email and a notice to everyone. He's pretty good about that."

"Well, I wanted you to hear it from me," Erica explained. "Walt will be one of the people who takes a turn down here."

"Ha!" Dan laughed. "You're in good hands, there."

"The best," Erica agreed.

Dan asked her about the gray pickup at the trailhead. "Is that one of your people?"

Erica considered it for a moment. "I doubt it," she said. "We're more Outback or 4Runner kinds of people. Probably just a local off-roadie. But I'll ask around."

"No worries," Dan said. "I was just curious."

And with that, Erica let Dan hang up and go home.

chapter 22

One Day Ago: News Feed: *Merced Standard and Bulletin*: Two young Merced men are missing and presumed drowned in the area above Pinecrest Lake, the Tuolumne County Sheriff reported. The two were part of a group hiking along the Stanislaus River in the section known as Cleo's Baths when they went swimming in the water and were swept downstream. Despite the efforts of their hiking partners and subsequent searches by Tuolumne County SAR, neither of the two have been found.

This story has been updated to include the names of the two victims: Bryan Balanza, 19, of Ripon, and Ashton Crabbe, 18, of Manteca. The two attended Ripon Christian High School together. Both were planning to attend Columbia College in the fall.

Dan and Kristen had just finished dinner when Dan's phone rang. He checked the number. It was Bruce Spielman, his ex-brother-in-law. Dan rolled his eyes at Kristen, then picked up the phone. After all, if the call lasted more than a few minutes, it might get him out of doing the dishes.

"Hey, Bruce. What's up?" Dan greeted him more cordially than usual.

"I think I'm making some real progress on this treasure thing, Dan," Bruce replied. "Got a minute to talk it through with me?"

Dan glanced at Kristen, who was now taking dishes into the kitchen. "Sure. What have you got?"

"I've read through almost all the books," Bruce explained.

"And I've done a bunch of checking online, too. I think I've got some of this worked out."

Dan grunted to show he was listening.

"See, each one of the books has a different set of clues in it," Bruce went on. "And you have to add them all together."

Bruce then went on to explain, book by book, the clues he had found in each one. By the third book, Dan wondered if Bruce was expecting him to take notes.

"No, I'm going to send you all of this in an email," he told Dan, "but I wanted to talk you through it first."

That suited Dan just fine. He could pay as little attention as he wanted.

Bruce had read all but the last two books and continued to explain to Dan how they worked together to create a solution to the puzzle. When he was done with his explanation, Dan asked him if the last two books might include something that changed it all.

"Oh, sure, that could happen," Bruce admitted. "But from what I'm reading online, I think I'm on the right track."

"That sounds great, Bruce," Dan said. He intentionally left any enthusiasm out of his voice.

"Well, that's where I'll need you," Bruce answered. "I've got this narrowed down to a couple of quadrants in the Sierra. One of them is up above Lake Thomas Edison, but another one is right up by you, on the Stanislaus."

Dan's stomach gave a small lurch. If others were using the same system as Bruce, that would explain why so many people were suddenly interested in his part of the National Forest.

"You said you're going to send me this stuff in an email," he reminded Bruce.

"As soon as we get off the phone," Bruce said. "And I'd

appreciate it if you could take a look at it as soon as possible."

"Sure, I'll do that," Dan agreed.

"Especially that section around where you are," Bruce said. "I'd like to nail that down and get your take on it."

Dan promised he would take a look that very evening.

"Because I'm not sure how much longer that treasure is going to be out there," Bruce said.

"You think somebody might find it?" Dan asked.

"Maybe, but I doubt it," Bruce answered. "But I just read that this guy McLeod is being sued by the family of some idiot who died looking for it. And if he gets sued, he may need the five mil to pay them off."

This got Dan's attention. "Can you send me a link to that story, too?" Dan asked.

"Yeah, sure," Bruce agreed. "Coming at you right after we get off the phone."

Dan put the phone down and allowed his mind to wander. In seconds his computer beeped to tell him he had mail.

He wondered what Martina Guzman might think of the news story about the lawsuit. And then it occurred to him that she might even have encouraged it. It seemed like the kind of thing she might do, from what he had seen of her. He found her email address and sent her the link, without any comment.

And he did the same for Steve Matson.

As he sat at the table, holding his phone, Kristen's voice called out from the backyard. "If you're done with your phone call, the dishes are waiting for you in the sink," she said.

"Yep," Dan answered her, his plot neatly foiled. "I'll get on them in a minute."

chapter 23

It wasn't until the next day that Dan finally read through Bruce's own email. With Kristen working late, he had the evening to himself.

What Bruce Spielman had sent Dan was more than ten pages of impenetrably dense speculation. Just the sight of the long paragraphs without any punctuation made Dan lose heart, and that was before he had tried to decipher the words themselves.

Bruce, for all his glib manner on the phone, had somehow resorted to a bizarre form of quasi-military bureaucratic language full of newly formed acronyms for various terms and theories that he had developed.

It was, Dan concluded, exactly the kind of writing that would tempt him to report Bruce to local law enforcement if there had been any inkling of aggression or violence in it. But there wasn't. There was just an unending stream of postulations and tenuous conclusions that seemed vaguely logical until you read them carefully.

The first page laid out Bruce's general conclusions and promised fuller explanations for each later in the document. Dan was skeptical, and the second page did nothing to convince him.

The text was full of expressions of confidence and clarity. "When you examine the two possibilities here, only one makes any sense at all," Bruce concluded in one section. But he gave no rationale for that. And Dan, with his greater knowledge of the Sierra, could easily identify two other possibilities that Bruce had missed entirely.

By the third page, the struggle to identify where one thought ended and the next began had taken its toll on Dan. He quickly scrolled through the remaining pages, hoping that there might be some summary, some outline, some improved structure to the words.

There was none.

Dan skipped to the last page. Here Bruce had finally come to some kind of point. There were two locations that he was interested in locating. The first was a lake five miles, or possibly seven, depending on how you solved one of Bruce's mystery equations, from a trailhead with eight letters in its name. It was surrounded by granite and had a notable dead snag towering above the shore, and if you stood at the base of the snag, you could see a notch in the granite above.

Bruce did not want to say more than that—either because he didn't trust the security of the internet to put all of the solutions in an email, or because he didn't trust Dan.

Not that Dan cared, either way. He didn't know the lakes well enough to know which ones had snags on the shore. In his mind, they all did, somewhere. Snags were a part of the Sierra landscape. And there were at least two obvious trailheads with eight letters. Both Gianelli and Crabtree fit that criteria. For that matter, so did Disaster Creek, if you left off the creek. And there was Bourland as well. And those were just the ones that came to mind near his ranger station.

And lakes within seven miles of those trailheads? There were quite a few. Dan toyed with the idea of explaining all this to Bruce, but then decided that it would be simpler to just list as many lakes as he could remember that might fit the criteria. With any luck at all, that would dishearten the guy enough that he would either drop this whole thing or spend another few weeks refining his brilliant solutions. He imagined Bruce spending hours on Google Earth, looking for the shadows of trees, searching the shores for notches.

It would keep him busy, at least.

Dan spent the rest of the evening fighting to stay awake as he finished Crevasse. As Dan expected, Jack Pulaski managed to single-handedly fight his way out of impossible situations against insurmountable odds, all the while struggling to come to grips with the guilt and memories of his most recent fight with his current love interest. The bad guys always put up a bombardment of shots that somehow missed Jack, while he carefully allocated each bullet in his gun to take out one evildoer. He never missed. It was both miraculous and heroic.

At the end, Pulaski's obnoxious boss grudgingly gave him a few days off to recover from his many wounds, and the worst of the crooked cops got shot up badly enough to take them out of the picture. We would never know who the evil genius was behind all of this, but Dan suspected there would be more to come in Death Zone.

Jack finally drove off to his cabin, listening to mournful tunes on his radio, with a bottle of bourbon in a bag on the seat beside him, to find that his love had moved out, and only his dog was there to greet him.

He broke out the bottle of bourbon, fed the dog, and went out on the porch to watch the sun go down.

Dan closed the book and realized that it was later than he thought. He took a quick tour of the kitchen to make sure it was tidy and began turning off a few lights. A quick check of his email. Martina Guzman sent him a short note: "Looks like they're serious. And they've named McLeod in the suit. They've asked for his real identity."

Out the front window Dan saw the headlights from Kristen's car pull into the driveway, and he went over to turn on the porchlight and open the front door.

"Hey," Kristen said. "Were you waiting up for me?"

"Of course," Dan lied. "That, and trying to finish that damn McLeod book."

Kristen laughed and gave him a hug and kiss.

"It's nice to have you home," he said.

"Ugh, I must smell of onions and grease," Kristen answered.

"With hints of rosemary and garlic," Dan said with a smile. "Just the way I like you."

chapter 24

Before Dan left for work the next day, his phone rang. He looked at the number—an area code that he didn't recognize. He was about to ignore it when he remembered Lindsay Warren, the writer from the New Yorker. Was this her number?

Dan answered.

"I hope I'm not calling too early," Lindsay offered.

Dan explained that he was about to walk out the door.

"Can I call you later?" she asked.

"What's on your mind?" Dan asked. If he could get out of it now, he didn't want to miss the chance.

"What do you know about the archeological dig out there?" she asked. "It sounds like it's right in your neighborhood. And maybe right up your alley."

Dan agreed that it was, but that he didn't know anything about it. He suggested that Linsday call Erica Fisher, and offered her number.

"She's not really saying much," the reporter told him. "I was hoping that you could give me a little info on background."

Dan knew how the system worked and wasn't biting. "I can only suggest that you try Erica again," he said. "There's nothing I can tell you that she didn't tell me. And it's exactly what she's told everyone else."

"Have you been asked to look into this at all?" Lindsay asked.

Dan chuckled. "No, and I won't be doing that. This is really an archeological dig by Dr. Fisher, and I don't have any place there."

"Well, I've been hearing a lot more than that," the writer said. "Some of it is pretty sensational."

"I can't help you," Dan insisted. "And there was nothing very sensational in what Erica Fisher told us. I'd take anything else you've heard with a huge grain of salt."

"Well, thanks." Lindsay Warren was clearly getting frustrated with Dan. "If you do hear anything, can I ask you to call me? I'd really appreciate it."

Dan was shaking his head. "Talk to Erica," he said. "She's really the only one who knows what's going on."

"Okay, thanks, Dan." The writer hung up.

Kristen looked over at him, eyebrows raised.

Dan shook his head. "A fishing expedition," he said.

"Sounds like she didn't catch much," Kristen suggested.

"Not my department," Dan said. "It's always easier when I can claim complete ignorance. Especially when it's true."

He kissed the top of her head and walked out the door.

"Don't forget our book meeting tonight," she called out as he left.

Dan waved to her to show he had heard. But they both knew that didn't mean he was planning to participate.

Up at the Summit Ranger Station, Doris was humming happily. Dan quickly learned that her grandson Travis was due home from his first year of college, and Doris was already levitating ever so slightly off the floor.

Dan asked if she knew what his plans were for the summer.

"Oh, he's already lined up an intern job with a tech company,"

Doris explained. "I guess he works remotely for them, somehow? But I'm sure he'll be very busy."

"Not too busy to visit with Grandma?" Dan asked.

"Well, he's already agreed to come over to set up a new computer system for me," Doris said. "And I'm sure we'll see him when he has time."

She continued in her good mood all day, and Dan found it infectious. And it seemed that the people coming into the office were more pleasant than usual. They had a visit from a local woman who brought cookies leftover from the bake sale to benefit the local volunteer fire department. Steve Matson called to make sure Dan was planning to get out on the trail later that week to "show a presence" to the hikers who were sure to come on the weekend.

It seemed all too good to be true.

A little after four, Martina Guzman called to let him know that Matthew McLeod had disappeared off the face of the earth. "We're trying to track him down, but that's proving more difficult than we expected," she said. "Someone doxxed him last week, and he's pulled into a shell."

"What do you mean?" Dan asked her.

"Somebody outed him on the internet," Martina explained. "Posted all his personal data, and his real name, Nathan Petrovski."

Dan reminded her of the call from the Stockton police about Petrovski. "Is this because he's being sued by Antonio Gemmeli's family?" Dan asked.

"Maybe. Someone certainly got on his case," Martina said.

There was an awkward silence as Dan wondered whether that someone was Martina Guzman.

"It wasn't me," she said, correctly reading his silence. "We don't play dirty like that. But it wouldn't be hard for someone who knows how to use the internet to track him down."

Dan remembered Doris' grandson and thought it better to keep quiet. "So the mystery writer has a mysterious disappearance," Dan said. "Just around the time that he's getting sued."

"I don't know if that is any connection, but it certainly seems like good theater right now."

She didn't sound pleased. Dan decided that he didn't want to ask her if she had anything to do with the lawsuit. Besides, he doubted if he would get a straight answer from her on that anyway.

"Maybe that will mean that we get fewer people up here," he suggested.

"I doubt it," Martina answered. "Right now, the internet is on fire with stories about how he had to go into hiding because there's a huge conspiracy to muzzle him."

"Who is supposed to be behind that?" Dan asked.

"Who else? The big bad government. The Forest Service. The swamp in Washington."

Dan wondered how much of that had been promulgated by McLeod himself.

"He claims that he was nearly run over by a truck, and then assaulted by thugs outside his home, and it's not safe for him to stick around, so he's going to hide out and leave the whole mess behind. Just letting you know that's going on," Martina continued. "And I don't think you will, but please let me know if you hear anything."

Dan promised he would. In the background of the office, he could hear Doris promising someone that she would make sure he would call them back.

He signed off with Martina and turned to look at Doris.

"Erica Fisher," she said quietly. "And she doesn't sound happy."

The afternoon had definitely taken a turn for the worse. Dan dialed Erica's number, and she picked up immediately.

Erica didn't wait for Dan to say hello. "Dan, I have to ask you. Did you talk to a reporter from New York about the dig?"

Dan took a deep breath and gave her a summary of the call.

"Shit," Erica said.

"I swear, I did not say anything other than that she should talk to you," Dan assured her.

"Well, she, or somebody else, got some information from someone," Erica said. The way she said it made it sound as if she still considered him a likely source. "And it is all wrong. This thing is completely out of control."

Dad repeated what he had told her.

"Okay, fine. Thanks, Dan," She was obviously still furious. "But she got this story from someone, and now the story is out there, and there is almost nothing in the story that's accurate."

"I promise you that none of that came from me," Dan said. "The only thing I told her was that she needed to talk to you."

"Okay. Thanks, Dan." Erica hung up abruptly.

Dan held the phone in his hand and looked at Doris.

"Not good?" she asked.

"Not good," Dan agreed. He couldn't decide which of the calls had bothered him more—the one from Martina Guzman, or the one from Erica.

It was only ten minutes later that Steve Matson called. He wanted to discuss a phone call he had just received from Erica Fisher.

Dan gave a sigh and summarized his conversation with Erica, and told Steve about the call from the reporter that morning.

"Jesus," Steve said. "It would help if you let me know about that kind of thing."

"If I had told her anything, I would have," Dan said. "But I didn't. So I didn't."

"I know," Steve said. "But it would have been nice to know about that before Erica called."

Dan agreed and apologized to his boss.

"Have you seen the story in the Post?" Steve asked.

"No," Dan said. "And the writer I talked to writes for the New Yorker."

"Thanks, Dan," Steve said. "But I don't think that is going to make the slightest difference to Erica."

chapter 25

It was the following day that the shit really hit the fan.

Dan had just arrived home after a long day at the ranger station when he glanced out the window to see his elderly neighbor Ruth trudging toward his house, a look of grim determination on her face.

For only a second, Dan considered hiding from her, and then he walked over to open the door.

Ruth didn't waste any time with a greeting.

"I thought you'd need to see this," she said, holding up her phone. "It's on all the news now."

She stared at her phone briefly, then tapped the screen and handed it to Dan.

Dan watched as the screen came to life, and he recognized the image as a major right wing news personality, Patty Harrison. The headline below her talking head said, "Major Coverup in California Massacre."

"Tonight, we bring you the news of another major coverup by this administration, so focused on being woke, about protecting everyone's snowflake feelings, that they won't even come to grips with some of the most damning evidence we've seen."

Dan swallowed weakly as he watched the screen.

"A professor at the University of California in Merced, and yes, that's a state university paid for by your tax dollars, has discovered the human remains of at least four individuals, an adult and at least three children, who were murdered and then scalped back in the day when that state still had bands of Native Americans roaming the countryside and attacking the settlers.

"The evidence is clear, and Professor Fisher admits that's what she's found. But she is so afraid of the ridiculous political powers that be, that she won't even hazard a guess as to what these discoveries really mean. All she will say is that she has dated these remains to between one hundred and three hundred years ago.

"Well, I guess we don't need to be professors of archeology to understand what happened here. By Professor Fisher's own estimation, some time ago, possibly as recently as the early 1900s a group of people--men, women, and children—were massacred and scalped right there in California. And I will give you just one guess as to who was responsible for that horror.

"Don't you think it's about time we stopped buying that ridiculous story about the noble savage, who loved the earth and lived in peace with all creation? Don't you think that it's about time that we brought these massacres out into the light of day? Why are Dr. Fisher and the rest of these academics so afraid of the obvious truths? They want to rewrite history to tell us how evil the white colonists were, but will they admit that those very settlers were fighting for their lives against savages who murdered and scalped women and children? Apparently not."

Dan's stomach was churning. He tried to hand the phone back to Ruth, but she pushed it back to him. "No, keep watching. There's more," she said.

As Dan looked at the phone again, there was an interview with a man named Marty Harrison, who was described as a local pastor. Dan glanced at Ruth. When were people in Sacramento considered locals up here in the mountains, he wondered.

Harrison was explaining to the interviewer that "My group was asking the US Forest Service and Tuolumne County to allow our church to provide a Christian burial for these brave souls who risked their lives to help make our state what it is today. It is their right as Christians to be received into heaven after all they suffered. We are asking that this site be forever preserved as a state park or national monument, as a testament to the courage and suffering that our forefathers showed in the making of America. This is the kind of story that should be taught to every child in every school in our state, and in the nation."

The broadcast cut back to Patty Harrison. "He makes a very good point there," she said. "We certainly celebrate and memorialize the Donner Party for their heroic struggles to head west in the face of all that Mother Nature could throw against them. It's only appropriate that we do the same for this brave family that fought for their lives, and lost, against the cruelty of native peoples in this area. All they wanted was a place to live in peace, and be free, and they were cruelly massacred and scalped, offered no mercy, no quarter. They should take their place among the bravest heroes of the West."

Off camera, a voice broke in to ask a question of Patty Harrison.

"Is this on government land? Is it National Forest land?" the voice asked.

"That's just it," Harrison continued. "It is National Forest land. It's our land. I don't know why some assistant professor gets to decide what happens on land that is owned by the American people, but I'd like to know why."

Ruth gestured at the phone, asking Dan to pay even closer attention now.

"And I can't keep from wondering what the Forest Service, our taxpayer-funded Forest Service, is doing about all of this. It's not like they couldn't get involved. Remember Dan Courtwright, that ranger who likes to solve crimes?"

Dan's heart sank hollowly into his shoes as he listened.

"Well, the Forest Service doesn't want him to get involved. When a journalist reached out to Mr. Courtwright, he made it very clear that this entire site was under the control of an assistant professor at the local university, and he wasn't being asked to get involved in any way. You got the idea, talking to Mr. Courtwright, that he had been told to keep his hands off. Now, why would they do that?"

The color had drained out of Dan's face. He really wanted to give the phone back to Ruth and find a place to sit down, but Ruth murmured, "Just a second, it's almost over."

The next face on the broadcast was identified as Jason Fletcher, of Willoughby Partners.

"Mr. Fletcher," Patty Harrison was asking, "I understand that your company has provided the funding for this project. What's your take on these findings?"

"We think this is a very important discovery," Fletcher said. "It really tells a narrative of what these early settlers endured to come west and help this country grow. We'd like to see this site honored by creating a state park like Donner Lake, or even a national monument to recognize its importance. "

Patty Harrison was back. "I think we can all agree with that, one hundred percent," she said. "And don't worry, this story is not going away. We will keep following this until we know exactly why such primitive savagery is being defended and covered up by university professors in California."

Ruth reached out for her phone, and Dan handed it back to her.

"There's a Mormon group that's leading prayers for the salvation of their souls," Ruth said drily. "So that should make everyone feel better."

Dan was still stunned. "What does Walt say about all this?" he asked weakly.

Ruth shook her head. "He's still down at the dig. I don't think he's seen it yet. But Erica Fisher left there yesterday, and they haven't heard a word from her since. She must be sick to her stomach."

"I sure as hell am," Dan said. "And in case you're interested, Matthew McLeod has done the same."

"What do you mean?" Ruth asked.

"Claims a truck tried to run him down, and then somebody tried to beat him up, so he's going into hiding," Dan explained.

"Give me a break," Ruth muttered with disgust. "How derivative."

Dan shot her a questioning look.

"Sherlock Holmes," Ruth replied. "He left London after being run down by a carriage and then attacked by hooligans outside 221B Baker Street. I wonder if McLeod is going to Reichenbach Falls."

Again, Dan looked confused.

"All part of the Holmes legacy," Ruth said. "A television adaptation of that has Holmes and Moriarty fighting on the edge of the falls, and both falling to their deaths. Supposedly."

Dan shook his head dismissively. "We can only hope," he said.

Ruth nodded. "Well, at least you got off lightly on this news story. At least you weren't accused of hiding the truth about brutal savages."

"This must be so hard on Erica," Dan said.

"Can't you do anything, Dan?" Ruth asked.

But they both knew the answer to that question.

<h1 style="text-align:center">chapter 26</h1>

Once Ruth left, Dan took a look at his answering machine on his landline. The light was blinking to indicate he had messages, but that didn't prepare him for the announcement that there were twenty-seven of the damn things. When the first one was from someone he'd never met, Dan turned the machine off and went into the kitchen.

That was when his cell phone rang, and Dan saw it was from Steve Matson. Dan let it ring three more times before he finally answered.

"I guess you've seen the news?" Matson began.

Dan grunted an affirmation.

"I have a suggestion," Steve continued. And before Dan could offer an objection, he asked if Dan would like to spend a few days far from any phone or computer. "I was thinking about that old trail up the Carson River," he said.

"The one that hasn't seen a trail crew in forty years?" Dan asked.

"Yeah, maybe fifty," Steve agreed. "Do you think you could spend a few days up there, checking things out for me?"

Dan didn't like the feeling that Steve was trying to get rid of him. But the more he thought about that area, far from any other trail, far from any media, long abandoned by hikers, the more it appealed to him. "So, just go up there and check it out?" Dan asked.

"How long do you think that would take?" Matson asked. "Maybe three or four days?"

"I mean, you're not asking me to restore the trail, just to check it out?" Dan asked.

"Exactly. You couldn't fix that trail if I gave you all summer. Just see what's still up there, and if there is anything worth restoring."

"Yeah," Dan said. "Maybe three days. It kinda depends on what I find."

"Exactly," Steve said. "Check it out."

"Okay. Yeah, I can do that," Dan agreed.

"And Dan?" Steve added. "Leave your phone down here."

"And my radio?" Dan asked hopefully.

"Take it along," Steve said. "Just so I can tell people I know you took it."

When Dan told Kristen about the phone call, she gave him a sad smile and patted his shoulder. "At least you have somewhere to go," she said. "I feel sorry for Erica."

Dan nodded. He didn't feel much like talking about it.

"And don't let the bears get you," Kristen said. "I want you back."

"The bears would probably go easier on me," Dan said.

Kristen began to rub his neck, then drew him close and kissed him. And kissed him again.

The next morning Dan drove to the trailhead with enough food in his pack for four days in the wilderness. There were only two other cars in the parking area. Dan guessed they might be fishermen. He parked his truck under a tree that should provide shade in the afternoon, if he had done his solar calculations correctly, and locked up.

With no tools to carry, his pack seemed light this time. He

hoisted it onto his shoulders and set out up the trail. The first half mile followed the course of the river, flat in this section, but still carrying a full load of spring snowmelt.

At the first junction, Dan took the left-hand trail and began to climb up the switchbacks that ascended alongside a tributary creek, each switchback revealing a new view of the creek as it cascaded down from pool to pool with whitewater in between. The trail climbed more quickly than the stream, and soon Dan was well above it, with views back down the canyon toward the main river.

As he stopped to enjoy the view, Dan spotted a lone man, crouching in the bushes near the stream below. Dan watched as the man expertly cast a fly line up into a small pool and then driftes it down. On the third cast the man jerked his rod up, and a flash of silver leapt out of the water. The man quickly hauled the fish in, unhooked it, and tossed it back into the stream below.

He was a tall, thin black man dressed in loose faded blue jeans and a plaid shirt. Dan had met him a few years ago and enjoyed their conversation. What was his name? Jackson? Jefferson? Some president's name starting with a J. He drove up from Stockton a few times a year, passing up the planted trout in the river to catch these wild fish in the small tributary creek.

The man wiped his hands on his pants, then looked up and caught sight of Dan. He smiled and Dan gave him a thumbs up. The man bowed and took a small ironic bow. And then they both went back to what they had been doing, Dan climbing the switchbacks up the side of the ridge, leaving the fishing to the man who knew it well.

After a few miles the trail flattened out and led Dan into a large meadow, now just ringed on the south side with a few white strips of snow. That was where the trees still shaded the meadow and kept things cool, even now.

The center of the meadow was saturated with water, and Dan picked his way around the right-hand side, where he could get above the water and keep his feet dry. From there he climbed the last ridge and stopped for lunch where the trail intersected with the Pacific Crest Trail. The sun was out, the air was sparkling clear, and Dan could see endless peaks extending for miles both north and south.

It was a great spot. Dan sat down on the trunk of a fallen tree and opened up his pack. He carefully laid out the food for lunch: salami, cheese, some crackers, some dried fruit. A handful of M&Ms for dessert. It was gourmet fare for the mountains. He took a long pull from his water bottle, feeling the icy water as it flowed down into his gut, so cold it made his teeth hurt.

A noise from the south made him turn his head, and he saw a young couple hiking toward him on the PCT. The girl, in front, wore a tank top and tights, with a big floppy hat providing shade for her head and shoulders. The young guy behind her was in shorts and a sleeveless T-shirt, a ball cap on his head. Dan wondered how they could bear the straps of the backpacks on their bare shoulders.

After a cheerful greeting, the young man asked Dan if he wanted to see their permit.

Dan smiled and shook his head. "Anybody out here right now probably has a pretty good idea of what they're doing," Dan said. "And nobody without a permit ever offers to show me one. Where have you been?"

The young man summarized their route and asked how far it was to the trailhead.

"I left there this morning," Dan said. "And it's all downhill. You'll make it in plenty of time before dark."

The young woman leaned on her hiking poles and smiled at

Dan. She nodded her head, flopping the big hat and flashing her sunglasses, and said she was dreaming of a hot shower.

"And pizza," her partner added.

Dan smiled and offered them a seat on the log. With a quick glance the two consulted with each other and decided that they would keep on hiking. As they took the trail down into the meadow, Dan called out, "Enjoy the hike!"

"And the shower!" the young woman replied, with a laugh.

Dan watched them go, realizing that theirs was probably the second car in the parking area. That meant that he had the place to himself. He finished off his lunch, saving a few M&Ms to munch on the trail, and pulled on his pack. From here on, he would be exploring new ground, and he would be doing it on his own. He couldn't help smiling to himself.

The trail crossed the PCT and then threaded its way down a narrow canyon, accompanied by a gurgling brook. Here there was more snow—this was the northeast side of the ridge, after all—and the trail occasionally crossed over or through a thick bank of the stuff. There were no footprints to show that anyone had been down here before Dan this year.

The trees down in the canyon were thicker, protected from the prevailing west winds, and there were already the first shoots of grass pushing up where there was no snow.

As Dan looked down into the canyon, he spied a tiny cascade, the white water of the brook tumbling some thirty-five feet down into a black pool nearly hidden behind a dense cloud of new green grass, ferns and bushes.

There was something down there, Dan realized. The tall grass was moving in places. Dan stopped to watch, trying to see what was ruffling the deep grass.

The head of a small black bear poked itself out of the green grass and looked around. Dan froze, holding his breath in suspense, hoping not to frighten the bear.

The bear slowly surveyed its surroundings, staring myopically in Dan's direction, and then, satisfied that all was in order, lowered its head and went back to burrowing in the ground for whatever it had been eating. Dan watched for another minute or two, but the bear made no further appearances, so he quietly slipped off down the trail.

By the end of the day, Dan had hiked down to the bottom of the Carson Canyon and was looking for a place to set up camp. He found a nice spot on a small rocky knoll above the river, with more than enough flat space for his tent and an area to cook as well. He prided himself on being quick and efficient at setting up camp, and this time was no different. Within minutes he had his three-man ultralight tent set up—Dan was far too tall for a regular one-man tent, and the extra ounces of the larger tent were more than compensated by the extra room it gave him.

He unpacked his gear, fluffing up his sleeping bag, inflating his sleeping pad, and taking the time to unpack his clothes and move into his tent. This was going to be his base camp for a couple of days, so he set everything up. Then he walked down to the river to filter and fill his water bottles, getting enough done for both that night and the next morning.

Down at the river, he enjoyed the sunlight of the late afternoon as it reflected off the surface of the water and added a golden glow to the sides of the canyon above him. This, he decided, was going to be a great trip.

He went to sleep that night with the rushing water of the river filling the air of his camp, whispering calm in his ears.

<h1 style="text-align:center">chapter 27</h1>

Dan woke up three times that night. The first time the discreet hooting of an owl in the forest greeted him. He rolled over onto his back and listened for a few minutes. The next thing he knew, it was hours later, and a gentle breeze was ruffling the fabric of his tent. He lay cocooned in his sleeping bag. He could hear the gentle scratch of his beard against the fabric of the bag as he breathed. The rush of the river was less now, as the cooler temperatures of night had slowed the melting of the snow. He allowed himself to melt down into the bag.

And then it was dawn. He could hear the birds in their early morning chorus, greeting each other and making sure that they had all made it through the night. Dan slowly opened his left eye and judged that the sun was just now beginning to dust the very top of the peaks above him. It would be more than an hour before it reached down into the canyon to warm his camp. He closed his eye and allowed himself to drift back into something between sleep and awake.

His mind began to lead him forward, and he started thinking through the route he might take up the canyon. Stay on this side of the river, or cross over? It would be easier to cross now, early in the morning, before the snowmelt picked up again. But if he did, how would he cross back in the afternoon? On the other hand, most trails would stay on this side of the river, unless there was a major problem upstream, some obstacle that the other side would avoid. Maybe there was a cliff that blocked this side, or a dense aspen thicket that would take hours to fight his way through.

He decided he would take his chances with this side, at least at first. He could always cross the river later, farther up the canyon, where it would be smaller.

And he would try to stay in the trees, looking for ancient blazes on their bark. After forty or fifty years, some of the trees would have fallen, and others might be hidden by younger trees that had grown up in the meantime. But if he could find a blaze, it would clearly indicate the trail. And fifty years ago, a blaze was the standard method of marking a trail. If he could find one, it would give him a reference point for the rest of the day. From there he could make concrete progress.

As he thought about it, Dan reflected that this process wasn't unlike solving McLeod's damn treasure hunt. But with McLeod, there were too many options, too many possibilities, and not enough information. He knew where trails were likely to lead. He had built them, faced the same problems, and knew the usual solutions. He had no idea how McLeod liked to do things.

And there was one more big difference. He knew where he wanted to end up in the canyon—far upriver, where the trees were tiny and the trail would be more obvious. And from there back down, maybe he could follow it more easily. It was a lot easier to follow a trail once you had part of it identified. That had certainly happened to him on trips like this before.

But with McLeod, he had no idea where the end of the trail was, or where it was leading. There was no way to work backwards. With a trail, he knew the general parameters and could take an educated guess about how it would go. He didn't have that with the books.

He didn't know enough about McLeod or the books to make any educated guesses. And there were too many possibilities, too many ways to go wrong. And, he decided with a start, he wasn't going to waste any more time thinking about it.

He opened his eyes, unzipped his sleeping bag, and sat up. It was time to get on with things. That did not include thinking about Matthew McLeod.

After breakfast he struck out from camp, aiming to stay in the forest and look for blazes on the trees. It was slow going, and it got a lot worse when he wandered into the path of an avalanche that had swept down and flattened the trees. By the age of the newer trees growing up in the ruins of the old forest, Dan estimated that it had happened twenty years ago or more—long enough ago that the young trees were dense and tall, but not long enough ago that the trunks of their fallen ancestors had completely decomposed.

Dan swore quietly to himself and tried to hike up the side of the canyon to get above the worst of the bushwhacking. When that didn't work, he surrendered and picked his way over the larger fallen trunks and through the thicket of young pines. Even with a good-sized trail crew, clearly this section would take days, if not weeks.

When he finally got past the avalanche damage the sun was well up in the sky, and Dan could see the wall of a moraine across the canyon in front of him. That meant a steep climb, and he picked his way upward, first past huge boulders and manzanita bushes, then, as he got higher on the moraine, through pines and smaller rocks and cobbles. Moraines always made trails more complicated, as the underlying rocks were such a jumble that it was hard to pick a clean, clear line up the slope.

Once he cleared the moraine, the hike got easier. Ahead he could see a few clearings in the trees, either wide spots in the river or a meadow or two. He had yet to see a tree blaze or a cairn, but now in the flat of the canyon floor he found a game trail that looked as if it could have been even wider and larger years ago. The clue that sealed its identity was an ancient log, cut through and marking the path of the original trail.

Dan grinned. He looked backwards to see where the trail might lie in that direction. On his way back, he would try to track it. He slipped off his pack, pulled out his water bottle, and took three deep swigs of water. This was more like it.

Ahead he could see the game trail leading out into a sunlit meadow, in all likelihood following the old hiking path. Clouds overhead told him that there was a chance of thunderstorms, but it was still well before noon. He could easily continue another two hours in this direction before he had to turn around, and by then he'd know if the clouds would continue to build.

On the far side of the meadow the trail disappeared into the forest, but Dan carefully examined the largest trees on the far side and was rewarded with an old blaze, nearly scarred over, that marked the way forward.

Now it was hunt and peck, looking for blazes, clambering over massive fallen trees at times, and trying to determine what was the original trail, what had been created by wildlife since then. As the wall of the canyon closed in on the right side, the trails all converged down by the river, and Dan was confronted with an aspen thicket that blocked his path.

He had learned long ago that aspen thickets were nearly impassable and made for lousy trail routes—the trees grew too quickly and too close together, which meant that they overgrew the trails faster than any trail crew could clear them. He made a tentative effort to penetrate the thicket but gave up when faced with numerous crossing branches and trunks only thirty feet in.

He turned around and climbed back out.

Above him, the canyon wall on the right was steep and rocky. He turned and faced the river. There, down on the boulders above the current, was a cairn: four large rocks, built into a stable pile.

That was the good news.

He hiked down to the cairn and looked around. On his side of the river, upstream, the aspens were dense to the point of being impenetrable and ran right down to the river. With the high water, there was no way past the aspens without swimming. Across the river, Dan could see another pile of rocks, set atop a boulder some fifteen feet above the river.

That was the bad news.

The old trail crossed the river here, and there was no way Dan was going to try that now, with the current near flood stage with snowmelt.

Which left him with only one conclusion: It was clearly time for lunch.

Dan sat on a large rock above the river, pulled off his daypack, and rummaged around inside for the food.

A shadow passing over him made him look up. The clouds were building now and covered most of the sky. As he pulled out his food, he also pulled out his rain shell. At least he was prepared for this.

He ate his lunch slowly, enjoying the sound of the river below him. He looked for trout, but the high water meant that most of them would be deep along the bottom, avoiding most of the fastest current.

The sky seemed to be lowering, and the peaks above him were now sometimes covered with cloud. Dan calculated it would take him a good two hours to get back to camp and the safety of his tent, and looking at the sky, he wasn't sure that was enough time. But he had his rain shell. He decided to take his time with his lunch.

By the time he had swigged the last of his water and eaten the last peanut M&M, Dan knew it was going to rain. He just didn't know how hard. He packed up, strapping his rain shell outside his daypack, and began to try to trace the old trail back down the canyon.

Dan found a blaze on the back of a large pine and stopped to get his bearings. That was when he felt what he thought were the first drops of rain. He pushed on through the forest, with the trees sheltering him from most of the drops. But then he came to the moraine. Here the trees were smaller, and the rain was picking up. He stopped to put on his rain shell, and then studied the terrain ahead.

He could see at least three options to follow, and chose the route that led most directly down the canyon along the river. It wasn't the easiest route, but he knew that most people would want to follow the river as much as possible, and that trails often followed that path.

He soon lost the trail in the rocks and trees on the slope of the moraine, but found it again fifty yards further down when he spotted a cairn still standing on a large rock. From there he found the tread of the trail—barely visible on the ground—that contoured along the slope back away from the river, and followed it for another seventy-five yards until he'd lost it again.

The rain was steady now and was dripping down off his hood in front of his face. He gave the hood a shake and was rewarded with a face full of raindrops.

Peering through the rain, he could see the avalanche path in front of him. In this rain he would get soaked clambering through that. Up to his left, the slope seemed more open, and he decided to take his chances in that direction.

The only trails here were narrow game trails created by deer, sometimes going underneath branches or trees that Dan had to avoid. The deer were a lot shorter than Dan. It was tough going, but it was better than the avalanche.

By the time Dan got back to camp, his pants and boots were soaked through, and his shirt was dripping with condensation. The rain was still coming down steadily, and he stripped out of his wet clothes in the vestibule of the tent, leaving them there to keep the inside of the tent dry. From his big pack he pulled out his towel and dried off as best he could, then climbed half into his sleeping bag, his body shivering.

He lay back, content to know he would soon be dry and warm, and watched the raindrops fall on his tent, collecting on the fabric of the roof in tiny pools, then racing down the side in little rivulets. He allowed his eyes to close and was soon drifting off to sleep.

When he woke, he checked his watch. He had only slept for twenty minutes, but his body and mind felt completely renewed. He folded his hands behind his head and relaxed in the tent, watching the raindrops and listening to the sounds of the water. There was nothing else to do.

The rain continued for another hour, and Dan rested in the tent, allowing his mind to wander over the possible routes of the trail. It would be a huge job, and one that would never get approved with the current funding. Thinking about the funding brought to mind the five million dollars that McLeod was supposed to have hidden in the Sierra. Dan let those thoughts mingle with the trail work, and soon he was drifting off to sleep again.

He woke up without a solution to either problem. Slowly, over the course of half an hour, the rain drops on the tent went from steady drumbeat to intermittent sprinkles and then stopped. He could hear the steady shower ease into a spattering patter of drops. When he stuck his head out of the tent, he could see sun on the canyon wall above him, and blue sky to the west. But the forest glistened and looked refreshed.

Ten minutes later, Dan had pulled on his boots and was digging through his bear canister, making plans for dinner.

chapter 28

The next morning, as he hiked back out, Dan mentally composed a note to Steve Matson on what he had found. It wouldn't be a long note, because it would be a huge project to restore the trail. And he knew that neither Steve nor the USFS would decide such a project would be a priority. There was no need to waste time or words on something that would never happen. By the time he reached the PCT he had written it mentally a dozen times.

Once across the PCT the trail was all downhill, and Dan increased his pace, swinging his long legs in big strides through the first meadow and across a tiny stream. When he got to the switchbacks alongside the creek, he looked for the fly fisherman, but the stream was still slightly milky with the runoff from the rain, and he didn't see anyone fishing. The air cleansed his brain and left a scent of rain and fresh earth.

At the trailhead, Dan's was the only car. He tossed his pack in the back, climbed into the driver's seat, and started down the road to home. With any luck at all, he would be in time to take a nice hot shower before dinner.

Farther down, Dan saw the turnoff to the track to Erica Fisher's dig. On a whim he turned off the highway and followed the side road down into the canyon. He had enough time to drive by and see what kind of signage had been put there.

But of course there was roadwork. One of the rules of travel in the mountains was that if you were ever in a hurry, you would run into roadwork. Today proved the rule yet again. Before he could find a wide spot to turn around, Dan came around another corner and found himself in front of a tattooed and sunburnt woman flagman with a long dirty blond ponytail, who waved him to a stop, a cigarette in the other hand. She looked tired and weatherbeaten, as if she'd spent her life out there.

The woman stared at Dan for a few seconds, then came over and asked Dan if he was there to inspect.

"Nope," Dan assured her. "I'm just passing through. How long is the wait?"

She gave a shrug. "Twenty minutes, maybe. I can call 'em if you want." Her voice was rough, and she pulled on her cigarette.

Dan looked down the road. He could see flashing lights down there, and a couple of big machines were roaring and beeping over the sounds of a chain saw. He checked his rearview mirror. Nobody was behind him. It would make more sense to just drive back to the highway and keep going. Down below, a group of men watching the work turned and looked at him. Maybe they would take pity on him and let him pass. He waved.

One of the guys waved back, and then gestured to someone further down the road. In a moment Dan saw Cal Healey, betrayed by his usual slight limp, walking up the road toward him.

Dan got out and went to meet his friend.

After shaking hands, Dan asked Cal, "What's going on?"

Cal pointed to his Tuolumne County Sheriff's car parked on the side of the road near the work. "See that squad car down there?" he asked Dan. "We're trying to find the driver," he deadpanned.

Dan grinned. "Been looking long?"

"Ever since I got here," Cal answered, face still deadpan.

Down below, the chain saw continued to drone away, and then a large Ponderosa pine began to slowly topple down. With a resounding whump it hammered onto the ground near the road, sending up a cloud of dust and small branches.

"We figured the easiest way to keep people out of that dig of yours was to take care of some tree work that needed to be done," Cal said. He looked around at the road behind Dan's car. There were no other cars. "Seems to be working. I guess if you can't get to the trailhead…"

"Good idea," Dan said. "I have to admit I didn't like hearing about some of the problems down there. They're kids. They're not exactly equipped to handle them."

"Isn't your friend Walt down there as well?" Cal asked. "He seems pretty solid."

"He's great," Dan agreed. "But he's also damn near eighty years old."

They stopped talking to watch as a large tree came crashing down alongside the road.

"Is that one of those rogue Ponderosas?" Dan asked, pointing to the felled tree.

"You need to do a better job of controlling these damn trees, Ranger Courtwright," Cal said. "They are a public nuisance and a positive menace."

Dan shook his head. "Not my trees," he said. "My trees are well-behaved. They stay on National Forest land. These are problem trees. They've become habituated to people, and that's when the trouble starts."

The two men stood together, watching the crew work on the fallen tree, cutting off the branches.

"I heard that now you're an honorary girl," Cal said quietly.

"Well, it's nothing official yet," Dan said. "I'm waiting until I get the confirmation letter."

Cal nodded. "Makes sense. Do you have a special outfit to wear for that?"

Dan asked if he had heard of the Royal Order of the Garter. Cal glanced up at him.

"It's a British thing," Dan said. "Over here we get two garters, and the stockings to match."

"Sounds great," Cal said.

"I don't think I'll shave my legs, though," Dan said. "It wouldn't look right."

"Good idea," Cal agreed. "People might talk."

Dan pointed to Cal's vehicle. "I thought your car might be one of these decoys. I've been seeing a lot of those recently."

"Oh yeah," Cal said. "We love them. We're getting rid of all our officers and just putting out the decoy cars, parking them anywhere there is a problem."

"Really?" Dan asked.

"Sure," Cal replied. "Those decoys are cheaper, and statistics show that wherever we put an empty car as a decoy, crime goes down fifteen percent. We figure if we can put out another seventy cars or so, it should disappear completely."

"Good idea," Dan said. "But I bet it would work even better if you could get some of those self-driving cars. They could patrol around."

"Already on it," Cal said. "The best part is that with those, you don't even need any officers at all, just a thirteen-year-old kid with a joystick."

"Seems like a perfect solution," Dan said.

Cal snorted. "Yeah. You should get some for the Forest Service," he suggested.

"Yeah, but I don't think we could get a car into the backcountry," Dan answered. "Too many rocks."

Cal considered this. "Maybe you should get some robotic bears," he said. "Can you imagine somebody camped up there and they see a bear walking over to their campsite?"

"A bear with cubs," Dan suggested, now grinning.

"Robotic cubs, right," Cal agreed. "And it comes and inspects their campsite, and if there's a violation, the bear craps out a citation and a fine, right then and there."

"Complete with photos, to document it," Dan said. "How soon can you have those delivered?"

"Do you have Amazon Prime?" Cal asked. "Two days. Otherwise, it might take a week. They come from China. And you'll need to specify color and size."

"I'd want to make sure they were native bears," Dan said. "Pandas won't cut it."

"I'll specifiy that on the order," Cal said.

They stood together watching the tree crew bring a loader over to lift up one of the logs.

"Maggie says you guys are making great progress," Cal said.

Dan shook his head. "Maybe we are, I don't know."

"She says you and Ruth are explaining it all," Cal insisted.

"Ruth's teaching me, that's for sure," Dan answered. "But there are so many different possibilities that it's like a whole lot of spaghetti thrown on the wall—a massive mess."

"You know," Cal said, "you're not supposed to put the sauce on the spaghetti before you throw it."

"That would explain why Kristen got so upset," Dan answered. That made him remember the time. He glanced at his watch and knew he'd better hurry. "Hey," he said. "If I see one of those self-driving cars, how do I know you're at the wheel?"

"Wave," Cal said. "If it's me, I'll blink the lights at you."

"One if by land, two if by sea?"

"Right," Cal agreed.

Dan pointed to Cal's car, with the lights flashing. "So what does that mean?" he asked.

Cal was quick with his response. "Danger. Rogue robotic bear ahead. Proceed with caution."

Dan grinned. He turned to walk back to his truck. "Stay safe," he called out. "Watch out for those rogue trees."

"Yep," Cal replied with a wave. "Same to you."

chapter 29

Dan did make it home in time for dinner, barely.

"I wasn't sure you were going to make it," Kristen said, "but I made enough for us both."

Dan tried to kiss her, but she protested, "Get in the shower. You just have time for a quick one before dinner is on the table."

Dan admitted defeat and within a minute was in the steaming water, letting it run over his head and pummel his shoulders. He stayed that way for minutes, until he heard Kristen bang on the door. "Dinner's ready!"

He quickly soaped up and rinsed off, toweled off his body and slipped on a clean pair of pants, commando, with no shirt. He arrived at the table still rubbing a towel on his head.

"Did you have fun?" Kristen asked, putting a plate in front of him.

Dan grinned. "Not exactly fun, but you know how John Muir was always revived and energized by his trips to the wilderness? Well, that's me. Consider me revived."

"Nice," Kristen smiled approvingly. Then a different look flickered across her face.

"What?" Dan asked. He glanced down at his plate. Italian sausages with garlic pasta, and fresh salad in the bowl in the middle of the table.

She grimaced. "You've been a popular guy while you've been

gone," she said. "Lots of people want to talk to you."

Dan took a mouthful of pasta and rolled his eyes.

"Good?" Kristen asked.

"Delicious," Dan mumbled through the food in his mouth.

"You could do what Napoleon did," Kristen suggested.

Dan looked at his plate, then back at Kristen.

"About the messages," Kristen explained. "Apparently, he never opened his mail until it was three weeks old. He said the important decisions could always wait, and the little stuff would take care of itself."

Dan grinned and sawed off a piece of the sausage. "Did he have email and voicemail?" he asked, and popped the sausage into his mouth.

"It was just a suggestion," Kristen said. "Or else you're going to be busy tonight."

Kristen watched him take a deep breath and let it out slowly, even as he was chewing the sausage. "Sorry," she said.

Dan shook his head. "I'll see how many of them I can delete," he said.

Kristen poured a little more wine into his glass. "You might need that," she said.

There were thirty-one messages.

Dan sighed and began to listen to the first one. It was from Erica Fisher. "Just wanted to apologize for the other day, Dan. I know it wasn't you who talked to the reporter. I'm sorry. I shouldn't have gone off on you like that. Please call me when you have a minute to allow me to apologize in person. Well, on the phone, anyway."

Dan kept that one to deal with later.

The next two were from reporters he'd never heard of. Both needed to talk to him urgently. He decided to delete the rest of those messages.

Lindsay Warren called to ask if he'd seen the story in the New York Post. She hoped Dan would find some time to tell her his side of the story, and maybe correct that one.

So it hadn't been his friend who wrote the story. That made Dan feel better. He'd forward the writer's contact information to Erica and let her have a go.

Two more from other reporters, and three telemarketing calls.

That Napoleon was beginning to sound like a smart character.

In between the chaff, there was an interesting message from someone named Kim Archer, who explained that he was a private detective working for the Gemmeli family and was hoping he could talk to Dan. Given what Dan knew, that the family was suing people over Tony's death, that sounded like something to avoid.

And then a call from Steve Matson, just making sure Dan got home safe, and checking in with him.

More chaff, and then Martina Guzman, with a note to give her a call. He would call both Steve and Martina and ask them about returning the call from Kim Archer.

The phone rang and Dan glanced at the number. It was not one he recognized. He considered the odds based on the voicemail and muttered something about Napoleon going to hell.

"Hello!" he said. "This is Dan."

There was a pause. Dan was about to hang up when he heard a woman's voice on the other end clear her throat. "Mr. Courtwright?" she asked. "I am hoping you might indulge me for a minute."

Dan was not in the mood to play games. "Can you tell me who this is?" he asked.

There was another pause. "Let's just say that my name is Jacqueline Pulaski," she said. "I am a friend of Matthew McLeod.

He gave me your number."

Now it was Dan's turn to pause. "Okay," he finally answered. "And what can I do for you, Ms. Pulaski?"

Another pause. "I am in a rather complicated situation," she said. "It isn't something I can go into on the phone, but I was wondering if you might be willing to meet me somewhere so that we could talk."

Dan's suspicions were now running full bore. "About finding five million dollars?" he asked, allowing a note of sarcasm to tinge the remark.

"No," she said. "I think it might more accurately be about ending the search for five million dollars."

"By helping you find it?" Dan asked.

"Only in a manner of speaking," the woman said. "I don't need help finding the treasure."

"But you do need my help?" Dan asked.

"I think so, at least in some way," she said. "If you want to end this nonsense. And I think you do."

Dan thought about this. "How do you know McLeod?" he asked.

"Your reputation precedes you," she said. "It's an honor to meet you. A signal honor."

Exactly the words McLeod had used on their phone call.

"Okay," Dan agreed. "You know McLeod. And you think you know a way to end this hidden treasure stuff?" he asked.

"I might. And I'm wondering if you might be willing to help me."

"Doing what, exactly?" Dan asked.

"Where can we meet to talk about this?" she asked. "I can be in Sonora tomorrow."

Dan thought it over. After his work on the trails, he could take at least half the day off. He wanted to go somewhere he wouldn't be noticed. He gave her the location of a Starbucks in a local mall. "Noon?"

"Thank you," she said. She sounded relieved. "I'll see you there."

chapter 30

Gold Country News, Angels Camp, CA. Two teenage boys survived a terrifying ordeal in the mountains yesterday, as they were swept off their feet by the swift current of the Calaveras River above Calaveras Big Trees State Park. The Calaveras County Sheriff Whitewater Search and Rescue team was able to pull them both from the river late yesterday afternoon.

The boys' names are being withheld because they are juveniles. One has been released to his parents, while the other is still in critical condition in the hospital. The Sheriff's office had no further comment, other than to urge the public to show caution and discretion with the very dangerous conditions in the mountains.

The next morning, Dan decided to start with a call to Steve Matson. He took his phone out into the backyard, settled into an Adirondack chair there, and gave Steve a call. He began by briefing Steve on the work he had done up on the long-abandoned trail, and promised to write up a report once he got back in the office. Steve agreed that Dan could take most of the day off, if he promised to write up the report at some point. That was a deal Dan was quick to accept. The following two days he had off anyway. Now it would almost be three in a row.

Before Dan hung up, he told Steve he had one more tale to tell. "You'll never guess who called me yesterday."

Steve didn't bother to guess.

"A woman calling herself Jacqueline Pulaski," Dan said.

Steve paused. "Is that someone I should know?" he asked.

Dan explained that the hero in the McLeod books was named Jack Pulaski. "This woman claims to know McLeod and has a plan on how to end this crazy treasure hunt."

"She sounds like one more nut case to me," Steve said. "I hope you got rid of her."

Dan cleared his throat. "She told me she had a way of ending this thing," he said. "I thought it might be worth talking to her."

"Not on behalf of the Forest Service," Steve said. "Absolutely not. If you want someone to talk to her, refer her to Martina Guzman."

"I'm just going to see what she has to say," Dan tried to explain. "If it makes any sense, I'll pass it on to Martina."

"Not a good idea, Dan," Steve said. "Leave it alone or put her in touch with Martina."

"Well," Dan filibustered, "I'll have to meet with her to do that anyway."

"You could just call her," Steve said. "Or send her a text message with Martina's contact info."

"Yeah, I guess I could do that," Dan agreed. "But I'd want to give Martina a heads-up, first."

"Right," Steve assured him. "Call Martina, tell her about it, and then just pass the woman on."

"In that case, I should call Martina now," Dan said, carefully avoiding making a promise to follow Steve's orders. "If I can get a hold of her."

"Do you still have her number?" Steve asked.

"Yep. I'll call her right now."

He was surprised that Martina Guzman answered his call immediately.

"Dan Courtwright!" she greeted him. "What can I do for you?"

Dan always had the impression that Martina Guzman was two steps ahead of him, but in this case, maybe not. He told her about Jacqueline Pulaski.

"Did she offer any real proof that she was associated with McLeod in any way?" Martina asked.

Dan told her about the quotes from their Zoom call. "And she had my number," he said.

"That really doesn't mean anything," the attorney answered. "Basically, there is no reason for you to meet with this woman. I can't see any real benefit at all, and I do see a number of potential risks, particularly since it will be just the two of you in conversation. There's a real potential that she can put you in some very awkward complications."

"She really seems like she wants to end this thing," Dan said. "Don't you think that's worth at least a short meeting?"

"If she has an idea about that, I would suggest that she put it in writing, and you can send it to me. Otherwise, I would strongly recommend that you have nothing to do with her. You have nothing to gain, and there are many ways that you could end up with a whole lot to lose."

"Isn't that what all attorneys tell their clients about every meeting?" Dan asked.

Martina Guzman sighed. "Yes, it probably is, for good reason. Because that is very good legal advice, and our job is to keep our clients out of trouble."

"Wow," Dan said. "I didn't realize that I was your client. Or, I guess, that you're my attorney."

"I'm not, and you're not," Martina clarified. "The US Forest Service is my client. And if you are working for them, I can give you legal advice."

Dan chuckled. "Steve Matson told me that if I met with this woman, it would not be in any way part of my job."

"Dan, this isn't a game," Martina said. "If she has some kind of offer to make, ask her to put it in writing, and we'll take a look at it. If not, there is no reason to pursue this any further."

"Okay," Dan said. "I'll suggest that to her."

After they ended the call, Dan was pleased to note that he could interpret the conversation to mean that Martina Guzman had given him permission to speak with Jacqueline McLeod, more or less. He would meet with her and find out if she had a plan that she could put in writing.

Dan carried his phone back into the house where Kristen was in the kitchen. He told her about the calls and what he considered his clever solution.

The look on her face told him she was not fooled.

"Steve is right," she said. "Sounds like a nutcase to me. And why would you want to meet with someone like that?"

"She just didn't seem crazy to me," Dan said. "At least on the phone."

"And if she is crazy?" Kristen asked.

"I'm meeting her in a very public place," Dan said. "Not much can happen there."

"I think you should call Cal and ask him what he thinks," she said. Cal was often the source of common sense for Dan, and Kristen knew how to play her cards.

"He'll just want to be there to make sure nothing happens," Dan said. "And who knows what this woman could do if she sees his car there."

"You mean, you're worried that law enforcement might scare her away?" Kristen asked. "That doesn't sound like you think she's very reasonable at all."

But before the discussion could escalate into something more serious, there was a knock on the door. Dan glanced over to see that Maggie and Ruth were waiting outside.

"We're meeting again today," Kristen explained.

Dan nodded. "I'll get out of your hair. Steve wants me to write the trail report."

Before Kristen could let the two women in, Dan had raced for the back of the house, his hands quickly grabbing his laptop computer.

chapter 31

It didn't take him more than forty-five minutes to write up his notes for Steve. He pulled out a previous trail report and used that for a template, with a lot of cutting and pasting. The trail was a mess, and he hadn't been able find most of it, or even explore most of the canyon. But he had seen enough to know that it would be a massive undertaking to reconstruct the trail, even if they could follow the old route. And the route was miles long. That would take weeks or months of work by a trail crew.

When he was done, Dan read through the report one more time, fixing a few typos that autocorrect had highlighted for him. He saved it, then decided to wait until later to send it to Steve. There was no need for Steve to know exactly how quickly he had finished the job.

Out in the living room Dan could hear the women talking. Maggie's voice always carried, and the quieter one was Ruth. But then Dan heard another voice that he recognized, and it surprised him. He decided it was time to go into the kitchen and get a drink of water.

Sure enough, as he walked out into the living room, he saw Maggie, Ruth and Kristen sitting with Doris.

Dan grinned. "I thought you were working with Travis," he said to Doris. "Aren't you the competition?"

Doris laughed. "The boys are doing some kind of computer analysis of everything," she said. "They think they can work the whole thing out without any human help."

"So they don't think they need Grandma?" Dan asked.

"I told them to call me when they did," Doris said. "But in the meantime, I'm going to see what we women can do on our own."

Dan nodded. "Well, if I were a betting man, I wouldn't bet against you guys," he said, taking in the whole group.

A gesture from Kristen caught his eye, and he looked at her.

"Do you want to talk about that phone call?" she asked.

The women all turned to Dan expectantly. Dan realized it was going to be hard to hold back the story, so he began.

"I got a call today from someone who says they know Matt McLeod and can help end this whole thing."

"How did she get your number?" Maggie interrupted him quickly.

"She said Matthew McLeod gave it to her," Dan answered, then waited to see the reaction. The women appeared satisfied.

He went on to explain the rest of his conversation with Jacqueline Pulaski. When he was done there was a moment of quiet.

Kristen was the first to break the silence. "I suggested that he give Cal a call about this," she said. "If this is some kind of swindle, he could back you up."

Maggie shook her head. "He's in court today," she said. "But you could always try to ask one of the other deputies."

Dan shook his head. "It's not that big of a deal," he said. "I'm meeting with her in public, and it will just be the two of us. I'm not worried."

"Where are you meeting?" Maggie asked, still not willing to let it go.

Dan told her about Starbucks.

Maggie nodded. "I can be there," she said. "I'll just sit over to the side and have a latte."

Dan shrugged. "I really don't think you need to do that."

But Maggie just smiled at him and said, "See you there."

That left an awkward silence. After a moment, Ruth spoke up. "You know," she said, "I am convinced that these books were written by more than one person."

The others looked at her expectantly.

"There are changes in style that I've noticed in these books. Some of them are intentional, like when they wrote those chapters on the various topics like presidents, or women, or mining. But sometimes they happen right in the middle of a page. It's been bothering me," she admitted.

There was another silence, only broken by Doris clearing her throat.

"The boys think that there are two authors," she said. "I don't think that's sharing too much information, now that Ruth has mentioned it. They say their computers analyzed it all, and that one person wrote most of it, and then another person did the rest."

Ruth was nodding. "Yes, I'd say only ten or twenty percent, from what I have seen," she said.

"You mean we have two authors?" Maggie asked. "No wonder these things are so complicated."

"I wonder," Ruth said quietly. When everyone was looking at her, she continued. "I wonder if Jacqueline Pulaski might be someone who worked on these books."

At which point the group erupted into a flurry of comments. Everyone except Dan was talking excitedly, nodding, smiling, and pointing fingers at Dan.

When they had all calmed down, Maggie spoke for the group. "Right, then we're agreed," she said. "Dan, you'll meet with this woman, and I'll be there as backup. I'll try to sit somewhere close."

Dan glanced at his watch, and Ruth noticed this.

"You still have lots of time, Dan," she said. "You might as well join us for the rest of the meeting."

Dan looked at the rest of the women, who were nodding. He shrugged, gave a sigh, and found a spot to sit down next to Kristen. She patted him on the leg, but kept her attention on Ruth, who was leading the discussion.

"The next topic is what I have come to call the introductory numerical notes," she said. "Did you notice these? At the beginning of each book, there is a short note."

"About the number of the book," Kristen answered. "I saw those. I thought they were just trying to be cute."

Maggie quickly grabbed Avalanche and started thumbing through it, finding the right page. "You mean this?" she asked. She started reading: "First of all—I have accumulated a wide range of place names in the Sierra based on the geology of the place, from Andesite Peak to Porphyry Lake."

Ruth picked up a piece of paper from her folder. "I have a list of them. Listen to this:

First of all—I have accumulated a wide range of place names in the Sierra based on the geology of the place, from Andesite Peak to Porphyry Lake.

Second to none—Presidents who have died in office somehow get more than their fair share of recognition, and it's something that has been true throughout the course of our history.

The third degree—Peaks are not hidden from sight, nor are lakes hard to find, if you know where to look for them.

The fourth estate is no longer in play—Gems, jewels and other rare stones are hard to find, but that doesn't mean they are not here.

A fifth column is waiting in the wings—Gold miners rarely found any treasure in the higher regions of the Sierra, and it was far more likely that bankers and middlemen profited most from the finds that the miners made.

Honor the Sixth commandment—Death is a rare event on Sierra Nevada trails today, but it was not always so unusual.

There is no reason to stand for the seventh inning stretch—one of the delights in the exploration of mountains and forests is the discovery of small places, places that enfold you in an embrace of intimacy.

There is no eighth wonder of the world—Towering peaks abound in many mountain ranges, but few ranges offer such benign conditions for the recreational hiker as does the Range of Light.

Cloud Nine—The forests of the West are far less complicated than those of the East, but they carry a majesty and power that is all their own.

It's over, for all in tenths and purposes—Women: they inspired the early explorers of these mountains, sometimes because they waited at home, sometimes because they joined in the adventures.

"Each one of them specifically refers to those academic chapters about the topics not related to the story," Ruth continued.

"Is that just to tell us that those chapters don't matter?" Maggie asked.

Ruth's face twisted into a wince. "I don't think it's that simple," she said.

Kristen gave a short chuckle. "Nothing in these books is simple."

"Those are unusual," Doris said. "Why does he say, 'There is no reason to stand for the seventh inning stretch?' And why does he mention that there is no eighth wonder of the world?"

Ruth was nodding now. "I think you're right, Doris," she said. "If you read these, the ones for books two, four…seven…and eight all have negatives in them. Second to none. No longer. There is no… I wonder if that's a way of telling us that we should ignore any clues in those books."

Maggie was shaking her head. "This is nuts. I give up. He just made these so complicated that there is no solution."

The others chorused in agreement.

Ruth held her finger up, and they grew quiet. "Let's look at what that eliminates," she said. "We wouldn't have to worry about the presidents, or the minerals." She paused. "I'm not sure what the seventh one means: 'There is no reason to stand for the seventh inning stretch—one of the delights in the exploration of mountains and forests is the discovery of small places, places that enfold you in an embrace of intimacy.' It's the odd one out, that's for sure."

"And what about number ten?" Kristen asked. "Bad pun intended."

"It's also an outlier," Ruth agreed. Then she looked straight at Dan. "Dan, you will need to ask this woman about these. If she is who she says she is, she probably knows the answer."

chapter 32

It was already blistering hot when Dan got out of his truck in the shopping center, and not a hint of shade anywhere to be found. How did they get these parking lots approved, without a tree in sight? He left the windows open a crack before locking up, but he knew he would be coming back to an oven.

He walked across the asphalt, passing acres of gleaming chrome and paint baking in the sun. He could feel the heat on his face and knew that he would wear a light coat of sweat on his body even before he made it inside the coffee shop.

His eyes took a moment to adjust from the bright sun outside to the relative gloom of Starbucks. He scanned the tables inside but didn't see anyone who might be waiting to meet him.

Suddenly, a short Asian woman waiting for her order turned and walked right up to him.

"I'll bet you're Dan Courtwright," she said.

Her head was level with Dan's chest, and the fact that her face turned up to greet his gave her a look that was somewhere between determined and pugnacious. She was smiling, but there was an energy in her gaze that went beyond mere friendliness, and tinged, maybe just a shade, towards manic. Horn rim glasses and short bobbed hair added to her no-nonsense look. Dan guessed that she was a few years younger than he, but he wasn't sure.

Dan gave her a courtesy smile and admitted it. "That's me."

She was wearing an ivory-colored t-shirt that was snug enough to show her stocky build. She didn't seem fat to Dan, only compact and slightly muscular. And her baby blue jeans were fitted without being tight.

"Latte for Susan!" the woman behind the counter called out.

She gave an apologetic shrug to Dan and went to collect her coffee.

Dan looked around. There were only a couple of tables free, and before he could choose one, Susan pointed to a single table for two in the back corner. Dan followed her there, knowing that it would now be harder for Maggie to drop by.

"You aren't going to order anything?" the woman asked.

Dan shook his head. "I'm fine."

Behind him, Maggie walked into the shop, took a quick glance around, and stepped up to the counter to order.

The woman sat down at the table, taking the chair that faced the door. Dan sat down in front of her and watched as she took a sip of her coffee.

She put the coffee down, leaned in toward Dan, and said, "I'm assuming that you're as tired of all this stuff as I am." She wasn't smiling.

Dan shrugged and nodded in agreement.

The woman leaned back. "I think we can make this all stop," she said. She looked at him. "If you want it to."

Dan hesitated. He still wasn't sure who this woman was, and what she wanted. He gave her a slight nod. Then he held up his hand.

"I'm sorry," he said, "but I don't know who you are, or what this is all about. Who are you? What do you have to do with Matthew McLeod?"

The woman gave a quick glance around at the room behind

Dan, then leaned in to speak quietly to him. "I'm kind of an assistant to Mr. McLeod," she said. "I help him with stuff. I helped him with these books."

Dan decided he'd had enough. "What's your name?" he asked bluntly.

She stared at him for a moment before answering.

"Okay," she said. Her eyes swept the room again. Behind him, Dan could hear someone talking loudly, mentioning Maggie's name. "This stays between the two of us." The woman's eyebrows went up in a question.

Dan nodded.

"Susan Chen," she said.

"And do you have any ID to show me?" Dan asked.

The woman paused for a moment, then said, "Fair enough." She reached into her purse and showed Dan a driver's license. It did say Susan Chen on it.

Dan nodded and handed it back to her. Susan thrust out her hand for Dan to shake. "Nice to meet you."

Dan shook her hand—she had a surprisingly firm grip—and unnecessarily told her that he was Dan Courtwright.

"I know," she said. "I know who you are."

They awkwardly broke off the handshake, and Dan waited expectantly for Susan to continue.

She took a sip of coffee, then slid the cup off to the side of the table.

"This whole thing has gone on long enough," she said. She pointed to Dan. "On your side, people are getting hurt, lost. You're having to organize search parties."

"Some people have died," Dan replied. He wanted to make sure she understood.

"Right," Susan agreed. "And on our end, things are getting crazy. Matthew has had to go underground. We're getting all kinds of crazy threats and stuff. It's insane." She stopped to shake her head.

She looked at Dan. "Somebody even doxxed Matthew, so now just about everyone knows who he is," she said. "That's nuts. And it's actually dangerous, with all these threats and everything. Some of the stuff they write is unbelievable."

Dan leaned back in his chair. "So why doesn't he just end the whole thing? Come out and tell people where the five million is, or that it doesn't exist?"

Susan Chen shook her head, her lips pressed together. "I don't know," she said.

"Have you asked him?" Dan asked.

"Actually, I don't even know where he is," Susan answered. "He's gone, incommunicado. But I've had enough."

Dan gave her a skeptical look.

Susan took a deep breath. "Look, I wrote a lot of the books, okay? I know what's in them, every clue, and every red herring. I know exactly what McLeod did in these books, because I did most of it."

Again, Dan raised an eyebrow. "So how much of the writing did you actually do?" he asked.

Her lower lip pushed up as she considered this. "Probably ninety percent, give or take." She met his gaze frankly.

Dan's face gave his incredulity away. "Ninety percent?"

She nodded. "Never underestimate the willingness of a college professor to exploit the talents of his graduate students," she said. "It started years ago, but still…"

Dan's mouth dropped open a bit. He could still hear that

woman's voice behind him, still talking to Maggie, from what he could tell.

"Oh, he paid me," Susan said. "Not a huge amount, but more than I could make working here." She waved her hand around the Starbucks. "Way more than an English major usually makes."

Dan leveled his gaze at her. "So, is there a five-million-dollar treasure hidden somewhere up in the Sierra?" he asked her.

She gave a sad smile and shook her head. "It's not that simple," she said. "Remember, these books were written over a series of years. When you write books, things change, things evolve. What seemed like a good idea at first might change as you get further into the series."

"So, there's no treasure?" Dan asked.

Susan sighed. "I don't actually know," she admitted. "It's possible that Nathan did something about it. I don't know. Maybe he did. Maybe it's out there somewhere. But I don't care. I want this to stop, and if he won't do anything about it, I will."

Dan noticed how she mentioned Nathan. "How do you plan to do that?" Dan kept his voice neutral, but he wasn't buying this.

Susan Chen put both of her hands on the table in front of herself. "There are only two people in the world who know that I worked on these books," she said. "Nathan Petrovski and me. Now three, with you. And if I can help someone announce that they have found the money, then the whole thing is over. Nathan can't point the finger at me without revealing that I wrote most of the books."

"And me?" Dan asked.

Susan smiled at him. "Why would you want to say anything that would keep this chaos going?"

<h1 style="text-align:center">chapter 33</h1>

"What I don't get," Dan said, "is what you need from me?"

Susan nodded at him. "How many people have come up here looking for that money?" she asked. "Lots, right? And lots more people have hiked all over these mountains in the last couple of years, right? Thousands and thousands, right? "

Dan agreed.

"The problem is, I can't find that treasure some place where lots of other people have already looked," she said. "That won't work. Somebody is sure to raise a stink about the fact that they were already there, and it can't have been there."

"Wait a minute," Dan said, holding up his hand. "Isn't it already somewhere? Don't you know where it is?"

Susan shrugged. "Maybe Matthew McLeod hid it somewhere in the mountains. I don't know. If he did, I don't know where it is. But I tend to think that he didn't. I don't think he even had that kind of money, although I could be wrong about that."

"So why not just explain that it was all a joke, or fake, and that there is no treasure?" Dan asked.

"I could do that," Susan agreed, "but nobody knows who I am, and nobody would believe me. Or, at least, many people would think I was lying. They would be sure it was a trick. And they'd keep looking. And some people would be really pissed. Dangerously pissed off."

"Yeah," Dan said, "but don't you have to know where it was hidden? I mean, the books have all those clues and references."

Susan waited a moment as she considered her answer. "I guess the easiest way to explain this is that we decided early on to leave our options open, to suggest a number of different possibilities that we could then deal with later."

Dan sat back in his chair. "So there's no five million, and it could be anywhere."

Susan nodded. "Pretty much. We had no idea it would take off the way it did. And once it did, we were kind of trapped by it."

Dan shook his head in dismay. He thought of trying to explain that to Kristen and Maggie, and all the other people who had spent time trying to solve the mystery. "That is disgusting," he said.

"Not really," Susan tried to argue. "We really did have a plan to hide it somewhere. Nathan's job was to get the bitcoin, and then we'd go ahead. We had a number of plans that might have worked."

"But he never got the money," Dan said.

"I'm not sure, but I don't think so," she answered. "Or he decided to keep it."

"So why not just say that?" Dan said. "Why not expose the fraud?"

Susan held up two fingers. "One, I'm not sure it's a fraud. Only Nathan knows that, wherever he is. And two, with the anger this thing has drummed up already, can you imagine what people might do if they found out?"

Dan thought that maybe Nathan would get what he deserved, but it probably wasn't for him, or even Susan, to make that call.

"So again, what do you want from me?" he asked. "Other than keeping my mouth shut."

"We have enough clues buried in those books to hide the

treasure just about anywhere," Susan said. "I mean, I know how to put them together in a bunch of different ways so that they can point to wherever I find the treasure. I even put in some clues that Nathan probably doesn't realize. So once I determine a place, I can show the clues later."

"Working backwards," Dan suggested.

"Exactly," she agreed. "But what I need from you is a place to hide the treasure that nobody's found yet. Where can I put it where nobody's already looked? And I need your experience, boots on the ground."

Dan thought about this. "But say you wrote these books," he said. "From what I've read, you must know a lot about the Sierra. Why not just pick a spot yourself?"

Susan smiled. "My dad was a big fan of the Sierra," she said. "But he wasn't a hiker or a backpacker. He loved to come up here to look for mushrooms. Every burn area, after every storm, we'd pack up the car and come on up for mushrooms. It's one of the great smells of my childhood—ashes. But we were not alone. There were always other people doing the same thing. I want a place where nobody goes."

Dan sat back in his chair and took a look around the coffee shop. Maggie was over by the door, still in conversation with someone. It was clear that she was going to be no help. At the very least, he could drag out the conversation.

"Okay," he began. "Let's start with where people go. They go to lakes and rivers. People always want to be near water. They like to fish, to swim, and they need the stuff to drink, so those are out. And the tops of mountains, too. They like to climb up and see the view, especially if the peak has a name."

Susan Chen had pulled out an iPad and was writing things

down. "Got it," she said.

"And for that matter, no place that has a trail," Dan said. His mind was trying to envision a way to explain to her how to get somewhere that didn't have any way to get there. "No big trees, or funny-shaped rocks, or anything of interest that someone might have taken a photo of."

She stopped taking notes and looked at him, waiting. "So that's where we don't go," she said.

"Right," Dan agreed.

"Okay. I've got that. So where do we go?" she asked.

"Canyons are good," Dan said. "They have rivers in the bottom, of course, but the sides of canyons are usually steep, and there are not a lot of trails. And they get hot in the summer, so people tend to avoid those."

"But they have rivers," Susan said. "And if they're too steep, there's no way to get there."

"That can be tough," Dan admitted. He told her about the archeological dig down in the canyon, and how once he got past the dig itself, the area was very isolated.

"But there's a dig down there," Susan said. "And there are people, so that won't work. Plus, don't fishermen always go to the rivers?"

"Yeah, you're right," Dan admitted. "And some nut cases have already gone down there. But you'll need some kind of markers to get people to wherever you decide this is going to be," he said. "You'll need to start with a trail to somewhere, and then turn off the trail and get away from people."

"Like, where could I do that?" Susan asked.

"I'd start with a remote trailhead," Dan said. "One that doesn't get that much traffic to begin with."

Susan looked at him, waiting for more explanation. "So, give me an example, Dan," she said.

"Something like Bourland Creek," Dan said. "It's at the end of a long dirt road, which discourages a lot of people. And there aren't any easy hikes out of there. You can get down into Cherry Creek Canyon from there, but it's a trek. And it's pretty wild country. A lot of bare granite."

Susan's face looked concerned. "How do we hide something on bare granite?" she asked.

Dan shrugged. "Well, there are lots of cracks and things, and loose rock. Erratics—boulders left out on the granite by glaciers."

Susan didn't sound convinced.

"And that's the only place to hike out of this Bourland trailhead?" she asked.

Dan shook his head. "No, there's also a trail to Chain Lakes," he said, "but it doesn't get a lot of use either. There are no fish in Chain Lakes, so…"

Susan nodded. "But people go there," she said. "There's water."

"Yeah, some people do," Dan agreed. "But there aren't a lot of trails or anything out there. The lakes are swampy in places. It's pretty without being really beautiful. People usually don't go there twice."

"But they go there," she said.

"They go there, but if you go beyond the trail, beyond the lakes, I don't think many people do that. There's just rocks and forest, and swamp and brush."

"Nothing to see," Susan said.

"It's pristine," Dan said. "And nothing back there has a name."

"And nobody goes there?" she asked again.

"Not really," Dan said. "Once they get to the lakes, they pretty much stop."

Susan nodded. "Okay. So that's a possibility. Can you show me where that is on this map?"

Dan watched as she pulled out a map. She handed him her coffee cup and unfolded the map out on the table. A couple of people nearby turned to see what they were doing.

Dan pointed out the trailhead and noted a few other points of reference for her: Highway 108, Long Barn, Pinecrest Lake.

'And the dig?" Susan asked. "Where's that?"

Dan showed her. "There will be people down there," he said. "Because of the dig."

She nodded. After studying the map for a minute longer, she started to fold it up.

Dan placed his hands on the map, pinning it to the table. Susan stopped and looked at him, startled.

"Before we're done here, I have a few questions of my own," he said. "Those chapters about presidents, and minerals, and place names," Dan said. "What is that all about?"

Susan shook her head. "Those were Nathan's idea," she said. "They're just window dressing, but he liked the idea of mimicking Moby Dick. He was always looking for the books to be taken more seriously."

"So they don't mean anything?" Dan asked.

Susan shrugged. "If we needed a clue, we could pull one from there, but no, they don't really mean anything."

"What about the start of each book, where you write about the third degree and the sixth commandment, and stuff?" Dan asked.

Susan smiled. "I wrote those," she said. "I thought it would be helpful to have a way to eliminate some of the clues if we needed to do that."

"But they don't really matter?" Dan asked.

Susan shook her head. "I don't know what Nathan had in mind, but I just added a bunch of stuff to give us options. And I'm glad I did, because wherever I find this famous treasure, I'm going to be able to show how the clues point to exactly how I got there."

Dan shook his head in disgust. After a moment, he lifted his hands up off the map and allowed her to fold it up.

"It wasn't my idea to begin with," Susan said, by way of apology. "It was all about Matthew McLeod. And he wanted to make a big splash."

"And you went along with it," Dan said.

"It was a job," she said, sounding tired. "I couldn't believe anyone would take it seriously. I thought that only crazy people would believe it."

Dan remembered his conversation with Bruce Spielman. "What about lollipops?"

Susan smiled. "My dad taught me that one. You know those trees that have no branches below and are kind of round on top? They look like a lollipop. When we went hiking, he promised me a sucker if I ever saw one of those on our hikes."

She packed up her bag, picked up her coffee cup, and dropped the cup off on a tray on her way out the door.

Maggie was still talking to the woman at her table. She looked up and waved at him, hoping for a rescue.

<h1 style="text-align:center">chapter 34</h1>

Dan walked over to Maggie. The other woman saw Dan and quickly stood up and excused herself. As she walked away, Maggie shook her head in exasperation.

"I guess you didn't hear much of that," he said.

Maggie made a face of pure frustration. "Of all the times to run into someone you haven't seen in months. And I couldn't get rid of her," she said. She shook herself, trying to rid herself of the memory. "What did you find out?"

Dan's face was full of frustration. "Not much," he said. "I don't think there's a treasure after all, and if there is, nobody is going to find it."

Maggie stared at him. "What do you mean?"

"What if it was all a hoax?" he said. "A hoax that just got out of hand."

"And that's it?" Maggie's face looked like she was ready to explode. Either that or go chasing down Susan Chen in the parking lot.

Dan shrugged. "If she is telling the truth, I don't think there ever was a treasure."

"And what is she going to do about it?" Maggie asked.

"I guess she has a plan," Dan said, remembering his promise to Susan Chen. "And I am going to let her deal with that all by herself."

Maggie stood up and grabbed her purse. She stopped and

looked at Dan. "I guess I have to tell the rest of the girls," she said. She gave a deep sigh. "They are not going to be happy."

"I promised her I'd keep this a secret," Dan said. "Can you just keep this quiet for a few days?"

Maggie smiled. "You are something else, Dan. But yes, I can do that."

Back out at his truck, Dan called Steve Matson. "I met with that woman," he told Steve. "The one who said her name was Jacqueline Pulaski. It turns out there may not be a treasure after all."

"You met with her?" Steve asked, clearly letting Dan know that he had not followed Steve's advice.

"Just a conversation in a coffee shop," Dan said. "After I called Martina Guzman. This woman seems to think she can do something about all this?"

"Like what?" Steve asked.

"I'll let her figure it out," Dan said, "but she thinks she has a plan."

Steve was silent. Dan thought maybe the phone connection was bad. Then Steve spoke. "Well, maybe she does. We sure haven't got anywhere with that agent, or with McLeod. The agent says she has no idea where he is, so that's a dead end. Keep me posted."

Dan agreed to do that and hung up. A quick glance at his phone showed that he had received another call from Kim Archer. What the hell, he might as well find out what the private eye wanted.

"Thanks for the call back, Dan," Archer answered his phone.

After some brief pleasantries, Archer got to the point. "I was wondering if you'd heard anything from Marco Gemmeli." Archer said.

"Isn't he your client?" Dan asked. "Why would he call me?"

"He is, or he was, my client," Archer explained. "I helped

him track down McLeod so that they could serve papers about the lawsuit. But now I can't seem to track him down."

Dan chuckled. "Aren't you a detective?" asked. "How hard can it be?"

"Very funny," Archer said. "The thing is, the guy owes me a fair amount of money. And it looks like he's trying to skip out on the bill."

Dan smiled. "And you can't track him down?"

"I will," Archer promised. "I can promise you that. But I just thought I'd give you a call. So if you hear anything from him, do me a favor and let me know."

"I don't know why he'd call me," Dan said, "but sure, if I hear from him, I'll give you a call."

"He's told me he thinks you're one of the few honest guys he knows," Archer said.

Dan snorted. "He doesn't get out much."

There were two more messages on the phone. He recognized one as coming from Doris.

He opened up the door of the truck and let the oven-hot air escape. While he waited, he dialed Doris.

"Dan, I've got some news for you," she said. Even more than usual, Doris sounded breathless with excitement. "Travis and the kids have been doing some computer work on those mysteries. They think that they've discovered a kind of plot."

Dan made a small noise to say that he was still listening.

"Those groups on the internet that are trying to solve the clues to the treasure," Doris continued. "Travis says they're all coming from the same place, somewhere in the computer lab at UOP."

"What do you mean?" Dan asked. "How are they coming from the same place?"

"Travis says it's all phony," Doris explained. "He says it's probably just a few people posting under a number of different names and all, but they're all coming from the same USB. No, wait, that isn't it. The same ISP."

Dan leaned on the cab of his truck, then quickly pulled back when he felt how hot it was. "No, yeah, that makes sense, Doris," he said. "I think this whole thing is a wild goose chase."

Doris gave a disapproving snort. "Then can we tell people it's all a mistake, it's all fake?"

"Wouldn't that be nice? I don't think we're quite there yet," Dan said. "But I have a feeling this is all going to come out pretty soon."

"Well, it had better," Doris said, her enthusiasm gone. "I am sick of it. Sick to death."

Dan was going to respond when his phone buzzed to let him know there was another call. He checked the ID. It read Martina Guzman.

"I've got to take this other call," he told Doris. "We can talk about this tomorrow."

chapter 35

"What did this Susan Chen say?" Martina asked over the phone, even before saying hello.

Dan tried to give her a summary of his conversation.

"No, no," Martina interrupted him. "I don't want the short version. I want you to tell me, as accurately as possible, exactly what she said."

Dan sighed. "I'm standing in the sun in a parking lot right now," Dan said. "Maybe I can call you later."

"Make it sooner, not later," she said. "This could be important."

Dan agreed to call her within the hour. He looked around at the cars, baking in the sun, and climbed into his truck. The seat was so hot he could feel it burning his legs through his pants. He started the truck, boosted the air conditioning up to high, turned on the fan full blast, and rolled down the windows on both sides. It would still take a couple of minutes before any of that made the truck cab bearable.

He slowly drove through the parking lot, waiting for cars to find a spot to park, letting shoppers walk across in front of him. At one point a kid from the supermarket pushed a long line of carts into the roadway, and Dan waited for him to clear.

By the time he exited the parking lot, the A/C was working, and he rolled up the windows. He had left the radio on, and the announcer was promising big news about a murder. He punched the button to change the station. This one had a cooking show on. He punched the button again and got a loud pop song. He turned off the radio and pulled out onto the street, and was soon driving up Highway 108 in silence, with cool air blowing on him.

He spent the rest of the drive to his house rehearsing what he would tell Martina Guzman. He decided that he didn't need to go into great detail. And if she pushed, he would just say that he didn't really remember, exactly, what Susan had said. Which was absolutely true, at least about some things.

When he called her back from his house, she answered with an apology.

"I was a little abrupt earlier," she said. "Sorry about that. I had just gotten off the phone with your boss, Steve Matson."

"He can have that effect on people," Dan said.

"I thought we had agreed that you wouldn't meet with this woman," Martina said.

"Huh," Dan answered. "And I thought we said that I would talk to her and ask her to put her suggestions in writing."

Martina Guzman was quiet for a moment. "Okay, let's move on," she said. "What were her suggestions? Did she agree to do that?"

"Nope," Dan told her. "But she also didn't ask me to do anything, either. She just told me she had a plan to stop this and wanted to know a little more about trails and destinations around here. She just wanted some information from me."

"And what kind of information was that?" Martina asked him.

Dan explained about looking for places that nobody ever visited.

"Did she say why she wanted to know that?" Martina asked.

"Can I ask a question here?" Dan asked. "Are you acting as my attorney? Does this conversation fall under some kind of attorney-client privilege?"

Martina waited for a moment before answering. "Why would

you need to ask that?" she said.

"I didn't break any laws," Dan assured her. "And I am not planning to break any laws. But there are parts of that conversation with her that I would rather not share, not unless it is absolutely essential."

"Well, I won't know that unless I know what they are, will I?"

Dan thought about Susan's plan to find the treasure and end the whole adventure. "I think I'm okay just letting you know that she really only wanted help in that one way." he said. "And there's not much else to say."

"And you think that she is in some way able to do that?"

"She might be," Dan said. "I don't know if she was telling me the truth about anything, but if she was, then she might be able to do that."

"And what was her name again?" Martina asked.

Dan paused. "She told me it was Jacqueline Pulaski," he said. That part was true, he thought, at least, at one time it was true.

"And do you think that's her real name?" Martina asked.

"Nope," Dan said. "I think it's a name she pulled out of the books. The hero of the books is Jack Pulaski."

"And did she give you any ideas or clues about her real identity?" Martina asked.

"Any and all of which could also be false," Dan pointed out. He had decided to give Susan Chen two days to put her plan into effect. At least two days, he told himself. If she could pull this off, he wasn't going to be the one to stop her.

He heard Martina Guzman sigh on the other end of the phone call. "Try to keep me in the loop, Dan, please," she said. "We're on the same team here."

"I know," Dan assured her. "I will let you know if I hear anything more from her."

chapter 36

It was the warmest part of the day, and Dan had already been given the rest of the day off. With Kristen at work, Dan had the place to himself. He sat down at his computer and sent off the trail report that Steve Matson had requested. That done, he looked around and noted McLeod's book Crevasse still on the table. He had never finished it.

He was curious, now that he knew there were two authors. Dan picked it up, made himself comfortable on the sofa, and started to read again, right where a major international drug cartel was running its West Coast operation out of an abandoned barn in the National Forest.

But he found it hard to concentrate. The book was full of hair-raising crises, but something was keeping Dan from fully embracing the story. He started to think about Susan Chen again. What was it Doris had said? That there was some kind of computer hacker group that started the whole hidden treasure hunt?

He looked for his phone. It was over by the computer. The whole thing really was Susan's problem, he reminded himself. And then he got up and walked over to get his phone. He called Doris.

"What did Travis and his friends say about this computer hacker group?" he asked her.

"Let me see if I can remember this right," Doris said. "They said it started some years ago, and it was a group at UOP, you know, University of the Pacific."

"I got that part," Dan said. "But what did they do?"

"Apparently, they are the ones who started this," she said. "They started posting a bunch of stories about the books and the clues to a hidden treasure. But they did it secretly, and it was all out of one ISP at UOP. They pretended to be a bunch of different people, so that it went trendy, or viral or something. Anyway, pretty soon after that, everyone was talking about it, and it got to be a big thing on the internet."

"So, a social media campaign," Dan said.

"Well, I guess so," Doris said. "But Travis and the kids were upset about it. They said it was all fake, that a lot of the posters didn't really exist. Like those Russian hackers who post fake stories, and then people believe them and pass them on."

"And people believed all this?" Dan asked.

"I guess they knew what they were doing," Doris said. "They found a bunch of those conspiracy nuts and survivalist guys who loved the story, and then they started passing it on, posting about it. Pretty soon, everyone knew about it."

"And a lot of them believed it," Dan said.

"Exactly," Doris said. "The boys say the whole thing is bogus. That's the word they used."

Dan thought of the emails and calls he had received from Bruce Spielman. "That makes a lot of sense," he said. He thought this over. "So, what are they going to do about it?" he asked her.

"Oh, I think they've already moved on," Doris said. "They were talking about some kind of plan to hack into the system at UOP, but they've decided it's not worth their time or energy."

Dan smiled. "Did you have to convince them?" he asked.

Doris laughed. "They wouldn't listen to an old lady like me anyway," she said. "I think they just found something more fun to do. Some kind of AI game they're working on."

After saying goodbye to Doris, Dan looked at his phone. Among the recent calls was the one from Susan Chen. She hadn't left a message. He wondered if she knew anything about the hackers. But when he dialed her number, the call went immediately to voicemail. He left her a short message, then hung up.

He picked up the book, started to read again, and allowed himself to fall asleep.

When his phone rang, his first reaction was to think it was Susan Chen, calling him back.

"Hello?" Dan knew his voice sounded sleepy.

"Am I ruining your beauty sleep?" Cal Healey asked.

"Hey, Cal. What's up?" Dan was still slowly coming up from the deep.

"I heard you had a conversation with somebody today about those mysteries and the hidden treasure of the Sierra Nevada," Cal said.

"News travels fast," Dan said. "Did Maggie tell you? It turns out that I think the whole thing is a silly game. A complete waste of time."

"Yeah, maybe not so silly," Cal said.

"What do you mean?" Dan asked.

"The guy who wrote those books," Cal continued. "Was his name Nathan Petrovski?"

"Yeah, at least he wrote part of them," Dan said. "But he called himself Matthew McLeod. Well, that's what we think."

"And you met with someone today who knows him?" Cal asked.

"Basically, yes," Dan agreed.

"I think you might want to give the Stockton Police Department a call," Cal said, "just to be on the safe side."

Dan was silent.

"You still there, Courtwright?" Cal asked.

"Yeah," Dan answered. "Why should I call them?"

"I think they'll be interested in what you have to say," Cal said. "Mr. Petrovski is no longer missing. They found him, at least what's left of him."

Dan's stomach lurched and he sat down on the sofa. "What happened?"

"I don't have all the details," Cal said. "But Mr. Petrovski met an untimely end. Not a pretty picture at all."

"Where?" Dan asked. "What happened?"

"I'll let the boys in Stockton fill you in," Cal said. "But if I were you, I'd call them sooner, rather than later."

chapter 37

Dan did call Detective Gregory but had to leave a message. He kept it simple. "I have some information about Nathan Petrovski that may be important. Give me a call back when you have time to talk about it."

With that off his conscience, he took stock of his mental to-do list. He should probably call Martina Guzman and give her the news, but it was well after office hours on the East Coast. He doubted that she would answer, which made it more attractive to leave her a message.

He called, got voicemail, and told her that he'd heard McLeod or Petrovski had been found dead. And no, he didn't know anything more about it. Just as he was going to hang up, he added that he had called the Stockton Police Department to tell them about his conversation with Susan Chen, revealing her name. That should take care of her, he figured.

Next in line was Steve Matson. He wasn't in either, but Sara in the office promised to have him give Dan a call as soon as he could.

Dan's mind was racing. With McLeod/Petrovski dead, Susan Chen was now in a position to end the treasure hunt all on her own, if she had told him the truth. She could say she found it, and Dan had no real proof that it wouldn't be true. Dan had believed her, but he had to admit that if she were lying, all kinds of things could now be true.

What if she simply knew the books really well, and was just trying to pick his brain for where the treasure could be believably buried? Possible, but she didn't really need Dan for that. But what if she not only knew Petrovski, what if she were involved in his killing? What if he'd never hidden the treasure? She could be part of a team that killed him and would now announce that they had found the treasure, even if he'd never hidden it. He might have kept it in his house, or somewhere else. The killers could well have found it already. They could keep the money because there was no one to argue they hadn't really found it. Nobody but Dan, that is.

Or she could have been working with the hackers at UOP. Maybe they had something to do with McLeod's death. They were certainly responsible for some of this craziness.

He checked his phone, trying to make it ring, without success.

What would he say if Susan Chen called him back? The words of Martina Guzman came back to him: "You have nothing to gain from this, and there are all sorts of bad complications…" He had to admit she was right about that.

What would he do if Susan Chen came out of the mountains tomorrow, or the next day, announcing that she had found the treasure? The Stockton cops would be all over that. But what if she waited a few months? If Susan Chen had told him the truth, the only person who knew about her plans, or her connection to Petrovski, or even her connection to the mysteries, was Dan Courtwright.

The thought hit Dan like a sledgehammer.

He was the only fly in the ointment, if she had planned all this. He had told her where she could claim to have found the hidden bitcoins, a place where nobody else would have looked.

He checked his phone again. Nothing.

He tried to remember what he had told Maggie or anyone else.

Had he told them that Susan claimed to be the author of the books? Had he even told them her name?

Now his mind was working at full speed. If Susan had lied to him about some or all of this, then what? If she were part of a plan to kill McLeod and steal the money, Dan was the only person who could connect her to the crime. And he didn't even know if he knew her real name.

Maggie was a witness. She had seen Dan talking to the woman. If they had killed McLeod, would they stop at killing him? Maybe not. But they wouldn't know about Maggie. At least, Dan hoped they wouldn't know.

A car drove by on the street in front of his house, and Dan found himself shrinking down into the sofa, trying to hide.

This was nuts.

Dan picked up his phone again. He wasn't going to wait. He dialed Cal Healey's number and hoped that at least Cal would answer.

"Did you get ahold of Stockton PD?" Cal answered the phone.

Dan let out a sigh of relief. "I left a message. I haven't heard back," Dan explained. "Do you have a minute?"

"Shoot," Cal said.

And so, Dan began to tell him the whole story. He told him everything he could remember about his meeting with Susan Chen. Cal listened and made Dan go back over several of the details. He made Dan try to remember exact words, and dates and times.

When Dan was done, Cal asked him, "Is that all?" He sounded like he thought that was enough.

And then Dan told him about Travis, and the hackers at UOP, and how there might be a larger group involved in the whole thing, and that it had apparently been going on for years.

Cal occasionally asked Dan to slow down or wait a minute. That made Dan realize that Cal had been taking notes.

Dan finally ran out of story to tell. "And I'm sitting here right now, thinking that I am not in the best situation," Dan said. "And I haven't heard back from Stockton PD."

"You got that right," Cal agreed. "Jesus, Dan, how do you get into these things?"

Dan gave a sigh. "Just lucky, I guess."

"Or not," Cal suggested.

"I mean, the reason that I called you is that if I'm the only one who knows this stuff," Dan said, "then…"

"Oh, I get that part," Cal replied. "So now I know about it, too. But if Susan Chen or whatever her name is, is a bad guy, she doesn't know that. She still might think that you're the only one who could blow her story. So she just might decide to take you out of the picture before they claim to have found the money. The money they found where nobody else looked."

"Yeah," Dan agreed, "but I don't think she's lying, you know."

"I don't need to remind you that it is possible for you to be wrong about that," Cal said, reminding him anyway. "And if she's not a bad guy, then the bad guys who got Petrovski might get her next. And she might very well point the finger at you and tell them that you know something about where it is. That's a another bad thing."

"Yeah," Dan said. "That's what I was thinking."

"And you're at home now?" Cal asked. "Anyone with you?"

"No," Dan said, "Kristen isn't home yet. She might not get home until late tonight."

Dan heard Cal let his breath out slowly. "Are Walt and Ruth home?" he asked.

Dan looked across the street. He couldn't see either of them. "I can't tell," he said. "Their car is there."

"Do you want to come over to the house?" Cal asked. "I can't send a car over to you, like they do in the movies. But you need to get out of there."

Dan did not like the idea of imposing on Cal and Maggie. "No, I just don't think it's that big a deal."

"Okay, a couple of things," Cal said. "One—if Susan, or whatever her name is, killed this guy McLeod, why would she take a chance on getting you involved in some way?"

"She said it was because I could help her find a place where nobody else had looked," Dan reminded him. "But maybe it's because she thinks I'm a good character witness or something?"

"I'm not buying it," Cal said. "The more people you involve in a crime, the more likely somebody is going to screw it up. Admittedly criminals aren't the brightest bulbs, but getting you involved seems like a completely unnecessary risk."

"Yeah, I see that," Dan said.

"And that's if she or they really did trust you to keep it quiet," Cal continued.

'Yeah," Dan agreed. "And what's number two?"

"Whoever killed Petrovski probably tortured the hell out of him first," Cal said.

"You know that?" Dan asked.

"No," Cal admitted. "But it would sure make sense, wouldn't it? Torture him to find out where the money is. Tortured or threatened or…"

"Yeah, I guess so," Dan agreed.

"And he might have told them," Cal continued. "Told them where the money is and told them about your friend Susan Chen."

Dan considered this. "Do you think I should give her a call?"

"Absolutely not," Cal said. "Because if she's involved, you don't want to be involved. She's already got your number on her phone. That's bad enough. Don't make it show up more than once. And if she's not involved, you don't want to be involved. What you want to do is turn this whole thing over to the Stockton PD. And you want to do that as soon as possible, so nobody else gets hurt. Especially you."

Across the street, Dan saw movement in the front window of Walt's house. "Right," he said. "And I called them. But they haven't called back. You know, I think I see Ruth over there."

"Good," Cal answered. "Why don't you go over there and hang out for a while? I'll get a call in to Stockton PD and get this pulled up on their radar."

"I could just invite her over here," Dan said.

"No," Cal answered. "Because if anyone bad does show up at your house, you want to be somewhere else, capisce?"

"Got it," Dan said. "I'm on my way."

"Call Kristen," Cal said. "Let her know what's going on."

"Got it. Will do." Dan was already walking out the door. "And thanks, Cal."

chapter 38

Kristen didn't answer her phone. She was probably too busy at work. Dan imagined her in her chef's clothes, hurrying around the kitchen, and left her a short message that unless she heard otherwise, he would be at Walt and Ruth's house when she got off work. And that she should call him before coming home. There was no need to worry her unnecessarily.

He slipped his phone into his pocket and walked across the street. He wasn't quite sure what he was going to tell Ruth and Walt, but he'd known them long enough over the years to know that it wasn't going to be a problem.

He knocked on the door and waited. Another car came driving by, and Dan was relieved to see that it was one of his neighbors from down the road.

Ruth answered the door, gave Dan a big smile, and waited expectantly for him to explain why he was there.

Dan cleared his throat and started in. "This business with the McLeod books has gotten a bit more complicated," he said. "Can I come in for a minute?"

Ruth threw the door open and waved him inside. He noticed that she took a quick look around out the door before she closed it behind him.

"You know that woman I met, the one who wanted to talk to me?" Dan began.

And then his phone rang. He quickly checked and saw it was

the Stockton Police Department. He glanced at Ruth, held up his finger for a moment, and answered the phone.

Detective Leroy Gregory of the Stockton PD introduced himself again and told him that the local Sheriff had insisted they talk.

"Yeah," Dan said. "That's Cal Healey."

"What's going on?" Gregory asked.

When Dan started to explain, Gregory interrupted him. "Sorry, but I need your full name and contact information."

Dan raised his eyebrows at Ruth and provided all the details requested by Gregory. When he was done, Gregory told him to continue.

"Do you know about this money that McLeod or Petrovski is supposed to have hidden in the Sierra?" Dan asked, as a way of starting.

"Why don't you tell me all about it," Gregory suggested. "And just to make sure, I'll be recording this if that's all right? Do I have your permission for that?"

"Yeah, fine," Dan said. "So, you know about Matthew McLeod being Nathan Petrovski?"

"I think we're aware of that, yes," Gregory answered. "Can I ask how you are involved in all of this?"

Ruth patted Dan on the arm and left him in the living room, while she discreetly wandered away toward the kitchen.

"We've had this conversation before," Dan reminded him. "Did you get the recording of the conversation I had with McLeod about ten days ago?"

"We did receive that," Gregory replied. He didn't sound convincing.

"And have you listened to it?" Dan asked.

"Parts of it," Gregory answered. Dan interpreted this to mean that he hadn't paid the least attention to it. He remembered saying something similar to McLeod about having read the man's books.

He took a deep breath. "Let's start all the way at the beginning, shall we?" Dan asked, allowing a hint of frustration to creep into his voice.

"That would be very helpful," Gregory agreed.

And so Dan began, with the hikers getting lost, and Karl Rahm telling him about the mystery books and the treasure. Detective Gregory interrupted to ask for contact information, specific dates, clarifications. Dan tried to answer the questions as well as he could remember.

Then he moved on to explain about the Forest Service's attempts to call off the hunt for the money: the conversations with the publisher and their lawyers, the failed attempt to get any response from McLeod's agent. Again, Gregory insisted on contact numbers for Martina Guzman, Steve Matson, the author's agent, and more dates and times. Dan had to check the calendar on his phone more than once, just to make sure he was being accurate.

By the time he had finished explaining about the Zoom call, Gregory interrupted him one more time. "I appreciate all this information," he said. "It's very helpful." He sounded as if he wanted to get off the phone.

"Yeah, but you have all of this already," Dan explained. "At least, you should have. We've told you about it before."

"And we are working on it, Mr. Courtwright." Gregory sounded frustrated as well.

And that was when Dan went on to tell him about his phone call from Jacqueline Pulaski.

Gregory listened, but he had stopped asking so many questions. He just wanted Dan to confirm the date and time of the call. Dan could almost hear him losing interest.

"Okay," Gregory said, when Dan finished telling him about the phone call.

"So, I met with her," Dan said. "And it turned out that she claimed to have written most of these books."

"Did she?" Gregory asked.

Dan told him about Ruth's analysis, and about the kids from Cal Poly who did the AI research.

"You're saying that it's possible that somebody helped write these books," Gregory concluded.

Dan agreed.

"And you think this woman Susan Chen might have done that?"

Dan agreed that it was possible. He could also hear Detective Gregory waking up.

"You'd better start again, where she claimed to have written the books, and how she needed your help," Gregory said.

Dan told him that part of the conversation again. They went over the key points three or four times.

After Dan had told the story enough times for Gregory to be satisfied, the detective had another question. "Does anyone else know about this?" he asked. "Or I guess I should ask, does Susan Chen think anyone else knows about this?"

"I don't think so," Dan said. "I've told you, obviously, and I told Sheriff Cal Healey up here about it."

"Yeah, he's the one who passed it on to us." Gregory replied. "Is there anything else you can tell us about this Susan Chen person? Do you know where she lives, where she works?"

Dan repeated the phone number as his only point of contact. He mentioned that Susan Chen told him she had been a graduate student, or maybe just a student at UOP. In the background, he could hear Gregory passing on some of the information to someone else.

"And you have no idea where she could be?" Gregory asked.

Dan repeated his story about Susan looking for a place to discover the money, and his suggestion of the area out of the Bourland Creek Trailhead.

"Do you think that's where she might go?" Gregory asked. "Did she say that? And did she say when she thought she would do this?"

"All I can tell you is what she told me," Dan insisted. "She wanted a place that didn't get a lot of traffic, because she wanted to be sure nobody else would claim they'd already searched there. And that's why I suggested somewhere around Chain Lakes."

Dan could hear conversations going on in the background behind Leroy Gregory. He heard Gregory place his hand over the phone for a moment. Dan waited.

"We're checking some of this out," Gregory came back to explain. "Looks like we have an address for a Susan Chen, so we'll run a car out there. She sounds like somebody we need to track down."

"Sounds good," Dan said, "Do you need anything else from me?"

Leroy Gregory thought this over for a minute. "No, I think we're good there," he said. "I want to thank you for your cooperation."

"Yeah, sure," Dan said. "If you want some help tracking down Bourland Creek or Chain Lakes, I'm happy to help."

"If we need help, we know where to get it," Gregory said. "And I would think that we'd want to keep you about as far away from all of this as we can get. This is a murder investigation. We'd appreciate it if you left it to us."

Dan gave a short chuckle. "You and me both," he said. "Anything else?"

"The guy who died, Petrovski, was worked over pretty well," Detective Gregory said. "Either he took a long time to die, or they kept him alive for a long time. We don't want that to happen to anyone else. And you sure as hell don't want it to happen to you. You have my direct line now. If you hear anything from this woman, anything at all, I want you to call me immediately."

"Got it," Dan said, "I'll do that."

"And you are not to have any contact with her at all," Gregory continued.

"Exactly," Dan agreed.

"Are you at home?" Gregory asked. He then surprised Dan by reading off Dan's address to him.

"No," Dan said. "I'm at a friend's house."

"Stay there," Gregory said. "And keep your phone on, and keep it charged."

When the call was over, Dan's phone showed that he had missed a call from Cal Healey, and he called Cal back.

"I guess you heard from Stockton PD that I talked to them," Dan said.

"Just checking up on you to make sure you don't get any stupid ideas," Cal said. "They're setting up a search area for Bourland Creek tomorrow, and you are definitely not going to participate."

"Yeah, I'm good with that," Dan agreed. "I'm glad that they're taking this seriously."

"Oh, they are," Cal said. "Seriously enough that you should probably stay as far away from there as you can."

"Yes, Ma'am," Dan answered him. "But I may have to work up at Summit tomorrow, if they pull a lot of people in for this search. Is that okay with you?"

"No," Cal answered. "Because you may actually be a target

here. You need to stay away from anywhere that you usually go, just in case the bad guys are looking for you."

Dan gave an exasperated grunt. "What am I supposed to do, stay here hiding in Ruth and Walt's house?"

Ruth caught Dan's eye and opened her arms in welcome.

"Just stay the hell out of the way," Cal said. "Go sit on a rock somewhere and do that forest bathing thing."

Dan's phone beeped, and he saw that he had a message from Tuolumne County Search and Rescue.

"Gotta go, Cal," Dan said. "I've got another call coming in."

But by the time he got off the phone with Cal, he had two messages from SAR. The first one had gone out to everyone and announced the need for a search team tomorrow at Bourland Creek. The second one was addressed to Dan specifically, and it said: "Dan Courtwright—you will not participate in the SAR operation tomorrow. Not under any circumstances. Stay away."

Dan smiled. Angela always did have a way with words, particularly when talking to Dan.

And less than a minute later, Steve Matson called to give Dan the same message.

"I already heard from Angela," Dan told him.

"Good. And now you are hearing it from me," Steve emphasized. "I told you that it would be a bad idea to see that woman, and you ignored that. Don't ignore this."

Dan was in the middle of assuring Steve that he had no intention of ignoring this when it occurred to him that Steve Matson was the reason Susan Chen even knew about him. "Hey," he said. "You were the one who got me involved in this. You wanted me to talk to McLeod. That's how this all started."

"And now I am telling you how it all ends," Steve said. "With you staying the hell out of it all. Do you agree?"

Dan assured him that he did.

chapter 39

When Dan got off the phone he looked around for Ruth. After a moment or two, she walked out from the kitchen.

"I'm going to see if there's a room at one of the hotels," he said.

"Don't be ridiculous, Dan." Ruth sounded almost angry. She pushed him back down. "Walt is down at the dig, and you and Kristen can keep me company. And don't make any silly noises about it. I insist."

Dan was smart enough to know when he was beaten. "At least let me take you out to dinner," he offered.

"I have too much food in the fridge right now," Ruth answered him. "You can take Walt and me both out to dinner later. Tonight we'll eat here."

While Ruth was barely five feet tall, it wasn't easy to stand up to her, Dan realized, not for the first time.

"Okay, that's a deal," he said.

"I hope you like meatloaf," she said, turning to walk back into the kitchen. "You can help by setting the table."

"Give me one second to call Kristen and let her know what's going on, and I'll be right there," Dan assured her.

Once he had left the message, Dan walked into the kitchen.

"I guess you heard all of that," Dan said.

"Not really," Ruth demurred. "I wasn't listening, anyway."

They both knew she was lying to be polite, but Ruth made small talk about the food, and Dan complimented her on that, and then they talked about the work Dan and Kristen had done on Dan's kitchen, and before they knew it, dinner was over and Dan was offering to do the dishes.

"We'll do them together," Ruth said. "You wash, and I'll dry and put them away. You wouldn't know where anything goes, anyway."

When they were done, Ruth suggested that they might as well set up the sofa bed in the living room.

Dan decided that the whole show had gone on long enough. So that they wouldn't have to pretend she hadn't heard everything, Dan gave her a quick summary of the call. And to make sure he had her attention, he sat on the sofa. Ruth settled into Walt's chair nearby.

Dan felt a sense of peace talking to the older woman. Ruth seemed like one of the massive pines in his forest, or one of those huge boulders that had been in place for centuries. She was grounded, stable. And Dan found himself trusting her completely.

He had now told the story often enough that it came out easily, tumbling along like a mountain stream, finding its way through the rocks and meadows, always knowing where it was going. Somehow it was all making more sense now. When he was done, they sat together in silence for a moment.

"Do you think that Susan Chen woman could actually be capable of murder?" Ruth asked.

Dan shrugged. "Who knows? She didn't strike me as being violent, but maybe she has violent friends. She certainly is smart enough to plan something complicated, from what I could see."

"So the police think she is involved?" Ruth asked.

"Involved?" Dan repeated. "If she didn't help murder Petrovski, then you have to figure that she might well be the next victim, based on what she knows about the books, at least the way she tells it.

Either way, she's involved."

"Well, if she is Moriarty, the evil genius, then you should be worried, Dan," Ruth said. "Because she thinks you are the only person who knows about her plan."

"I think it's more likely she's a victim or a pawn," Dan said.

"And that leaves you in kind of the same place, doesn't it, Dan?" Ruth asked. "If she is the murderer, then you are in danger. If she's a potential victim, then you could be next."

Dan grimaced. "I don't think that necessarily follows," he said.

"But the police do, don't they?" Ruth insisted.

"Yeah," Dan said. "They do."

"But you know," Ruth said, "Five million dollars is a lot of money. It makes sense that someone might want to break the rules to get it."

Dan smiled. "You have a grim opinion of mystery readers," he said. "Although, I guess if they read about it all the time…"

"Who said anything about reading books?" Ruth asked him. The sun was down now, and Ruth turned on a floor lamp by the chair where she was sitting. "Five million dollars is more than most people would see in a lifetime. And this has been in the news enough that anybody might know about it."

"Yeah, but they'd have to know about the books first," Dan said.

"Would they, Dan?" Ruth asked. "You said that somebody exposed McLeod's identity on the internet. Doesn't that mean that anyone could have seen that, heard about the five million, and just tracked him down?"

Dan admitted that this was probably correct.

"With all these stories about gangs stealing catalytic converters, or solar panels, how hard would it be to find a couple of people who would rough someone up to get five million dollars?" Ruth asked.

Dan nodded. "Yeah, that's true. For someone who writes murder mysteries, I don't think McLeod thought this through very well."

"Well, he writes fiction," Ruth said. "That doesn't mean he knows much about real life. There's really not much difference between this idea and Roald Dahl and Charlie and the Chocolate Factory. When you put a plan like this in motion, some people are going to want to cheat."

"And as you say, the stakes are a lot higher with this one," Dan said.

"That poor man," Ruth said. "You can imagine how terrified he must have been, someone breaking into his house and doing who knows what to him. I'm sure he would have said anything to get them to stop."

"And probably told them about Susan," Dan added.

"If she told you the truth, that she had written most of the books?" Ruth asked. "Of course. And if I were Susan, I would be terrified that they would come after me and do the same."

"Which is a good reason for her to want that treasure found," Dan said. "Once it's found, she's safe."

"But until it is, she is right to be worried. And I think the Stockton Police must have a much longer list of suspects," Ruth said.

Dan nodded. "Yeah, although you still would have to be looking for someone who is willing to kill for five million dollars." Even as he said it, he realized that there were certainly people in the country who fit that description.

They sat quietly together, both lost in thought.

Ruth looked at Dan. "Do you miss being part of it?" she asked him.

Dan shook his head. "Not this one. I'm fine leaving all this to the pros."

"But you're still thinking about it, aren't you?" she asked.

Dan smiled. "Yeah, and so are you."

Ruth let out a long sigh. "Well, at least it will give us something to think about as we fall asleep tonight," she said. "Now get off that sofa so we can make up the bed."

chapter 40

As they were just finishing up putting the pillowcases on the pillows, Dan saw a car pull up out front, and was relieved to see Kristen arrive. Ruth immediately went to open the door and ushered Kristen into the house.

"What is going on?" Kristen asked, looking from one to the other. Then, looking at the sofabed, she turned to Dan. "Dan, why are we here?"

Ruth discreetly left for the kitchen while Dan started to explain, for what seemed like the tenth time that day, what had happened since he had last seen Kristen. Once again, his words came out easily. Each time he told the story, the narrative became clearer to him.

As his story went on, Dan watched Kristen slowly put her purse down on an end table and then, still listening to Dan, sit down on the edge of the sofa bed.

Dan was still talking when Ruth arrived with a set of towels for them to use. She placed them quietly on the seat of Walt's chair, and stayed, just a moment, to hear how it was going.

From the skeptical look on Kristen's face, Dan knew he could use some help. He mentioned the conversation with the Stockton Police Department. As he explained the need to stay out of their home, Ruth interrupted. "You are welcome to stay here for as long as you need," she said.

Kristen let out a gasp. "I don't even have anything to sleep in tonight," she said. Her eyes scanned over to her house across the street. "Can't I at least go get a few clothes?"

Dan and Ruth exchanged glances. "I know it seems stupid," Dan said, "but…"

"I'll get one of Walt's shirts for you to sleep in," Ruth interrupted. "And tomorrow we'll come up with something. Maybe you and I can go over and get you some things. Or better yet, we can go shopping."

Kristen let her shoulders slump and gave Ruth a tired smile.

Dan sat down next to Kristen, and Ruth offered to bring her something to drink. "Tea? Or would you like a glass of water? Or wine? It's nothing special, but I have some white wine."

Kristen shook her head and leaned slowly into Dan's body. "No, thank you, Ruth. I think I just need to call it a day."

Dan put his arm around Kristen and pulled her closer. He inhaled the smell of her hair and kissed the top of her head.

"I'm sorry," he said. "We'll get this figured out. I promise."

Ruth returned and held up a man's extra-large shirt in front of Kristen. "Will this do?" she asked. "It should be large enough."

Kristen nodded and thanked her.

"I'll let you two get some sleep," Ruth said. "If you need anything, just holler. But you know where the kitchen is, so feel free to help yourself there."

Dan and Kristen thanked her and waited to hear her close the door to her bedroom, then turned to each other. Dan rested his forehead on hers.

"Are you okay?" Dan whispered.

He could feel her gently nodding her head against his. "Yeah. Let's get some sleep."

Dan kissed her, then walked over to the front window to close the curtains. Across the street, their own house was dark. He stood there, watching. Down the street, one of his neighbors turned off their porch light. A dog barked somewhere in the distance.

He could see the towering pine that cast a deep shadow in the corner of his yard. It would be easy for someone to be hiding there.

From behind him, he could hear Kristen ask quietly. "Do you see anything?"

He shook his head. He stayed there another minute, then overlapped the curtains closed and turned to find Kristen already in bed, her clothes piled neatly on the coffee table. He stripped down to his boxers and joined her.

Kristen rolled toward him and nestled her head on his chest. After a moment she gave a deep sigh and patted him gently on the stomach.

Dan smiled. "Sorry," he said again. He hoped he was saying it often enough.

"Mm, mm," she mumbled sleepily in response.

Dan closed his eyes and allowed himself to drift off to sleep.

He awoke with a start. At first, he could not remember where he was, or why. He felt Kristen reach over to touch his arm. He realized that it was a noise that woke him, a car outside. Outside his house.

Dan slipped out of bed and crept up to the front window. The car was still there. He cracked open the curtains, holding them close to his face. He could see a light playing across the front of his house. The light flickered across the trees in his yard.

He realized that he was holding his breath. The light flashed back and forth, playing on both the house and the yard, looking for something? Looking for Dan? Behind him he heard Kristen moving, and then steps. The light kept searching from one side to the other. It paused on the front door, then on the window to the side.

He felt the warmth of Kristen's body as she came up behind him. "What is it?" she whispered.

"A car," he whispered back. The car slowly eased forward, and Dan could see the white panel of the door. He let out his breath. "A Sheriff's car."

"Are you sure?" she asked.

Dan nodded. The logo was now clearly visible. "They must be checking up on us."

They watched as the car drove up the road, then turned and drove back by again. It slowed again in front of the house.

Dan asked Kristen if she wanted to get some clothes.

She shook her head. "Not now."

The car flashed the spotlight over the house one more time, then accelerated off down the road.

And Dan and Kristen went back to bed.

chapter 41

It was just getting light outside when Dan woke again. In the backcountry, he would have heard the dawn chorus of birds welcoming the day, but here it was quieter. He resisted the urge to get up. He didn't want to wake Kristen, and he didn't want Ruth to hear him either. Kristen was curled up, her back to him. He reached out and gently put a hand on her hip. He wasn't sure if that was to comfort her, or himself.

He closed his eyes and lay there, letting the silence wash over him. After a few minutes he heard a door open, and then the smell of coffee came wafting out to him. He hopped up, slipped on a pair of pants, and went to help Ruth in the kitchen.

"What do you like for breakfast?" She whispered the question to him.

He shook his head. "No, you don't have to do anything. We'll go to our place."

Ruth gently pushed him backwards into a chair. Once he had sat down, she stood over him with her hands on her hips. "Waffles," she said.

From the door, he heard the words, "That sounds wonderful," and Kristen joined them, still wearing Walt's giant shirt. She looked rumpled and sleepy, and Dan could barely stand how beautiful she was.

"Good," Ruth said firmly. "You two get yourselves ready for

the day, and I'll whip up some waffles for us. Is banana and walnut okay?"

"Heaven," Kristen replied, and carried a clutch of clothes with her when she went down the hall to the bathroom.

Ruth looked at Dan. "She is really something, Dan, isn't she?"

Dan smiled and nodded, feeling just a bit as if he had a responsibility to Ruth not to screw up his relationship with Kristen.

"Go get dressed," Ruth said. "Waffles will be ready before you know it."

Over breakfast, Dan listened as Ruth and Kristen rehashed the details of Matthew McLeod, Susan Chen, and the strange developments over the past few days. He was happy to be a spectator. It wasn't his case, it wasn't his problem, and he didn't want to think about it anymore. It was too much like that old trail he had tracked: too many loose ends, not enough hard information.

As they finished up breakfast, Dan's phone rang, and he had a quick chat with Cal Healey.

"Just wanted you to know that we've got a major team out at Bourland Creek," Cal said. "But I've got a car headed your way, in case you want to get into your house and pick up a few things."

Dan assured him that they did.

"I figured," Cal said. "With any luck, we'll track down this Susan Chen today, and your life should get a little simpler. But until we do, you need to keep your head down. Got any plans?"

Dan hadn't really thought about it. Apparently, going to work was not one of his options, nor was staying home.

"You could always come down to the office and hang out with me," Cal offered. "I might even buy you a donut."

Dan suggested that he might pick up his laptop and do some work for the Forest Service.

"You mean, work remote as a wilderness ranger?" Cal asked. "If that isn't government double-speak, I don't know what is."

"You can never spend too much time filling out reports," Dan said. "Not if you work in government."

Cal told him that the car was on its way and hung up.

Back in the kitchen, Ruth and Kristen were still talking.

"What are you going to do today?" Kristen asked him.

"Stay out of the way, stay out of trouble," Dan said. "Those are my instructions."

"Sounds like Walt," Ruth said. "He's been down at that dig for almost a week now."

"I thought he was supposed to be trading off with the students," Dan said.

Ruth gave him a sad smile. "They spend a lot more time on social media, apparently," she said. "From what they see there, they've decided they're going to lay low until this other thing cools down."

"So Walt is there all alone?" Kristen asked.

"Oh, he loves it," Ruth said. "He's taken a stack of books down there and spends the day reading and listening to the river."

"Sounds pretty good to me," Dan admitted. "Although I'm not sure I have that many books."

"Well, you could always take a few of the McLeod mysteries," Ruth said with a chuckle.

"Dan, you should go see Walt," Kristen said. "It would sure get you out of town, and I'm sure he'd be happy to see you."

"Why not?" Ruth asked. "He would like to see you, Dan."

"What about all those books?" Dan asked.

"After six days, I'll bet even Walt would welcome a break," Ruth said.

Just to make sure, Dan gave Steve Matson a call and explained his plan.

"Sounds perfect," Steve said. "See if you can't find a nice arrowhead as a souvenir."

chapter 42

There were only two other cars parked near the trailhead this time: Walt's old green Forester, and a minivan with a big decal across the back window. Dan drove past them, parked in the last flat spot before the road plummeted down the hill like a bobsled run, and grabbed his day pack.

After breakfast and the process of getting in and out of his house, Dan knew he was making a late start. It was warm. Dan wove his way down the road, chasing the shade where he could find it. He was already thinking about how hot it was going to be on the way back up. Sweaty hot. But he could fill up his water bottles down at the dig, so he would have plenty to drink. Plenty to sweat.

What had been mud a few weeks ago was now dusty clay, and he could see it already clinging to his boots and working its way up the legs of his pants. But one large pine had fallen since the last time Dan had hiked down here, and someone had done him the favor of cutting it through and moving it off the old logging road. The air smelled of fresh sawdust and pine.

Farther down, Dan kept his eyes open for the rattlesnake, but it was nowhere to be seen. He could begin to hear the river now, less powerful than earlier in the spring. Some of the white water had slowed to take on the deep green of the rest of the river.

The big shade shelter had been taken down, but the rest of the dig looked unchanged. Dan took a quick stroll through the camp, looking for Walt, but came up empty.

He stopped in the shade of the big oak and looked out over the sun-washed area of the dig. There was no sign of Walt, so he walked out into the glare of the sunlight, following the path the team had worn into the dirt through the grass that was turning from green to brown. The tape and grid were still there, although there were a few stretches where the tape was now lying twisted on the ground, the bright yellow showing through the dust and dirt.

"You looking for me?" he heard a voice call out from the forest above the dig.

Dan turned to see Walt come out of the shade of the trees, carrying a book. "Hey, how are you doing?" Dan greeted him. "I thought you might like some company."

Walt shook Dan's hand. "Normally, no," he said. "But your company? That's a different story."

Dan waved his hand at the dig. "It doesn't look much different," he said.

"No, we really did stop work on it," Walt said. He held up a book, Guardians of the Valley. "Gives me time to read this."

Dan smiled, then turned his eyes back to the dig. "So where did you find all this stuff?" he asked.

"Want the cook's tour?" Walt asked. "Come on."

He led Dan over to the edge of the dig and started pointing out various trenches and holes. "That's where we found the button," he said. "And over here is where most of the human remains were."

To Dan it looked more like a building site before they poured the concrete foundation, but he followed along as Walk talked him through the story of the dig.

Dan nodded and acted impressed, but he wasn't sure that Walt believed him.

Sure enough, once Walt had narrated the outline of the dig, he looked at Dan and said, "Want to see something cool?"

When Dan agreed, Walt led him up river past the dig itself, and up onto a large smooth ledge of granite that stood above the river. They scrambled up a couple of larger boulders to get up on top of the granite slab, as big as a large patio. From here, the dig was laid out almost like a schematic.

"Nice," Dan said appreciatively.

"Look at your feet," Walt suggested.

When he looked down, Dan saw a series of deep holes and depressions in the granite.

"Grinding stones," Walt said. "Can you imagine how many hours, how many years, it took to grind those out of the granite?"

"Unbelievable," Dan agreed. "They're beautiful." He looked around and wondered if the pestles, what they called the "manos" in the Southwest, were to be seen.

"We only found one," Walt said, "over by the dig. I think they must have carried those smaller stones with them. But it fit that hole over there perfectly."

The two men stood on the dark gray, almost black granite. The river ran alongside, a deep pool where the water ran up against the granite under their feet.

"You can almost hear them talking to each other, can't you?" Walt asked quietly. "Some days, I swear I hear voices, and there's nobody here."

Dan nodded. "Yeah, the noise of the river does that to me, too."

Walt smiled. "If it's the river," he said.

The two stood in silence for a few minutes.

"I can see why you stay down here," Dan said. "But I think Ruth wishes you could come home from time to time."

"Well, the place seems to spook the kids," Walt said. "And they see more of the nasty stuff people have been posting on the internet, so they worry more."

"You don't worry about that?" Dan asked.

Walt looked around, his eyes taking in the deep canyon, the river, and the forested hills above. "Here?" he asked. He turned to look at Dan. "I don't get many visitors here. And I generally see them coming a long way off." He pointed to where the traces of the logging road entered by the tents of the camp. "It's a long way down here, and that tends to discourage most hooligans. They may talk big, but they don't like to work that hard."

Dan chuckled. "Yeah, I know what you mean."

"Present company excepted," Walt said with a grin. "Still, I do appreciate the company. So tell me, is this an official visit, or did you just take the day off? Or did Ruth send you down here to check up on me?"

Dan laughed. "None of the above," he said. "But it's a long story."

chapter 43

Walt pointed to a log lying back in the forest, in the shade of a towering pine tree. "I've got all day," he said. "Let's make ourselves comfortable."

Dan followed Walt over into the shade, considering exactly how much he should tell his old friend. He wasn't sure how much he wanted to think about it today.

He sat down next to Walt and stared out over the river, watching the roiling water roll by.

"You don't have to tell me," Walt said, putting his hands out in front of himself. "I'm happy to remain ignorant."

"Are you still getting unwanted visitors down here?" Dan asked.

"Not really," Walt assured him. "Since those signs went up, things have quieted down a lot."

"But you're still down here?" Dan continued.

"Just to keep an eye on things," Walt said. "And to make sure nobody takes advantage. My imposing presence seems to do the trick." His weathered face gave just a hint of a grin.

Dan chuckled. "I bet it does," he said. "How many times have you had to do that?"

Walt smiled. "Maybe a couple of times. I'm not sure. I had a couple of hikers through here yesterday, but they just moved on through."

"One look at you is all it took, huh?" Dan asked.

Walt laughed quietly. "They never saw me. I was up at the latrine, answering a call of nature. By the time I was presentable, they had already passed on through up the river."

Dan looked up the canyon. "Up that?" he asked. "Not a lot of places you can get to up there."

"Well," Walt answered. "You can get away. Maybe that's all they wanted to do."

"Or fishing," Dan added.

Walt nodded in agreement. The two men looked up the canyon. The only thing moving was the river. The pools and riffles certainly held fish. Dan knew that.

Walt looked at Dan's backpack. "Did you bring a rod in there?"

"It didn't even occur to me," Dan said. "I was thinking about other stuff."

And that was how he began to tell Walt about his last two weeks. He knew the story well enough by now that he could simplify a lot of the details—less white water now. "Has Ruth been telling you about these mysteries by Matthew McLeod?" he asked.

"Only briefly," Walt answered him. "I've been focused on what we've been doing down here."

"Then I guess I should start at the beginning," Dan said. "We started seeing a lot of hikers up here this year, really early in the season. And some of them were completely unprepared."

He proceeded to tell Walt about the searches, and the rumors of a treasure hidden in the Sierra. From there he moved on to his conversation with McLeod. "The sonovabitch wouldn't do a thing for us," he said.

He was expecting Walt to comment, but the older man just sat quietly, waiting for Dan to continue.

Dan went on to explain about the group of women, including

Ruth, trying to solve the mysteries. He looked at Walt but got no reaction.

Dan continued with Doris and her grandson and the kids at Cal Poly, and then how McLeod went missing. As he talked, Dan realized that he was able to put some distance between himself and the story. He was starting to make sense of it all, to see the pattern.

He told Walt about McLeod's true identity, and the missing person phone call from the Stockton police department.

He told him about the call from Susan Chen, and his meeting with her. He described her determined look, the sense that she was not someone who is easily diverted from her plan.

And then the second call from Stockton, this time about the murder of Nathan Petrovski. Now Dan had Walt's full attention. Walt adjusted his seat on the log so that he could face Dan more directly.

"So that's why I spent last night at your house," Dan said. "And why I'm down here today."

"It's not often that someone confesses to me that he spent the night with my wife," Walt said with a smile. "And expects to live to tell the tale."

Dan laughed. "You've been gone a lot, Walt," he said with a grin. "Ruth is getting lonely."

Walt briefly joined in the laughter. Then he asked Dan, "So what happens now?"

"If we're lucky," Dan said, "Susan Chen comes walking out of these mountains in a day or two with a thumb drive worth five million bucks."

"Let's take a little walk," he said. "There's something I'd like to show you."

chapter 44

Walt led Dan back into the meadow of the dig. They could feel the heat of the sun now, beating down on them. The thought of the icy water nearby wasn't enough to keep them from sweating. Dan admired Walt's ancient straw hat, which looked cooler in every way than his own ball cap.

They crossed through the meadow and Walt headed straight for the camp.

"Boy, it's going to be hot today," Dan said.

Walt grunted an assent and kept walking ahead of him.

Once they reached the camp, Walt asked Dan to wait for a moment. Now that they were in the shade, Dan looked back at the meadow. It wasn't even noon, and it was already hotter than hell.

Walt ducked into a bright yellow tent and came out holding an expensive-looking black camera. He handed it to Dan and said, "Follow me."

They walked up to the old logging road. For a second Dan thought they might be walking back up the road, but Walt stopped at a tree on the uphill side of the road and reached up to open a wildlife camera.

"Our high-tech seeing-eye doorbell," he said to Dan. "You don't even have to ring it. All you have to do is walk by."

Walt pulled out the photo card and took the camera from Dan. He popped open the back of the camera and removed the card there, handing it to Dan. "Try not to lose that," he said. "Erica would not be pleased about that."

Dan carefully slipped the card into his shirt pocket, hoping it wouldn't be too hard to pull out later.

Walt slipped the card from the wildlife cam into the camera and started pushing buttons. A beep, another beep, and then Walt nodded and handed the camera to Dan.

"Is this anybody you know?" he asked.

Dan squinted at the tiny image on the camera.

Walt reached out and took the camera from him, pushed a button that gave a different beep about four times, and handed the camera back to Dan.

Now the image was larger and clearer. Walking down the road toward the dig, there could be very little doubt about it, was Susan Chen.

Dan stared at the image. No, there was no doubt.

Dan kept looking at the photo. "When was this?" he asked.

"Yesterday morning," Walt told him. "Right around nine o'clock."

"And there was someone with her?"

Walt nodded. "She was in front. I think you can just see his leg there."

Dan shook his head. "Nope."

Walt took the camera from him and zoomed back out. "Now you can."

Dan could now see a boot and part of a leg on the left-hand side of the photo.

"Do you have any more photos?" Dan asked, "How do you scroll through these?"

Walt pointed out the button on the back of the camera that

allowed Dan to look through the images. The next photo only showed the back of the other hiker. And the image after that was a close look at Walt's face. Dan scrolled the other direction, only to find a deer walking through the view.

Dan muttered a curse under his breath.

"It has a time lag," Walt explained. "It's motion sensitive, but it only takes a photo about every ten seconds or so."

Dan handed the camera back to Walt. "Any idea who was with her?" Dan asked.

Walt shook his head. "Like I said, I didn't even talk to them."

Dan took a deep breath and let it out slowly.

"They were dressed kind of different," Walt said. When Dan looked at him, he continued. "She was all REI and Patagonia. He was," Walt paused here, searching for the right word. "He was more camo and tactical."

"Do you have a radio?" Dan asked. He had left his own at home, assuming he wouldn't be needing it.

Walt shook his head. "Not the kind you want," he said. "I've got a couple walkie-talkies, but that won't help. I do have a PLB, though."

"Can it send messages? Or does it just send out an SOS?"

"No, I can send a text message to Erica, for example. Well, I think I can send one to any cell phone." As he watched Dan think this through, he said quietly. "Don't tell Ruth about that part."

Dan walked over to the folding table in the camp and sat down. Walt followed and joined him at the table.

"Here's what I think we need to do," Dan said. His mind was flying through the options. "Get word to the Stockton PD ASAP," he said.

"Got a number?" Walt asked.

Dan shook his head. "No, but can you text Erica and ask her to call them? And maybe call Tuolumne County Sheriff, too."

Walt's face twisted into a grimace. "If she's checking her phone," he said. "She's been leaving it off a lot these days."

Dan muttered another quiet oath. "Got a pencil and paper?" he asked.

Walt pulled a ballpoint pen out of his shirt pocket and opened his book to the back page. "I think we can use this."

Dan wrote down the numbers for Steve Matson and Cal Healey. And he drafted a short message for Walt to type to them. "Susan Chen @ UC Merced dig yesterday a.m. Likely still in the area. Advise Stockton PD and Tuolumne CO Sheriff ASAP."

Walk took the book, read the message and nodded to Dan.

Dan asked for the book back and wrote in another number. "This one is for Doris," he said.

Walt took the book and pulled out his emergency beacon. "I'll send one to Ruth, too," he said. "I guess it's time she learned about this little thing."

Dan stood up and stared up the canyon. He glanced back down at Walt, who was busy typing in the message, letter by letter. There were a million reasons why he should stay in camp with Walt. He knew that. He remembered the photo card in his pocket and dug it out and placed it on the table next to Walt. Then he started walking out across the sunbaked grass of the meadow.

"Where the hell do you think you're going?" Walt called out to him.

Dan gave him a casual wave and kept walking.

"Hey," Walt called out after him. "Are you nuts?"

Dan stopped and turned around. "Just going to take a quick look," he said. "Don't worry."

Even though Walt muttered it, Dan heard Walt clearly call him a dumbshit. Then he kept walking.

<h1 style="text-align:center">chapter 45</h1>

The top of the granite slab with the grinding holes was now shaded by a large ponderosa pine. Dan stopped there and looked up the canyon. There was a gentle breeze coming down, as if catching a lift from the river. Dan could feel it in his face.

In front of him a jumble of large boulders sat at the base of the canyon wall on his side of the river. Some had tumbled into the riverbed, maybe a thousand years ago, and had created the first big rapid above the dig site. Dan knew that there would be many more.

At the top of the rapid Dan could see trees, standing tall into the sky. Where the canyon went, and what happened up there, was hidden behind the imposing wall of rocks.

He glanced down at the granite slab. On the upriver side it sloped down and away to the right, away from the river, steep enough to make him think, but not steep enough to stop him from easing his way down to the dirt of the forest. Once there he could reconsider.

He knew he should wait for the mass of people who were going to arrive, once they received Walt's message and organized themselves. How long would that take? At least two hours, more like four.

Dan eased down the sloping rock and checked the ground for footprints, but saw only pine needles, littered with a few cones from last year.

He walked slowly upriver towards the wall of boulders, eyes

more on the ground than looking around. Next to one small knuckle of granite sticking out of the ground, he saw what might have been part of a boot print, or a mark made by a hiking pole. Or not. Maybe it had been left by a deer.

The rushing of the river covered any sounds, and Dan looked at the boulders facing him. They were huge, some as tall as a house. Away from the river, against the wall of the canyon, they were overgrown with massive poison oak vines. He could see huge logs, trees that had fallen down the slope and come to rest among the boulders there. It was a morass of rock and vegetation.

No point in exploring that, he knew.

Down closer to the river, two massive boulders leaned against each other, making a small doorway between them.

Dan walked forward, noting the game path that seemed to lead to and through the passage. Contrasted with the brilliant sunlight, the shadows in the passage were dark enough to be almost impenetrable. But they also promised to be cool.

Dan stepped forward, ducked his head, and eased between the two rocks.

He came out into a small space surrounded by boulders, no larger than an average living room. A fire ring had been built up against the face of one of the boulders, and two logs were in place as benches in front of the fire ring.

The campsite had obviously been used for years, probably by fishermen. The blackened granite behind the fire ring told him that much. There were bits of tin foil in the ashes, and on one side what looked like a used container for salmon eggs. It was illegal—far too close to the river to pass muster. On another day he would have taken the time to break up the fire ring and move the logs to discourage anyone from using it again. But the ground here was dirt and dust.

And in that dirt and dust, Dan could clearly see footprints leading upriver, through the next passage between the towering boulders. He followed them.

It was wider than the previous one and led to the face of another massive boulder. To the left was nothing but a twenty-foot-high granite cliff and, behind that cliff, the river. But to the right there was a series of smaller boulders that made what looked like a staircase designed by a cubist leading upwards around the side of the boulder.

They were large steps, and Dan wondered how hard it might have been for Susan Chen to clamber up these. At the top of the stairs, the boulders led to a narrow chute, really nothing more than a crack with steeply sloping sides, rising tightly between two more large rocks. This time his feet were too wide. He was afraid they would get jammed in the crack. He wedged himself against one side, planted his feet against the other side, and squeezed up to the next level.

Now he was close to being on top of one of the largest boulders, the size of a house, with a roof that sloped upwards. He tested the rock and found that his boots held. There was enough friction that he didn't slide. Using both hands and feet, he carefully climbed up the roof to where the boulder topped out.

He stopped to catch his breath. Not that he had been working hard, but this had been nervous work, and he wanted to settle his heart rate for a minute. He could see the cascades of the river, not forty feet to his left. They were pure white water, roaring in his ears. The rocks here wore a slight sheen from the mist of the cascades. And the air was cool, chilled by the water racing nearby.

He looked around. On three sides, the boulder sloped off steeply. He already knew about the part behind him, but also towards the river, and ahead of him. But the side away from the river was flatter and led to a ledge that overlooked the top of another, smaller rock. He hopped down onto the smaller rock, not sure where he would go next. He checked back the way he had come and realized that it was going to be a struggle to get back up to the top of that boulder from his new perch.

He decided that he needed to check that and saw a ledge that might work as a foothold. He felt around with his hands, found decent handholds, and put his right foot on the ledge. He leaned into the rock and tried to put his weight on the ledge. His foot held and he was able to rise up enough to reach higher with his hands. He pulled himself halfway back up onto the boulder, then let himself back down again.

Yep. That would work.

He stepped back down on the smaller rock and turned upriver. A cluster of rocks in a narrow chute led back down to dirt, and Dan scrambled down, discovering a small opening in the rocks that was too small even for a single tent campsite. A steep dirt chute led up the side of the canyon wall, obviously unstable and full of poison oak. Dan could imagine a deer going that way, but not a human.

But now it looked like he was on a game trail through the rocks. It led him around one side of one boulder, past another, weaving through the labyrinth between these huge granite monoliths. There was no sound except the rushing water of the river.

He couldn't see past the granite walls that penned him in as if in a maze. But the game trail led on, through the boulders, slowly and steeply uphill. At one point there was a large tree blocking the trail at chest height—any deer would walk right under it. Dan slipped off his backpack, but it still required careful contortions. He managed to scrape his shoulder blade badly on a stub sticking out the far side of the tree. That hurt like hell. He hoped it hadn't torn his shirt or broken the skin too badly. He massaged the spot for a moment. At least for now he couldn't feel any blood seeping through.

More than once Dan had to stop to consider where it might lead next. In every case, just as he thought there was no way past the confusion of rocks, a single option appeared, often unlikely. There was another narrow chute. And once a thin ledge of rock angled up to get him to the next big boulder. In each case it worked out somehow. It took him further up the jumble, further up the river.

Near the top of the cascade, Dan came to a wide ledge that intersected with the river itself, and a small stream of water caught on the ledge and followed it away from the river to pool up at Dan's feet. The wall in front of him was a good ten feet high and presented no obvious route to the top.

But on the right-hand side, a huge old pine had fallen down the slope, its branches like the arms of an octopus extending in crazy twists in all directions. Dan walked over to inspect it. He looked at the lowest branch, the one he would use to begin to climb it. There was dried mud on it, right where it met the trunk, right where he would have placed his foot.

Dan took a step back, scouted his route up the fallen tree, and took a deep breath. And then he climbed up the tree, up the wall, and found himself on top of the cascade.

He turned around and looked back the way he had come. Much of the cascade was invisible to him, falling too steeply for him to see. But far below he could see the meadow and the dig. And yes, there was Walt, standing at the dig, and looking up toward Dan.

Dan gave him a wave but got no response from Walt. It would have been difficult for the older man to see Dan up here among the trees at the top of the cascade. There were no other people with Walt, and Dan knew they wouldn't arrive for some time.

Dan took one more look down the way he had come, making sure he could remember the route he would need to take back down. He was sweating, adrenaline pumping after the climb up the log. He wondered if Susan Chen could have made it this far.

Turning upriver, he scanned the ground and soon found footprints. Some of them were small enough to be Susan Chen's.

chapter 46

He felt his stomach grumble, protesting that even though he'd had a larger than average breakfast, it was still time to eat again.

Dan turned and looked back down the canyon. He couldn't see much, but he also didn't see anyone that looked like a law enforcement team.

He took a quick look around and spotted a nice flat rock in the shade just a few yards up the side of the canyon. He eased his pack off and settled himself down on the rock, the daypack in the dirt between his feet.

He took a moment to appreciate where he was. Despite the hot weather, the river still helped keep this part of the canyon cool. As he sat facing the river it rushed by from right to left, the deep pool at the top of the cascade gave him only a frisson of a clue to the energy that exploded into white water just beyond. He could hear the roar and see a light mist, but the white water itself was out of sight just over the edge.

Further up the canyon the river looked like a stairway as it poured down through a series of pools and rapids. From his vantage point he was looking up at them, and the upper pools were hidden behind whitewater powering over boulders and ledges.

The trees down in the canyon were huge—towering pines that soared into the sky, massive oaks with their blue-green foliage that clouded in among them, the branches soaring out to seek the sun.

But through the trees Dan could also see the sides of the canyon, rising up a thousand feet or more above him. And up there it was all pines and cedars. Down where he sat, it was the transition zone, oaks and pines competing for water and sun. Higher up, the colder temperatures in winter would keep the oaks from flourishing.

Dan pulled out a deli sandwich and packet of potato chips he'd picked up at a convenience store on the way to the trailhead earlier in the day. It wasn't what he would normally have eaten for lunch, but these were unusual times. He peeled the plastic wrap off the sandwich and took a bite. Bland, he decided, both in taste and texture.

He tore open the bag of chips and tossed a couple into his mouth, adding both salt and crunch to the sandwich. That was better.

He knew he'd have to make a decision, and he was using the lunch to procrastinate. As he ran through the facts, he knew that he didn't have enough of them. He didn't know if Susan Chen was capable of murder, even though he had his doubts. He didn't know who was with her, nor did he know if that guy was capable of murder. He didn't know if either of them were armed.

He took another bite of the sandwich, added a few more chips, and admitted that he really didn't know very much at all.

He did know that it would be an hour or two, and more likely three hours, before anyone from the Sheriff or police departments would arrive at the dig. And he added at least another hour for them to arrive up at the top of the cascade. He thought it through one more time and decided closer to four hours, total.

That would still give them plenty of time to continue up the canyon, but who knew what Susan Chen and her pal would be doing in the meantime?

He took a swig from his water bottle to wash down the sandwich and took another bite. As he chewed, he peeked into the bag of chips. There were plenty of them—enough to season every bite of sandwich, and still have some left over. He took another handful out of the bag and tossed them into his mouth.

He also knew that every procedure manual in the world would tell him to stay put and wait for backup. That made him think of Cal Healey, and what Cal would tell him. And that made him smile. Cal would not mince words. "Don't be the guy who goes in without backup," he'd say. "You're just as big an idiot as that girl in the horror movie who decides to open the door to the basement, when everybody knows what's going to happen."

He took another bit of the sandwich—only two more to go—and added in the chips. He leaned forward on his rock, trying to see further up the canyon, but didn't have much luck. And turning back to look down the canyon, he could see only the top of the boulders and the mist, now making a rainbow in the hot sun.

Another swig of water, and Dan checked his pack for the banana he'd brought along. As usual, even though he'd left it carefully positioned in the pack, it had become bruised and was now quickly turning various shades of brown.

He stuffed the rest of the sandwich into his mouth, put the plastic wrapper in his daypack, and considered the bag of chips. He put the banana on the rock and proceeded to finish off the bag of chips, pouring the last crumbs into his hand, and then tossing them into his mouth.

He wiped the salt and oil from the chips off on the back of his pant leg and peeled the banana. Far overhead, Dan could see a hawk slowly patrolling, looking for movement in the forest below. A red-tailed hawk, he decided. Even from here he could see that tail.

He finished the banana and drank the rest of the water in his water bottle. He had one more in the pack. And with the dig just a short hike away, there was no reason to hoard the water. He could get more from Walt on his way out.

He took the banana peel and put it into the empty potato chip bag, and dragged out the plastic wrap from the sandwich and did the same with it. He zipped up the daypack and decided it was time to answer a call of nature.

That would require him to walk away from the river—at least a hundred feet, according to the regulations.

Dan liked to be on the cautious side, and hiked up well more than that, carefully picking his way to avoid poison oak while still managing to find a viable route up the side of the canyon.

He peed, facing the hillside, with his back to the river. When he was done, he turned around, and used the higher elevation to look up the canyon again. The next half-mile or so didn't look too steep or demanding. And then the canyon took a turn, running out of sight around the bend.

Dan checked his watch. It was still only a few minutes before one. He sidled down the side of the canyon, back to his daypack, and picked it up. He took a short stroll over to the top of the cascade and looked down.

He knew it was still too early to expect to see any backup.

He turned and looked upriver. Other than the water, he didn't see anything moving up there, either. A couple of ravens sailed across the sky, from his side of the river to the other.

Dan took a deep breath and let it out slowly. Then he started walking slowly, picking his way through the rocks along the river, and up the canyon. The river still rushed through the canyon, and the sky above was still that startling blue of the Sierra.

Besides, this wasn't a horror movie, and there was no basement.

chapter 47

He told himself that he wouldn't go far, or fast. He was just doing a little preliminary scouting work before the real team arrived. As he walked, he imagined the conversation with them. Dan would explain what he had learned, and how they would use the information to track down Susan Chen and her friend.

They would insist that Dan stay behind while they proceeded, and he would be fine with that. He might even get home in time for dinner. He checked his watch again and decided that, maybe not.

The next set of boulders created a series of short waterfalls. Hiking on the bank, Dan had to turn his back to the river and hike directly up the side of the canyon to find a way past the huge rocks.

There was a small seep or spring here, he realized, as he waded through waist high ferns that covered the ground and hid both rocks and tree trunks from sight. It was a bushwhack, as he stumbled first one way, then another, trying to find his footing underneath the ferns.

If there was any wildlife in the area, he had certainly cleared it out now. He stepped over the last log in the ferns, and now he could see a path past the granite. It looked like the going got easier up there, and he checked his footing one more time before clearing the ferns.

When he looked up again, a man was staring at him from the far end of the trail.

Dan froze.

As he stood there, he took note of the fact that the other man had stopped, too. Wearing camo pants and shirt, Dan noted.

Somehow, they both started forward again. Dan found a wider spot in the trail and stepped out of the way to let the man pass. The guy walked with an odd rhythm, something between a limp and stumble.

"How ya doin'"? Dan called out to him.

The man nodded firmly but didn't speak.

Dan was sure this was the same guy he saw on the camera, hiking with Susan Chen.

"Where's your partner?" he asked.

The man startled, stopped, then continued walking toward Dan. "Up the river," he said, pointing over his shoulder with his thumb. "She decided to stay for a few days. Panning for gold."

Dan nodded and let the man stump past him. He didn't see any gun, but that didn't mean the guy didn't have one in his pack or somewhere else. There was something familiar about him, though. Dan couldn't place it, but he knew he had met him before.

It was the way he walked. Dan had seen it before. As Dan turned to hike up the river, he remembered that awkward, clumping walk. It was Marco Gemmeli.

He spun around to find Marco standing in the middle of the trail, pointing a gun at him.

"Marco Gemmeli," Dan said.

"You should have kept walking," Marco said. "I was willing to just let you go. But you stopped."

Dan now began to put the pieces together. "Where's Susan?" he asked. He was sure Marco wouldn't be working with her. So that meant…

"On her way straight to hell, where she belongs," Marco said.

He kept the pistol pointed right at Dan, finger on the trigger.

"What are you doing, Marco?" Dan asked, his arms out at his sides, pleading. "She's up here trying to end this whole stupid thing."

"She should have done that a long time ago," Marco said. "Before she and her pal killed Tony."

Dan considered his next move. He didn't want to make Marco any angrier. He gave a deep sigh and slowly sat down on a rock by the side of the trail. "That isn't the way it happened, Marco," he said. "You know. You and I know what happened. We were in the middle of that blizzard together. Three days."

Marco wasn't moving, his eyes hidden from Dan behind chrome sunglasses. He didn't lower the gun.

"We were out here for days," Dan said. "And you saw the weather. We couldn't see fifty feet in that stuff."

"Shut up," Marco said, waving the gun slightly.

Dan shut up.

They stayed there, looking at each other, for twenty seconds, maybe more. For Dan it seemed closer to an hour.

Dan started shaking his head. Finally, he broke the silence. "I always thought that vengeance was supposed to be the Lord's," Dan said. He was remembering Marco's family, united in prayer at the trailhead.

Marco reacted with a start. "What the fuck do you know about that?" he asked Dan.

"Isn't that what the Bible says?" Dan asked.

"I doubt you have any idea what the Bible says," Marco answered.

"Well, I know it says that thou shalt not kill."

Marco snorted at him. "Yeah, well, maybe a few other people should have read that."

"But now it's you, Marco," Dan said. "What about you? You're the one in charge, you get to decide."

"I already decided," Marco said.

That didn't sound good to Dan. "I mean, what about you? Are you going to heaven or hell? That's what you get to decide. There's still time for that."

"Oh, I'm going to hell," Marco said, seriously and far too loudly. "I'm going to hell, and when I get there, I am going to make them even more miserable. That asshole Petrovski and this bitch up here, too."

Dan was out of ideas. He didn't want to provoke Marco any more. Maybe he should tell him about Karl Rahm, who was also lost, but got found. No, that might just make Marco angrier. And Walt? He could tell Marco that Walt was down below, waiting for him, but then Marco might just decide to kill Walt, too. "So what now, Marco? What are your parents going to think about all this? They are going to lose two sons now."

"I told you to shut up!" Marco yelled at him. His face was red now, tinged with white around his eyes and lips.

"All I ever did was try like hell to find your brother," Dan said. "Are you going to shoot me, too?"

A flicker of motion behind Marco distracted Dan. and he glanced over to see someone coming up the trail behind Marco. He tried to conceal his surprise, looking back at Marco.

"That isn't going to work," Marco said, noting the change. He shook his head and gave Dan a skeptical sneer. "There's nobody up here. You know it and I know it."

Dan looked again. The man behind Marco was holding a gun, pointing it at Marco. Medium height, slight build. He was wearing a plaid shirt that looked hot and chinos that were dirty at the knees.

"Drop the gun, Marco!" the man said, somewhat calmly, in Dan's opinion. Then he repeated, "Drop it. Now."

chapter 48

Much to Dan's consternation, Marco kept the gun pointed at Dan. Marco's breathing was faster, deeper, and Dan had no idea what he would do.

"Drop the gun." The man behind wasn't yelling, just speaking quietly, firmly. He was walking up quickly behind Marco.

Dan tried to make himself smaller, sinking down on the rock, thinking somehow that he was making himself tiny. Invisible. Unhittable.

The man walked quickly and quietly up to Marco from behind and struck him on the side of the head with the butt of his gun.

Dan flinched as Marco dropped to the ground like a rag doll. But the gun was still in his hand, resting now on the ground. His other hand clutched at his head.

The man leaned down and said to Marco in almost a whisper, "Drop. The. Gun." Dan barely heard the words over the thunder of the river—more likely, he read the man's lips.

Marco hesitated, and Dan saw the man push his own pistol deep into Marco's neck. "Now," the man said quietly.

Marco's hand slowly relaxed, letting the gun lie on the ground at his side. The man reached down and took the gun away.

Dan started breathing again.

The man pushed Marco down toward the ground. "On your stomach," he said.

Marco rolled over as if someone had let the air out, face in the dirt.

The man took Marco Gemmeli's gun, checked it quickly, clicked on the safety, and stuck it behind his back in the waistband of his pants. He looked at Dan. "You can't argue with a guy like this," he said.

Dan mumbled something about seeing how that might be true.

The man was staring at Dan. "Are you Dan Courtwright?" he asked.

"Yep," Dan nodded. Walt must have given the man his name.

"Why aren't you in uniform?"

"It's supposed to be my day off," Dan explained.

"Are you armed?" he asked.

Dan shook his head.

"Why the hell not?"

Dan shook his head again. It would take too long to explain, and he doubted this guy would understand.

He tilted his head a touch to the side. "And you are?"

"Kim Archer," the man replied.

The detective that had been looking for Marco.

"Looks like you found him," Dan said to the detective, pointing at Marco Gemmeli.

"Looks like it," Archer replied. "Lucky for you."

Dan gave a slight nod. Even if Archer was right, Dan didn't want to feed the guy's obvious ego. "Given the situation," Dan said, "would you mind showing me some kind of ID?"

Archer didn't hesitate. He pulled out his wallet and tossed it toward Dan. It landed at his feet, and Dan leaned over to pick it up.

"CDL is in the plastic," Archer explained. "PI license is in the other side."

Dan checked them both. He also noted plenty of cash in the wallet. He folded the wallet up, stood up, and carried it back over to Kim Archer.

Marco hadn't moved. He was lying at Archer's feet, staring at the ground.

Archer took his wallet back from Dan and put it back in his pants pocket. Dan could see Marco's gun back there, too.

"Now what?" he asked Archer.

Archer did not have the kind of face Dan expected to see on a private eye. Roughly Dan's age, he was thin, but his face had a softness to it, an innocence, and it was pale. That was accented by the wire rim glasses he wore, and the soft bulge around his middle. He was wearing a ball cap tight on his head. When he took it off to wipe the sweat from his face on the sleeve of his shirt, Dan saw he was bald, with just a thin shading of blond hair around the sides of his head. He looked more like a middle-aged engineer than a detective.

Archer put the ball cap back on his head and looked at Dan.

"I guess we walk him out of here," he said.

Dan tilted his head to point upriver. "There's still one more person up there," he said. "Susan Chen."

Archer looked at Marco Gemmeli and nudged him with his foot. "Is she up there?" he asked. "What did you do with her? Where is she, Marco?"

Marco strained his head upwards to look up at both of them. "Maybe she's up there," he said. There was a wild gleam in his eye. He was enjoying the confusion he was creating. "Maybe she's still alive. Maybe she's dead. But you'll never find her. Not in time, anyway." He was grinning by the time he finished.

Dan looked back down the canyon, then checked his watch. It

would be at least two hours before the backup would arrive.

"There should be a team coming in here soon," he lied to Archer. "I don't know if Walt told you about that?"

"Yeah, he mentioned that," Archer said. "Not for a while yet, though."

Dan nodded, then turned to look back up the canyon. "Someone needs to go up there and see if they can find Susan," he said.

"If she's alive," Archer said. The man's face was oddly unemotional. He'd caught his man, Dan thought, and he didn't care about anyone else.

"You don't sound hopeful," Dan said.

Archer stared at him before speaking again. When he did, it was in a tight voice. "Nathan Petrovski was burned, repeatedly, over much of his body. Then he was taped into a large garbage bag. Large enough that he had plenty of air at first. Plenty of time to struggle and suffer before he died. It must have taken quite a while."

"And Marco did that?" Dan asked. It was bizarre to discuss this just feet above the man's head, as if they were in a parent-teacher conference. Marco gave no indication that he was even listening to them.

"That's what it looks like, from what the Stockton PD told me" Archer said. "I don't know who Susan Chen is, but if he went up here with her, there's no reason to think he was taking her on a date."

Dan looked at him. Something was bothering him. "How did you track him down?"

"I told you we would," Archer said with a shrug. "We were lucky enough to put a tracking device on his van two days ago, but it was hard to catch up with him until today. When we saw it finally stop up here, I knew we had him."

"And did you tell Stockton PD about it?" Dan asked.

Archer nodded. "Yeah, but they told us they already knew where he was."

Dan wondered If that was true. Or was Archer working with Marco? Was this all part of a more complicated plan? If he stayed with them, any chance that Susan Chen was alive would slowly melt away. If Dan left them alone, would they both bolt before the backup team arrived? And if they did, would they kill him? Would they kill Walt? The backup team would already be at the trailhead. Dan decided that there was no way they could somehow get out of here past the team coming in.

"I have an idea," Dan said, pointing to Archer's waistband. "Why don't you give me Marco's gun?"

Archer looked at him. "I thought you didn't like to carry," he said.

Dan shrugged. "Circumstances change," he answered.

There was an instant when Dan didn't know what was going to happen next. The two men looked at each other.

"Just to be on the straight and narrow," Archer said, "do you have ID on you?"

Dan pulled out his wallet and showed his driver's license to Archer. While he was still looking at it, Kim Archer reached behind himself, pulled out Marco's pistol, and handed it, grip first, to Dan.

"You know how to use that?" he asked.

Dan checked the safety, clicking it on and off. He checked the magazine. It was full. Dan sniffed the barrel. It hadn't been fired recently. Maybe that was a good thing for Susan Chen.

He looked at Kim Archer and nodded. "I think so," he said. "There should be a team of about ten LEO's here in the next hour or two. Can you manage to hang on to him until then?"

In answer, Archer pulled out a handful of zip-ties from his pocket. "Slip a couple of these on him, would you?" he asked. "I don't want to have to work too hard."

Dan pulled Marco's arms back and zip-tied his wrists together, showing Archer how he had done it.

Archer nodded in approval and pointed his gun up the canyon. "You going up there?" he asked.

"If you can manage our friend here," Dan said.

Archer pointed at the man at his feet, arms tied behind his back. "Go for it," Archer encouraged him with a shrug.

For some reason, Dan didn't want to turn his back on the two men. He watched over one shoulder as he walked over to his pack, still resting near the rock. He turned to face the men and picked it up. He thought about slipping the gun inside, but decided to wait until he was farther up the canyon.

He pulled the pack over one shoulder, gave a casual salute to Kim Archer, and started walking up the canyon, up to where Marco Gemmeli had been. When he got to the end of the straight section of trail, he stopped and turned around.

Marco Gemmeli was still lying on the ground, staring at Archer's feet. Kim Archer was now sitting on the rock that Dan had used for a chair, facing Marco, and looking like he was planning to stay for a while.

Dan turned and started walking up the canyon.

chapter 49

Dan knew that the canyon ran for another twelve miles up into the mountains before it crossed another trail. He also knew that there was no way he could search all that anyway. But as he hiked up alongside the river, he worked through a process of elimination.

She wasn't on the far side of the river. There was no way they could have crossed that raging torrent. And there was no way that they could have hiked all the way up to meet the other trail. So, she must be on this side of the river, but the real question was, how far had they hiked?

Marco obviously wasn't any help. But when Dan thought about meeting him by the river, Marco hadn't seemed tired, hot or sweaty. And it was a hot day today. Dan had hiked at a slow pace, partly because he was waiting for the backup to arrive. But when Kim Archer arrived, he was sweating from every pore. Marco was not.

In that case, either Marco hadn't hiked very far, or he hadn't hiked very fast. And possibly both. That gave Dan hope.

He also remembered Marco's clothes. They had seemed relatively clean. They certainly didn't look as if Gemmeli had done a lot of bushwhacking in them. If that was true, then Dan didn't have to worry about exploring some of the side canyons.

He was facing a series of granite slabs that came down into the river from the right. This part looked easy, and he followed a network of ledges and cracks that quickly led him up to the top of the rocks. On the far side, as they had with the grinding rocks near the dig, they sloped back down into the forest.

Dan gave a quick check but didn't see any grinding holes on this one. But the tilt of the slabs was the same—the geology was consistent through here. He knew that if he could see the rocks in the canyon wall above him, they, too, would share that same tilt.

The pine duff below the rocks made Dan feel as if he were walking on a soft brown carpet. Sure enough, Dan could see footprints here. He stopped to make sure. Yes, some were coming back down the river, but they were over the top of footprints that led up the canyon.

Up ahead he could see that his side of the river opened up, and a small meadow appeared. That would make the hiking easier. And hotter.

Dan dropped down into a gully from a small side canyon, hopped across three rocks over the stream, then struggled up the far side to reach the meadow. The air in the gully had been cooled by the little stream, but now he was in the full heat of the sun. Even with his hat on, his head was baking.

He scanned the meadow for tracks. There were so many trails running through the dry grass that it was hard to pick one. The ground was soft and sandy but littered with cobbles. At some point in the past, the river had run through here. The sand made footprints hard to identify. Deer, bears, coyotes had all come through here at times, adding their imprint. On one small flat rock, Dan noted some fox scat, and added that animal to the list.

He stopped partway into the meadow and turned around. He could see from here that Susan wasn't in the meadow. It was too flat, too thinly covered with dry grass to hide her. If Marco and Susan had come this way, it didn't matter what they did in the meadow. It only mattered where they went after they came out of it.

Dan went back to where he had first entered the meadow and started walking along the right-hand edge of the grass, keeping a sharp eye out for any footprints. His track led him along the base of the canyon wall, with forest above him and the glare of the meadow off to his left.

He resisted the temptation to climb up into the shade of the trees, but halfway along the length of the meadow, he stopped, took out his water bottle and drank deeply. He checked the level in the bottle and saw that it was more than half full.

Out in the meadow there was a darker lump in the grass. Was it a body? Dan decided he had to go look. But when he was thirty feet away, he saw that it was the rusted remains of an old piece of mining equipment, half-buried in the sand and slowly decaying in the sun. It looked like part of a boiler or tank. The old iron was blisteringly hot in the sun.

Dan looked around. Who had managed to manhandle this massive weight down into the canyon? How many people and mules had struggled to get it here?

He traced his route back to the side of the canyon and started hiking again, going slowly not to miss any tracks. Now that he knew there had been miners here, he noticed more traces. A cache of rusted tin cans was lying behind a rock. Up in that tree, someone had strung a steel cable, now frayed and hanging like a lock of some monster's hair.

At the upper end of the meadow Dan found three massive wheels, part of some kind of pulley system, lying where they had fallen a century ago. And here he could see dim traces of rock work as well, a tumbled-down wall over there, and what looked like the bottom half of a chimney in those bushes.

At his feet the ground was now covered with small pieces of quartz, shining brightly in the sun. It took Dan a moment to realize that the quartz was almost certainly the tailings of a mine. This was not a placer site. That would have had piles of cobbles. This had been a hard rock mine—a shaft into the hillside to find a vein of gold-bearing ore. As they brought the ore out, they had crushed it into this quartz debris.

In the forest beyond the broken chimney, Dan now spotted the steel beams of a stamp mill, still standing, its rusted steel blending in against the trunks of the trees.

Dan stopped to think about the mine. It had been a sizable operation and would certainly appear on the local topo maps. He wondered how they had moved the ore. Had they used some kind of aerial tramway, with the cable he had seen in the tree? Or had they built a small railway for the ore carts?

As his mind wandered through the site, it occurred to him that a hard rock mine would have had a shaft. And a mineshaft would be a very good place to hide a body. Or, for that matter, five million dollars on a thumb drive.

But where was the shaft?

Dan stepped back out into the meadow and tried to piece the puzzle together. On his right he located the stamp mill. That was where the rock was crushed, and that explained the low flat hill of white quartz below the line of trees.

But to dig the shaft, they would have had to remove tons of other rock as well—rock that had no ore, and served no purpose. Dan looked around the meadow and decided that one hill, upriver from the stamp mill, had a curiously even appearance. If that was where the miners dumped the rock, then the shaft would not be far.

It was hot in the sun, and the climb up the hill made Dan pay attention to every step. It was composed of rough, sharp-edged granite talus, just what you would expect from a mine, with just enough grass and brush to make it difficult to see where to put his feet. When he finally got to the top, he was happy to see that he had been right. There was an old ore bucket on the ground, right where it had been left. And from the bucket a cable led back into the woods, back up into the side of the canyon.

chapter 50

Dan followed the cable until it came to a frayed and twisted end a hundred feet later. But if it hadn't been moved, (and who would have moved it?) then it must be pointing in the right direction. Dan pushed on up the hill.

He soon discovered why the miners had used the cable and bucket. The side of the hill became steeper, and the footing less sure. Dan was now sliding with every step. He took two steps up and slid back down. Dirt and pine needles had now worked their way into his socks and boots.

He stopped to take a breath. He realized that this couldn't be right. Marco Gemmeli would never have climbed this hill.

Dan turned around and looked back at the meadow and the rest of the mining relics. Once again, he tried to lay out the schematic of the mine. Stamp mill there, boiler out in the meadow, but maybe it had been moved by the river. Quartz debris over by the stamp mill, and the rest of the tailings in that big hill.

Dan's eyes tracked the twisted cable back toward the bucket on top of the hill. Dan had only seen a cable snap once, when he had overloaded a cable and winch with a big tree. He remembered the snap of the cable, and the loose end flying past his head while he dove for cover.

Shaking his head, he walked back along the cable to the bucket and then kept going. Fifty feet on the other side of the bucket the hill dropped off again, and Dan descended through the mess of rock and brush. And there, near the bottom of the hill, he found more cable.

Even better, Dan found a bent piece of narrow-gauge railroad track. All he had to do was find the rest of it.

It didn't take long.

A small streambed came out of another side canyon, and Dan could see that it had been altered. There was stonework there, and what looked like a platform of some kind. But when he climbed up to it he found it was the bed of the old narrow railroad. And it led straight away from the river, straight into the small side canyon.

As he walked up the rails, Dan noted a dented ore cart down in the stream bed. The rails curved around a rock wall, and Dan was face to face with the entrance to the mine. He felt a slight chill. He wasn't sure if it came from the cool air escaping the mineshaft, or from his own nerves about entering the shaft.

This was definitely not approved procedure. He knew that.

The railbed was crushed rock. There was no way to see if there were any footprints there. And the interior of the mine was pitch black, sloping slowly downwards into the hillside.

Dan called out into the darkness, "Hello?" But there was no answer. Nor was there an echo. He waited. How deep was this thing, anyway?

The shaft was narrow, and a good foot shorter than Dan was tall. He waited for his eyes to adapt to the darkness of the shaft. He could see there were at least two big beams running across the top of the shaft further inside. He had no confidence that they were still solid. Beyond that, he could see only darkness.

He took a step forward, and now he had to bend at the waist. The roof was rough and jagged over his head. Dan knelt on the ground and took off his backpack. Inside he had a small headlamp.

He pulled it out, turned it on, and pointed it into the shaft. What the light showed was two or three more beams across the roof. On the left side, part of the wall had collapsed, and the shaft was half-blocked by the rocky debris.

"Hello?" he called out again. Still no answer.

He pointed his light at the floor of the shaft and started to creep forward. There was something odd about the floor. The crushed rocks gave way to what looked like a very smooth surface, almost polished. It wasn't until Dan took another step that he realized he was looking at water—a thin layer of water over mud. Now that he understood, he could see that the water got deeper the further you went into the shaft. He didn't like to think how deep.

And there were no footprints. The mud was undisturbed, as it had been for decades, if not more.

Still bent over carefully, Dan turned around and started to walk out of the mine shaft, disappointed that he hadn't found Susan Chen. But also enormously relieved that he didn't have to go any deeper into that black hole.

The sun outside was blinding. Dan held his hand up in front of his face to ease the shock of it. He walked back to the top of the tailings, and slowly allowed his eyes to adjust. He turned off the headlamp and put it back into the backpack. As he did so, his hand felt the wrapper of a granola bar, and he pulled that out.

He slipped his backpack on and looked for a quiet spot to eat the bar. Down nearer the river there was a nice-looking log, with a bit of shade from a nearby oak. That would do the job nicely.

Dan carefully eased his way down the nasty hill of tailings, and across the sand to the log. He sat down with his back to the river, facing up the canyon, and unwrapped the bar. Before he took a bite he checked his watch. It would still be another hour, probably two, before he could expect any help.

He took a bite and leaned back to enjoy the view. The river was calmer here because of the flat terrain of the meadow. It had carved a deep channel, and the water was a delicious dark green in the pools. As Dan looked up the river he could see the sides of the canyon, ridge after ridge, leading up to the Sierra crest miles and miles away.

The nearest ridge rose steeply from the river and was topped by a small granite knoll. Dan looked at the knoll and stopped chewing. He put the rest of the granola bar in his shirt pocket, grabbed his backpack and slung it over his shoulder, and started walking briskly up towards the knoll.

On top of the knoll was a lone pine tree, its branches battered by exposure on the rock. The lower branches had fallen away, leaving just a round cloud of foliage at the top of a tall trunk.

A lollipop tree.

chapter 51

The slopes up to the rounded granite knob were gentle, and Dan picked his way up, following the odd wrinkle or crack in the rock. Twice he stepped up over ledges, where the conchoidal fractures of the dome had left a broken layer of granite overlapping another, much like the skin of an onion.

He was hurrying, and even at this low elevation, he was starting to breathe hard. And sweat. The heat off the granite was fierce in the middle of the afternoon. It wasn't until he neared the top that he was able to notice how the top of the dome leveled off, allowing him to see the base of the tree.

And that was where he saw Susan Chen.

At least, he thought it must be Susan Chen. A body was slumped at the base of the tree, its arms back behind, the head rolling forward onto the chest.

Dan raced forward, now gasping for breath. "Susan?" he called out to her,

But there was no answer.

Dan knelt down beside the body. Susan's arms had been tied behind her, pinning her to the tree. Dan felt her neck for a pulse, and thought he detected a very faint, very fast one. He gently lifted her head and heard a groan, but he wasn't sure it wasn't just the body, reacting to the motion. He watched carefully for a moment, trying to detect a breath.

Yes. At least one, and very shallow.

Dan slipped off his pack and pulled out his knife. He cut through the tape that had bound Susan's arms behind her. Her wrists were horribly mangled underneath, but he didn't have time to worry about that right now.

He put his pack down and gently laid Susan down on the rock, cushioning her head with the pack. Another moan came from her lips, and he realized his water bottle was in the pack. He reached in, jostling her head as little as possible, and pulled out the water bottle.

He tilted her head and poured a tiny splash of water towards her mouth. Very little of the water went in, but he was encouraged to see that it got a reaction. She coughed and spit some of the water out.

"Susan?" he called gently to her. "Can you hear me? Can you try to drink some water?"

He waited. The sun was beating down, and Dan wondered if he should get out his emergency blanket, to try to give her some shade. Instead, he just moved his body between the sun and her face.

Her eyelids fluttered. At least Dan thought they did.

He poured a little water into his hand, and gently splashed it on her face and hair, hoping to cool her down.

Another moan, this time clearly made with an effort, and her eyes opened. They were unfocused, rolling a bit in her head.

"Susan, try to drink some of this water," Dan said. He began to look around for a place to move her, somewhere flat and most important, out of the sun. Just a few feet away, the shade of the lollipop tree fell on a nearby section of the granite.

Dan looked back at Susan. "Drink," he said, pouring another tiny sip into her mouth.

This time there was a slight reaction. Her mouth moved, almost like a baby searching for something to suck.

Dan pulled out his bandanna and splashed some water on it, then dipped a corner of the bandanna into her mouth.

Susan's lips reached out for the water. She sucked, tentatively, the water out of the bandanna.

Dan poured a little more on the bandanna and gave it back to her. Now she knew what to do, and attacked it greedily, her eyes closed again.

"Good," Dan encouraged her. "That's good." He wanted to move her out of the sun, but he wasn't sure if he could lift her. He thought about sliding her along the granite over to the shade, and that's when he registered that she was completely naked. The granite would scrape her skin like a rasp. He looked over at the shade and decided that a scraped backside would be the least of her problems.

"I'm going to move you," he told her. "Over into the shade where it's cooler."

Susan had no reaction to that. Dan carefully lifted from behind her shoulders and her head fell back. That wasn't going to work. He crossed his arms, cradling her head between his forearms, and tried that. He had meant to try to get as much of her body off the ground as he could, but that was now impossible. He simply slid her across the granite, the backpack catching on her feet as he pulled her away.

Once in the shade, Dan poured more water and gave her the bandanna again.

She sucked on it briefly, then choked out a painful sob. Dan patted her face with the damp cloth. He wondered if he should pour some of the water over her body, to try to cool her off. He didn't have that much left. Instead, he remembered that he had his buff in a shirt pocket. He poured a bit of water on it and wiped it gently over her skin. He noticed she wasn't sweating, which was a bad sign. He also noticed her body was covered in sores. At first he thought they were insect bites, but then immediately realized to his horror that they were burns—cigarette burns. And they were everywhere.

The thought sickened him.

The river, seventy-five yards away, offered the obvious solution. But Dan didn't want to leave the poor woman alone, not until she could better understand what was going on. He tried pouring a little water directly into her mouth and was relieved to see that she tried to drink it this time. Most of it dribbled out.

"Susan," he called to her again, "can you hear me? I am going to get some more water from the river."

There was no reaction. Dan checked his bottle. There were only a few sips left. "I'm going now, but I will be right back, with some nice cold water for you, okay?"

It looked as if her eyes opened again, and this time she tried to focus. Dan wasn't sure she was successful. "I'll be right back with more water," he said. As he gently let her head back down on the granite. He had zipped off the legs to his cargo pants and put them in one of the side pockets. He pulled them out and placed one over her chest, another across her hips. She deserved that dignity. He reached down, grabbed the backpack, slid it under her head, and stood up.

Which was the closest, fastest, route to the river and back?

chapter 52

He knew that without water he couldn't do much for Susan, but he still felt guilty leaving her there under the tree, alone.

He hurried down to the river, picking a spot where there was a bit of current, so that he could fill his bottles more easily. Those folding plastic bottles needed a bit of help. In still water they didn't hold their shape, and seemed like it took forever to fill them.

He knew the river would be icy, but he was still shocked by the cold water. As he held the first bottle in the rushing torrent, he nearly lost his grip, and bottle. And in reacting quickly, he nearly fell into the river himself. Dan stood up abruptly and reset his feet on the wet rocks.

This was better. He filled the first bottle, and then the second one with the snowmelt from the river. His hands were now chilled by the water, and he could feel the cold of the bottles as he held them against his body to climb back up from the river.

As he started up the granite to Susan he noticed a campsite off to his left, a few yards upriver. A backpack was propped against one of the logs, and there were a few more items strewn about the area. Dan took a quick detour to grab the backpack and slipped one of his arms through a strap. Slinging it over his right shoulder, he held the two water bottles by the neck in his left hand, and strode up the granite.

Susan was still there, of course. She hadn't moved, but it

seemed to Dan that she reacted slightly to his arrival. He dropped the backpack and knelt down next to her.

Dan took one of the water bottles and poured a tiny bit over her face and into her hair. She gave her head a short jerk, which Dan also took as a good sign. He poured new, icy water into the bandanna and put it to her lips. This time she sucked on the material fervently.

Dan poured a small amount of water on his buff, and laid it softly on her stomach, eliciting a moan from her.

Dan took a deep breath. He noticed that his knees were sending up flares of pain as he knelt on the bare rock. He shifted his weight and sat down next to Susan, still trying to keep her in the shade as much as possible.

A little more water in the bandanna, and now her lips, her face, were straining for the bottle itself. Dan allowed himself a tiny smile and held her head up with one hand while offering her lips the bottle with the other. She sucked at the cold water, and he struggled with the folding bottle, sending too much water into her mouth.

Susan choked badly on that, and the water spilled over her neck and chest.

"Let's stick with the bandanna for now," Dan suggested, and Susan lay back, accepting her fate.

But the fact that she was moving and reacting gave Dan hope. He kept loading the bandanna with water and she kept sucking away on it. Every once in a while, he would sprinkle a bit more on her head, or moisten the buff on her stomach.

After a few more minutes Susan lay back flat on the ground, no longer straining for the bandanna, and closed her eyes. Dan had a spasm of panic, thinking she had given up, and he called out to her. "Don't leave me here, Susan. Stick with me."

She opened her eyes, and this time they seemed to be focused on him. "You're going to be okay," he said.

He thought she might have given a slight nod to this, but he wasn't sure.

Dan poured more water on her head, on the buff, and on his pant legs covering her body. He even sprinkled a bit over her legs, hoping to cool them down as well. If he could get her down to the river, he could let her cool off in the water, bit by bit. But for now, that was too much to ask of her and of him.

He added more water to the bandanna and held it to her lips. She knew the routine now and was sucking up the water as quickly as he could saturate the cloth.

"You're doing great," he encouraged her. Dan could feel an intense force in his body and mind, all focused on Susan, willing her to fight forward. He measured every milliliter of water down her throat as a victory, every cooling wash of her body as a tiny step up. Slowly, almost imperceptibly, he was going to make this work. She was going to live. He was determined to make that happen.

He poured the rest of the first bottle of water onto the bandanna and watched as she sucked it in. The second bottle was nearly empty from his attempts to cool down her body.

"I'm going to get more water," he told her. "It won't take long." He sprinkled the last bit of the second bottle over her body. The buff and pant legs were now nicely saturated.

Susan's eyes opened in terror and she tried to grab at Dan, but her arms fell awkwardly short. She choked out something, a word or two, that Dan couldn't understand.

He stopped and bent over her. "What's wrong?" he asked. "I won't be gone but a minute or two."

Her lips strained to form words, but her voice couldn't make them into sounds. Finally, after three tries, Dan understood.

"He'll come back," she was saying. And her eyes spoke of horror, streaming tears across her face.

Dan gave her what he hoped was a reassuring smile and shook his head. "He won't come back," Dan said. He glanced at his watch. "We've got him. He's under arrest." Close enough, Dan thought. He would be as soon as the SAR team reached Kim Archer. That could happen at any moment now.

He looked at her, trying to determine if she believed him. "He can't come back now," Dan said. "I promise."

Her eyes closed, still streaming tears, but her mouth had relaxed, and the furrows on her face were fading away.

"Hey," Dan said. "Save those tears. You need the hydration." It was a poor joke, and Susan didn't react. But she lay still, resting, when he stood, picked up the water bottles, and headed off to the river again.

chapter 53

This time he knew right where he was going, and it didn't take him more than a minute or two to fill the bottles. The water was still icy cold, and it shocked him again. That made him realize how the heat of the day had warmed the previous bottles over time. The new ones were freshly chilled. He figured that Susan had drunk at least a liter of water. That should start making a difference in her dehydrated body.

As he knelt over her, Susan's eyes opened and fixed on the water bottles. Dan lifted her head up and tried to pour some into her mouth. This time she helped him, straining with her lips to meet the bottle. He poured gently, resting the bottle on her chest, where it could also cool her off. She drank a few swallows, then began to choke. He quickly lifted up the bottle and turned her on her side, where she could cough the water out.

After a couple of short spasms, she groaned and rolled onto her back again. He offered her more water, but she shook her head.

"You need to drink," he said. "Seriously. You are totally dehydrated."

She looked at him without expression, and slowly shook her head.

"You have to," he said.

She shook her head again. "I can't," she whispered.

Dan nodded. "Yeah, but you have to."

She took a deep breath and gave a sigh but didn't move toward the water.

While he waited, Dan remembered a packet of electrolytes in his pack. The pack was under Susan's head, and he lifted her up, pulled out the pack, and gently let her back down on the rock. "Just for a second," he said.

He dug around, not finding the packet at first, then remembered it was in the outside pocket. He held it up to her. "These will help, too," he said.

She stared, still not reacting.

Dan opened the packet and held one of the little jellies out for her. She didn't open her mouth. "Come on," Dan said. "Just one."

Susan allowed her lips to open just enough for Dan to squeeze the jelly into her mouth. She made a face and shook her head but didn't spit it out.

Dan sat back on his heels and looked around. The sun continued to move, and Susan's legs were now fully exposed again. He slid them over a bit, getting them back into the shade, but it was a losing battle. The sun was sinking lower in the sky now, and the shade of the lollipop tree was beginning to drop off the edge of the granite, down towards the river.

Dan glanced at Susan's pack, wondering if he could use it for shade. That was when he noticed the emergency beacon on the pack strap. He was immediately angry with himself for not having noticed it sooner.

He'd used the same model before, and quickly hit the SOS button. That would at least give the SAR team a specific location and would let Dan off the hook for making sure they found him. He thought about sending a message. It would make sense, because he didn't think Susan was going to be able to hike out of the canyon, and the search team would have a hard time getting her out.

He laboriously worked through the system to type in the words "send chopper," hit send, and left it at that.

He turned his attention back to Susan. She was resting now, eyes closed. He couldn't tell if she had swallowed the electrolyte jelly, but he didn't see it anywhere. At least she hadn't spit it out. He gently nudged the water bottle up to her lips again.

Susan opened her eyes and looked at him, then at the bottle. She opened her mouth and took a tiny sip, then turned her head away.

"You have to drink more," he said. "You need the water."

She shook her head. "No, I feel sick," she said. It was the most she had spoken since he arrived, and that was a good sign.

"You feel sick because you are dehydrated," Dan said. "And if you drink more, you'll feel better."

He waited. After a moment, she leaned forward to take another sip; this one was two short swallows.

"Good," Dan encouraged her. "Take a little more, and then have another one of these jellies."

She waited, gathering her strength, then leaned forward and drank a few more sips.

Dan fussed with the packet and worked out another jelly. This one was stuck in the plastic, and it took him a minute to get it free. While he struggled, he heard Susan strangle out a cry, and felt her hand grab his leg.

He turned to look at her and saw that she was looking off into the forest behind him, and terror was written all over her face.

The hairs on the back of Dan's neck stood up, and a chill ran down his spine. Susan was making strange moaning squeals now.

There was no way Marco could have escaped from Kim Archer, was there?

Dan slowly turned around to look behind him. At first, he saw nothing, and glanced back at Susan, who nodded a bit and made sure he looked again.

There it was, behind that tree down by the river. Something moving. Something dark brown.

A bear. A small bear. Maybe two years old. It was poking around in the brush, looking for something to eat.

Dan patted Susan on the shoulder. "Nothing to worry about," he said. "It won't bother us."

The look on her face told him that she didn't believe him. She was trembling. It was energy she couldn't afford to use.

Dan stood up and waved his arms at the bear. At first it didn't notice him. Susan, behind him, whined again. Then the bear saw Dan. It stared at him for no more than two seconds, then bolted up the side of the canyon at a dead run. Within seconds it was out of sight, racing up the steep slope over rocks and bushes at a pace that no human could ever match.

Dan whispered an apology to the bear. It was a lousy way to treat such a lovely animal. Then he turned and looked at Susan. There was relief in her face, and just a touch of a smile on her lips.

He took advantage of the moment to stick another jelly in her mouth and follow it with the water bottle. She took three more sips and then let her head rest against the backpack again.

chapter 54

It was another hour and a half before the rescue team arrived.

By then Dan had managed to give Susan nearly two liters of water and the entire package of electrolyte jellies, as well as a couple of pain pills. And he could see the difference. She had felt well enough first to sit up, and even ask him to find some of her clothes to put on. She didn't bother with underwear, and only rolled her eyes when he offered to leave her for a few minutes for privacy.

They were now in the shade, off the granite dome, and Dan had helped her down to the river, where he could more easily put water on her clothes to cool her off. He knew she was in pain. The burns on her skin must hurt terribly, and having clothes rub against them only made it worse.

But she was able to focus now. Not always, but sometimes. She heard and understood what he was saying to her, that the rescue team should be arriving soon, and they would find a way to get her out.

She had even been able to talk to him about what had happened. "He killed Nathan," she said.

Dan nodded. "Yeah, I figured that."

"He wanted to kill me, but I told him I knew where the money was."

Dan's eyebrows went up. "Did you find it?" he asked. He was not expecting that.

"It was just a way to put him off," she said. "I was expecting to see people at that archeology place."

Dan explained what had happened with Walt.

"When there was nobody there, I just kept telling him it was up here, a little farther."

"I guess he ran out of patience," Dan said.

It was the wrong thing to say. Her face contorted into a grimace, and she started sobbing. "He hurt me…so bad."

Dan felt like an idiot. "You don't have to explain," he said. "He's gone now, and you're safe."

She kept crying, and Dan wiped away her tears. He gave her some water to drink. It was many minutes before she spoke again. Each time she tried, she started to cry again.

"How did you find me?" she finally asked him.

Dan explained about Walt and the camera, and how he had hiked up the canyon. "When I saw that old mine, I thought you might be there," he said. "And then I saw the tree."

She gave him a tired smile. "The lollipop tree," she said.

Dan grinned. "Yeah, I remembered about your dad."

They sat in silence for a few minutes. Dan checked his watch again. Where the hell were these guys?

"He left me here to die," Susan said quietly.

Dan turned and looked at her.

"He wanted me to die, just like his brother," she said.

Dan nodded. "I know. But he's gone now, and you're safe."

Susan wiggled her toes a bit. Dan dipped his hand into the water and let the icy liquid dribble on her legs, then splashed a bit on her body. Two ravens squawked loudly and flew up the river past them.

"Do you want to drink some more?" Dan asked. "You probably should."

"Is it filtered?" she asked. Her face showed deep concern.

Dan chuckled. "Nope. Straight from the river. I don't have a filter with me, and I figured it was more important to get some liquid into you."

Susan made a face to show concern.

"If you get giardia, it will be days from now," Dan said "By then you'll be someplace where you can get medicine."

Susan nodded. He put his hand in the water and dribbled some over her head, into her hair.

"Do you want to try to drink more water?" Dan asked.

But he never heard her answer, because behind him he heard noises, shouts. He turned and saw a crew of SAR team members up on the granite, outlined silhouettes against the late afternoon sun.

"Got 'em!" he heard someone yell. And then the crowd came galloping down the hill.

chapter 55

Dan stood up so quickly that he stumbled and nearly fell over on Susan Chen. By the time he had stabilized himself, the SAR team was there, pushing in close.

He wanted to give them a status report on Susan, but as he tried, some of them pushed past him, kneeling down to tend to her.

Dan managed to corral one of the team, Bob Tschida, and told him when he had found Susan, and what he had done: the water, the electrolytes, the pain pills, and trying to cool her off. He tried to provide an accurate timeline for it all.

Bob nodded and wrote it all down in a little notebook.

Dan explained how Susan had been tied to the tree, and that she was having trouble moving her arms.

One of the women was talking to Susan now, asking her how she felt, what her symptoms were.

Dan mentioned the burns, how they were all over her body, and heard someone behind him mutter the words "sick fuck."

There were suddenly a lot of people around Susan. So many that Dan couldn't see her face any more. One woman near him had opened a large backpack and was pulling medical supplies out of it: bandages and tubes of some kind of ointment.

They were talking quietly, urgently to each other, and paying no attention to Dan. His own tiny first aid kit would have fit in one of the outside pockets of one of their backpacks with plenty of room to spare. Dan watched, now feeling completely unnecessary.

One of the women asked Dan to move back a bit, so she could position herself better.

Dan stepped back. He stood watching, realizing he couldn't do anything to help. Finally he walked a few yards away and sat on a nearby log.

They had radios. They were calling for a chopper. Dan wondered if it was already on its way, due to his message, or if it had waited for more information or a confirmation.

The scene around Susan had gone from urgency to focused calm. The team had done what it could do for her; now it was time to wait for the chopper and get her out.

Bob Tschida walked over to Dan.

"How is she doing?" Dan asked. Bob was one of the senior members of SAR, and Dad knew him from many rescues, including, once, his own.

Bob nodded, then gave a shrug. "She's got a long way to go," he said.

"When I got here, she was really out of it," Dan said. "Dehydrated, shock, sunburned."

"Not to mention the other shit," Bob said, referring to the burns.

"And terrified the sonofabitch would come back," Dan said.

Bob gave him a tight smile. "That won't happen," he said. "Not from what I saw."

"The sheriffs took him?" Dan asked.

"Oh, yeah," Bob assured him. "And he had quite an escort."

Bob turned to check on the team. Somebody's radio squawked, and a minute later Dan heard that the chopper was on its way. He thought he heard that it was thirty minutes out. Bob Tschida turned back to Dan. "You did good, Dan," he said.

"I didn't have much to work with," Dan said. "I wish I could have done more or done it more quickly."

"No, you did fine," Bob said. "The most important thing was to get her hydrated and out of the sun."

"You know," Dan said. "She might have been there all night. Tied to that tree."

Bob's eyebrows shot up. "Shit," he said. He looked up at the tree, perched on the rock above. "What a sick…" He didn't finish the sentence.

"I don't know all he did," Dan said. "I didn't ask her. It just occurred to me."

Bob shook his head, lost in thought.

Someone said something down by Susan, and they both turned to look at her.

"You're fine," they heard one of the SAR team say. "We'll get you out of here soon."

Bob looked down at Dan. "You can take off," he said. "You've had a long day, and it's still a good hike out of here."

Dan considered it. "I can wait until the chopper gets here," he said.

"Don't think we can handle it, eh?" Bob asked with a smile.

Dan chuckled. "No. I just don't feel right about leaving her."

Bob waved his hand, indicating the SAR team clustered around Susan Chen. "I think we have it under control," he said.

"I know you do," Dan agreed. "I just don't want to leave yet."

Bob smiled, but didn't mention it again.

chapter 56

Once the chopper had taken Susan Chen out of the canyon, Dan helped the SAR team pack up. And while he was at it, he packed up Susan's gear as well. He managed to get most of it, and his daypack, into her backpack, but it wasn't surprising that her pack didn't fit him worth a damn. She was a foot shorter than he was.

Bob Tschida saw him struggling with it and came over to help out.

In the end they divvied up her gear between a few of the SAR team members who were willing to lend a hand, and Dan took the rest, crammed into his day pack. His poor pack looked like someone had inflated a balloon inside. Unfortunately for Dan, it wasn't full of helium, and the straps were straining for all they were worth. He told himself that he only had a few miles to cover that way.

The team had water treatment tablets, and everyone was encouraged to "camel up" for the hike out. Dan was happy to oblige and filled one of his water bottles as well. It wouldn't fit in his pack and he carried it in his hand. It would be easier to drink that way, anyway.

The mood was subdued. It was clear that the team was still trying to process what they had seen that afternoon, and the cruelty that had caused Susan's injuries. Low voices, and the rare attempt at a joke, received only the quietest of chuckles.

Dan had asked Bob, out of Susan's earshot, what her prognosis was, but Bob didn't, or couldn't, give him a quick answer. "It's going to be a day or two before we'll really know," he said. "They'll give her more IVs in the hospital and that should help."

The way he said it did not reassure Dan much.

They packed up and marched out single file, Dan in fifth place in line. They had asked him if he wanted to lead the way, but he just shook his head. He was happy to take his place as just one more hiker on the trail. He had done what he could for Susan, and it had somehow exhausted him.

It was a relief to follow the group, listening to them as they chatted quietly. As they worked their way down the canyon, he could hear them regain their spirits. Two of the team up front were now talking away, discussing a workshop they'd done a few weeks ago.

Behind him, Dan heard someone comment about the rapids on their right, and then ask about a whitewater training that was scheduled. He listened to the answer without paying attention. It was all just a background soundtrack to his thoughts about the day.

They climbed down the log to get past the one big rock face, and that was enough to brighten the mood some. Climbing down is always harder than climbing up, and those who went first helped guide the rest down, sometimes offering a hand or a word of advice, sometimes helping place a foot in a key spot.

The care that they showed each other in the process seemed to reconnect them somehow. They talked to each other, touched each other, and slowly came back into the world of humanity.

Dan could see and hear it happening. When they left the steep rocks to hike back through the mine area, he was now last in line. As tall as he was, he could see the rest of them lined up in front on the trail. And he could see them turn, from time to time, to talk to each other. He also noticed that a few turned around enough to check on him.

Bob Tschida was next to last and did that more than anyone else.

"You doing okay back there?" Bob asked as they hiked along the river, now making good progress toward the trailhead.

"Yeah," Dan said. "I'm fine."

He looked across the river at the canyon walls, soaring green walls high above them. The sun was now lower, and the light was beginning to reach the golden hour when it picked up a warmer tone and made the forest glow.

A breeze was beginning to blow up the canyon, taking the edge off the heat. Dan popped the cap on his water bottle and took a long drink.

Bob turned again to check on him. "You must hike a lot faster than this when you are on your own," he said.

"This is fine," Dan answered. "We're in no hurry, and we'll get to the trailhead in plenty of time."

Bob looked around at the scenery. "It's a beautiful place," he said. "I might have to come back here just for fun."

"Pretty peaceful," Dan said, "when people don't fuck it up." He told Bob about the young bear they had seen.

"I'll leave that part out when I tell my wife," Bob chuckled. "She's not a big fan of bears."

Dan smiled. "If nothing else, they help keep some people away from places like this," he said. "And that's not a bad thing."

When they got to the dig, Walt was waiting for them.

"I saw the chopper, so I guess you found her?" he asked the group.

A woman in the front pointed her thumb over her shoulder at Dan. "Courtwright did," she said.

Walt searched the line of hikers until his eyes met Dan's. "Howdy, stranger," he called out.

Someone in the group called a short rest halt, and the others seemed to have agreed. They headed over to the camp in the shade.

Dan walked up and shook hands with Walt. "Did they get Marco bundled up and out of here?" he asked.

Walt nodded. "That fellow Archer came along at the right time, I guess."

Dan nodded.

Walt chuckled. "He was a character," he said. "Kept complaining about how he probably never would get paid."

A small smile played across Dan's face. The two stood there for a moment in silence. Walt face contorted as he sucked on a tooth for a moment. Finally, shaking his head slightly back and forth, he said, "You do manage to get yourself into some interesting situations."

Dan looked back up the canyon, and he gave a gentle shrug of his shoulders. "Thanks for helping get me out of this one," he said to Walt.

Walt snorted. "I didn't do anything," he said. "That Susan Chen, is she going to be okay?"

Dan gave him a quick summary of Susan's condition and what had caused it. "I'll guess we'll find out more once she gets to the hospital," he said.

"Are you going to go there?" Walt asked.

Dan started to say that there was no reason for him to do that, but somehow the words didn't come out. He remembered Susan on the granite, in such pain and distress. He remembered how hard he had willed her to fight back, to struggle. And of how she had tried. How hard they had both tried, in different ways.

"Yeah," he said. "I probably will."

The SAR team was standing up, ready to move on. They asked Dan if he was going to join them.

Dan looked at Walt, who nodded. "I'm fine here," Walt said. "I'm set for the next couple of days anyway. Give my love to Ruth."

The two men shook hands, and Dan took his place at the back of the line as the group started the hike back up out of the canyon to the trailhead.

He was going to need the whole hike out, and more, to clear his head and settle his mind.

chapter 57

There was nothing about the hospital that Dan found reassuring. None of the colors were found in nature—a sad sack of mealy pastel plastics and metals that seemed to be based on the elementary schools of decades ago. And the air assaulted him with a combination of chemicals and cleaning solutions with just enough hint of something animal to be distressing.

In the twenty minutes it took him to navigate the staff and hallways to find Susan Chen's room, he could feel himself coming down with something. A nasty case of claustrophobia, if nothing else.

When he finally found her room, he noticed someone already there, a young woman sitting quietly in a chair by the bed, and it was enough to make him stop and think about leaving. But before he could do so, she noticed him and, after a moment's hesitation, waved him into the room.

A quick glance told him that Susan was asleep.

"You must be Mr. Courtwright," the young woman whispered. "Susan has told us about you."

Dan admitted that this was true and handed her a greeting card he had selected for Susan. He had struggled to find something appropriate to bring her. Flowers were not allowed because of the pollen. He thought of bringing a book, but then remembered that she was a writer, and he was sure he would fail at picking out something she would like. And he had found enough of those damned mylar balloons in the backcountry to make him swear that he would never, ever support that industry.

And so it had been just a card, a simple one wishing her a speedy recovery. He had tried to think of something clever to write inside and had failed.

"Thank you so much for coming," the woman whispered to him. "My parents are getting a bite to eat, but they should be back soon."

Dan held up his hands in front of himself. "I don't want to be in the way, I just thought I'd stop in to see how she's doing."

"She's okay," the woman said, in a tone that indicated there was still cause for worry. "I'm Clare, her sister."

Dan shook her hand and looked again at Susan. There were numerous tubes connected to the poor woman.

"The doctors are worried about her kidneys," Clare said. "We just have to wait to see how they respond."

Dan nodded to show he understood. "She is tough," he told Clare.

When he looked back at Clare, she had tears in her eyes. Dan reached out with his arms, and she leaned into his embrace.

"She is tough," he repeated, his lips just inches from the top of her head. "It's going to be okay."

But Clare didn't answer him.

They were still standing that way when Dan sensed someone else had entered the room. He turned his head to see Susan's parents standing in the doorway.

He let go of Clare, and she wiped her eyes with her sleeve while trying to introduce everyone.

Susan's mother was a tiny woman who stared at Dan with what

might have been a hint, of fear or at least caution. But her father stepped forward quickly and took Dan's hand in both of his.

"Thank you," he said fervently. "Thank you so much for what you have done for our daughter." He was bowing a bit as he said it, and Dan found himself returning the favor with a deep nod of his head.

The room now seemed too small. Dan tried to maneuver into a position to leave, but before he could do so, Susan woke up. And every face in the room turned to her.

She gazed around sleepily, confusion on her face. Her eyes finally settled on Dan, and a smile drifted across her face.

"My hero," she said. Her voice was soft and distant.

Dan flushed and tried to protest, but the rest of Susan's family was now beaming and making approving noises at him.

"I just came by to see how you are doing," Dan said. Clare handed Susan his card.

Susan read the card quickly and put it down. "Thanks," she said. Then she closed her eyes.

Dan looked at the rest of the family and indicated that he would be leaving now.

"Thanks," Susan said again, her eyes still closed. "Thanks for getting me out of there."

"I didn't do that," Dan said. "That was the SAR team."

Susan opened her eyes and looked straight at Dan. "I know what you did," she said, her voice stronger now. "And thank you."

"You're welcome," Dan smiled at her. "You look a lot better than you did two days ago."

"Liar," Susan answered him. "But I appreciate the thought."

She turned to Clare and asked for her phone. Clare pulled a phone out of her purse and handed it to Susan. As she fussed with the phone, Susan said, "I thought you might want to see this."

Another minute of fiddling with the phone, and she handed it to Dan.

On the screen was an email to Susan from Bolton Hall Publishing. Dan scrolled through the email, which was sent to notify Susan that the treasure hidden in the Sierra by Matthew McLeod had been found. They could verify this to the satisfaction of their legal team, as would become clear.

The person who had found the treasure had requested anonymity, for what were obvious reasons, but the finder had provided the secret code that had been attached to the USB drive. If Susan had any questions about this development, the email gave her a contact person to call.

Dan read through the email, then looked at Susan. "Are they announcing this?" he asked.

She nodded. "I got it this morning," she said. "I think they go public sometime this afternoon or maybe tomorrow."

She closed her eyes again. Dan wanted to ask her, but he didn't.

A nurse came in to check on Susan, and Dan took this as his cue to leave. Clare and Susan's parents tried to talk him into staying, but he could see their hearts weren't really in it. He accepted their thanks one more time and slipped out of the room.

He took a last look at Susan from the doorway. Her family was clustered around her, watching the nurse tend to her. Susan's eyes were closed, and Dan couldn't really tell if there was a hint of a smile on her lips.

chapter 58

When Dan got home that afternoon he noticed, as he had for many months, the weeds that had grown up along the street in front of his house. And today he decided it was time to do something about it—no matter how hot the day. He needed a project.

Within fifteen minutes he was in his grubbiest clothes, wearing gloves, and carrying a pick and shovel out to the street. These were no normal weeds. They were wild pea vines, and the rhizomes below the ground just came back, year after year, unless he dug them out one at a time. Over time they would take over the whole yard, and Dan was not going to let that happen.

It was sweaty, mindless work, and he threw himself into the chore with vigor. He slammed the pick down into the rocky dirt over and over again, satisfied when it bit deeply into the ground. And he was feeling around with his fingers when he couldn't see the roots. Yanking them hard, and when they didn't come up, he used the pick again with a vengeance. When the dirt was looser, he used the shovel to scrape out some of the rhizomes and clear the way for another pick attack.

When his eyes were so filled with sweat that he couldn't see, he went inside and drank two glasses of water, then came back with a half-gallon of the same in a plastic jug. He tossed the jug into the shade and got back to digging.

It was a good hundred feet of work when he began, and he

was determined to finish it that day. After two hours, his back was beginning to ache and the gloves were wearing thin. He had a hole in the left-hand glove on one finger, worn out by his constant probing and digging in the dirt. And his mind was blissfully clear of any thoughts of Marco Gemmeli or Matthew McLeod.

Occasionally a car would drive by, and Dan would stop for a second. If the driver waved, he would nod back. But if not, he just stood there, resting for a minute, letting the sweat drip off him before he got back to work again.

It was slow going. But behind him he left a growing pile of weeds that made a leafy green berm alongside the road, a stark contrast to the bare ground he had cleared of weeds.

He was down to the last eight feet or so when another car drove up the street, but this one didn't pass him by. Instead, it pulled into Walt and Ruth's driveway. and even so it took Dan a second or two to recognize Walt at the wheel.

Dan leaned on his shovel and watched Walt get out of his car.

"You picked a hot day for that job," Walt said to him.

"Yeah," Dan agreed. "I thought you'd still be down at the dig."

"I am no longer needed," Walt said, sounding just a little disappointed.

"You got fired?" Dan asked incredulously.

"In a manner of speaking," Walt said. "I was made redundant."

Dan chuckled. "That's fancy talk for getting fired, Walt."

"Yes and no," Walt replied. "The dig's been shut down, and the whole team has been sent home. So no work for me, or anyone else."

"What do you mean, shut down?" Dan asked.

"Erica got the analysis of the remains we found there," Walt explained. "All Native American."

"So, they got turned over to the local tribe?" Dan asked.

Walt shook his head. "Not turned over. We replaced them where we had found them, covered everything up, and turned the whole site over to them. They'll manage it from here on."

Dan took a moment to consider how this might affect the US Forest Service in the area. He decided that it wasn't his job to worry about that. He said to Walt, "How is Erica with all that? Did she lose her big project?"

"She seems okay with it," Walt said. "She's got a really good relationship with the Tuolumne Band, and everybody seems to be on the same wavelength on this. She'll work with them on anything they need. The grad students are a little bent out of shape."

"They lost their thesis material?" Dan asked.

"Maybe," Walt agreed. "But there is still plenty of data they can use. And there's not really any question about what happened down there."

"What do you mean?" Dan asked.

"Well, you heard, or maybe you read, that all of them had been scalped."

Dan nodded. "Yeah. And if they were Indians, then it was the cowboys who were doing the scalping. Didn't the State of California have a bounty on Indian scalps for a while?"

Walt shook his head. "Not exactly. The state never paid a bounty, but some of the local communities certainly did. And the state had a budget to reimburse people for any expenses they incurred while fighting against the Indians."

"Which in those days meant trying to wipe them out completely." Dan said.

Walt nodded. "In this case, it wasn't much of a fight."

"How so?" Dan asked.

"From what Erica got back, the remains were from a group of six individuals: a man, two women, and three juveniles, ages between about two and eight. The two women were mother and daughter, and the juveniles were the children of the younger woman. The man was the father." He stopped to let this sink in. "It was just a family in the woods."

"Jesus," Dan said. He turned to look at his weed project. There wasn't enough left to take his mind off that news.

"We are a strange species," Walt said.

Dan blew out a deep sigh. "Strange, and violent," he replied.

"Sometimes," Walt agreed. "Happily, not all the time. How's your writer friend? What was her name?"

"Susan," Dan answered him. "Susan Chen. And she's still in the hospital. They're worried about her kidneys."

"That will happen with severe dehydration." Walt replied.

"Yeah," Dan agreed. "And she's better than she was, although that's not saying much."

"But a step in the right direction," Walt said.

"Sure. And let's hope there are many more," Dan said. "But the really good news is that Bolton Hall, the publisher of those mysteries, has announced that the treasure hunt is over. Somebody found the five million, and everyone else can go home."

Walt searched Dan's face for a moment. "That's kind of a coincidence isn't it"?" he asked. "It gets found right around when she goes looking for it?"

Dan nodded slowly. "Yes, it is," he said, looking Walt right in the eyes.

"Do you think it's for real?" Walt asked. "Or did she…"

"Don't know and don't care," Dan interrupted him. "It got found. And that means people can stop looking for it."

Walt smiled. "If they believe that it was found," he said. "These days who knows what people will believe."

"Yeah," Dan agreed. "We are a strange species."

"Well, I believe that I will go in and say hello to the love of my life," Walt said.

"Good idea," Dan grinned. "I hope to do the same when she gets home. And in the meantime, I believe I am going to beat the crap out of these weeds."

afterword

Attentive readers, or those truly afflicted, might notice a few details about this book. Twelve of the minor characters share a common theme that ties them, somewhat tenuously, to the legendary Tower of Babel. And for those who are still wondering if that treasure ever did really exist, the answer can be found, coded carefully, in the text. Good luck finding that one.

ALSO AVAILABLE:

When a Wall Street tycoon insists that his family join him for an annual backpacking trip into the Sierra Nevada, some of his children are not enthusiastic about the idea.

And that's before people start turning up dead. Ranger Dan Courtwright is first on the scene. And with his friend Sheriff Cal Healey, he sticks with it to the terrifying finish, which is a real cliffhanger. Literally.

DANGER: FALLING ROCKS is available on Amazon.com.

ALSO AVAILABLE:

There are five trails that lead into the Granite Gorge of the Mokelumne River, but none of them connect to each other. It seems as if there are five ways in, and no way out.

But when Ranger Dan Courtwright offers to help restore some of those old trails, he discovers more than he expected. And is lucky to get out alive.

GRANITE GORGE is available on Amazon.com.

Acknowledgments

My books are invented, whole cloth, from my memories of adventures in the mountains, both real and imagined. But they would not be possible without the help of some key players. My two daughters, Liz and Estelle, both read the first draft and make helpful and insightful comments. Robin Lewis is a prince and manages the design and production of these books with patience and style.

Karen Johnson adds her wonderful suggestions to the text. Finally, a note of thanks to my wife Margaret, who is kind enough to proof my work, and tries to keep me from making the most egregious errors. She is often successful.